WHAT THE  EYE
DOESN'T
See

A NOVEL BY
GRETCHEN RICKER

Mariners
Chapel
Series

Copyright

Published by Full Sail Books

ISBN-13: 978-0615506296
ISBN-10: 0615506291

Cover design by: Marjorie Hill

http://iTagStudios.com

Visit the author website:

http://gretchenricker.net/

version 2011.6.25

Praise for

What the Eye Doesn't See

"An exciting and promising debut of things to come. Gretchen Ricker knows all to well 'What the Eye Doesn't See' the heart won't grieve over, and she leads the reader into a novel of romantic suspense that captures the essence of what it means to be a Christian in today's world."

--RICHARD HERMAN, author of bestselling *Warbirds*
http://richardhermanbooks.com/

Every way of a man is right in his own eyes:

but the Lord pondereth the hearts.

Prov 21:2

KJV

To Dan,
My love and my life.

Chapter One

"What the eye doesn't see, the heart won't grieve over." Holly's Uncle Nikko slumped in his wheelchair and repeated the words like a mantra. Holly approached her uncle on tiptoe, stunned at how he had deteriorated in just three days. The morning light coming through the patio doors cast him in deep shadow. She cocked her ear, listening to what he was saying. It was the same phrase over and over. She bent and kissed his balding head. "Shalom, Uncle Nikko, how are you today?"

"What?" He started and looked up, his eyes vacant.

Her lips trembled as she waited for his mind to register. His knobby fingers wove themselves into an orange afghan her aunt had crocheted years ago, clutching it. His ever-present journal lay tucked beside his hip.

He's leaving me.

The thought unnerved her. She set a gentle hand on his shoulder. "So . . . how did you sleep last night, Uncle Nikko?" The words caught on stifled tears. She took a slow breath, willing the swelling emotion to retreat.

She already knew the answer. Three times the aides at Hibiscus House had found him sitting here, looking out across the facility garden to Morro Bay and the deep blue Pacific Ocean beyond, rocking and muttering.

He looked up and their eyes met. "They won't let me sleep, Holly." He reached out and grabbed her arm, his hand cold and soft, the strength fading.

"The nurses?"

"No. Them." His gaze drifted back to the garden. His face flushed pink and his hands shook. "I'm *tame,* and there is no one to cleanse me."

A single tear escaped and followed a wrinkled path to his chin and he began to rock again.

"No, Uncle Nikko. You are *not* unclean, you are *tahowr*, clean, washed by the blood of the Messiah, remember?" The words rushed from her, but he was gone again, leaving her alone in a cruel, twisted way. She sighed and rubbed his back, her fingers tumbling down the knobs of his spine. Just last month he had chided *her* for being too thin. Now he was the one wasting away. His thin, red hair, a family trademark, was now a mere wisp plastered to his age-spotted head.

A low moan rose from him and his rocking became more agitated. "There are no ashes with which to wash. There is no red heifer."

Dropping down on her knees in front of him, Holly looked up into her dear uncle's face. His eyes seemed flat and distant, looking through her into the wisps and shadows of the past. "Yeshua is your atonement, Uncle Nikko. You told me that."

She laid her hands over his and placed her cheek on his knee, shutting her eyes and squeezing her tears into the afghan. *"Ruach hakodesh,* Holy Spirit, touch Uncle Nikko," she whispered. "Clear his mind and ease his fears."

Long moments slid by as the two of them sat bathed in sunlight, her heart aching at the impending loss of her precious uncle. Her time with him was slipping through her fingers. Soon she would be alone.

Holly's mind drifted back to the years when he had comforted her through loss and heartache. Now the tables had turned. She needed to help him, but to do that she needed to know one thing.

How had he come in contact with a dead body?

Holly stood and wheeled her uncle down the long hallway to his private room. She glanced at an LVN who nodded and retrieved a tray with a teapot and a cup from the counter. Her uncle had refused any sleeping aid that might ease his troubled mutterings and lull him into a much-needed rest. They had agreed to try to get him to drink a warm cup of his favorite herbal tea. Perhaps she could read to him and he would doze off.

The nurse preceded them into the room and went to work. She set the tea on the bedside table, closed the blinds, and folded back the covers on Uncle Nikko's bed. "There you go."

Uncle Nikko looked at the cup. "I don't want a sleeping pill." He pulled his journal up to his chest, holding it like a small leather- bound shield.

"Uncle, it's not a sleeping pill. It's your favorite tea. Just drink some and lie back. You don't have to sleep, just rest."

"With sleep come dreams, Holly." Perspiration glistened on his forehead. He reached out a shaking hand toward her. "They find me in my dreams. I don't want to go there." He looked up at her, his eyes wide with terror.

She took his hand. "Who finds you, Uncle Nikko?"

He pulled the journal closer to his chest. "Holly, I want you to ..." He stopped himself with a conspiratorial nod toward the nurse.

Holly turned to her. "Thanks, Marjorie. We'll be fine now."

After the door closed, Holly poured a cup of tea and handed it to Uncle Nikko. He turned his head, refusing to look at the mug. How could she get him to drink it?

She set the tea back on the tray. "Who finds you, Uncle Nikko?" She kept her voice gentle and reassuring as she stepped around him and sat on his bed, where she could be at eye level with him in his wheelchair.

"They come in my dreams. They know what I've done. They want to kill me. But if I die, all is lost."

Holly's heart ached. Her dear uncle had been her spiritual mentor and guide all her life. Losing him would be like dropping the last line that held her firm to the dock, allowing the wind and waves to buffet her. She searched for a way to comfort him the way he had been there for her all those years.

"Uncle Nikko, in Christ Jesus you are clean, washed as white as snow. This you know and have known. Say it with me, for God so loved the world that he ..." she waited for him to pick up the familiar verse.

"... gave his only begotten son, that whosoever believeth in Him ..."

They finished together. "... should not perish but have eternal life."

"Do you believe this?" Her young green eyes held his old gray ones, waiting. "Do you, Uncle Nikko?"

For a moment, his eyes focused, and the man she knew and loved was with her. "Yes, Holly. Yes I do."

Holly stood and helped him from his wheelchair into bed. He lay back with an exhausted groan. She patted his arm. She handed him the mug of tea. He hesitated for a moment. Her heart quickened. Then breathing a sigh, he started to sip the tea.

"I'll read to you till you're asleep, Uncle Nikko." She pulled up a bedside chair and placed his worn black Bible on her lap. "What would you like to hear?"

"This week's Torah portion."

She paused for a moment, recalling the order of the readings, then pulled his Bible to her. *"Acharei Mot?"*

"Yes, After the Death." He nodded, his eyelids dropping shut.

Holly lifted the Bible and began to read. "The Lord spoke to Moses after the death of the two sons of Aaron who died when they approached the Lord. The Lord said to Moses, 'Tell your brother Aaron not to come whenever he chooses into the Most Holy Place behind the curtain in front of the atonement cover on the ark, or else he will die, because I appear in the cloud over the atonement cover. This is how Aaron is to enter the sanctuary area ...'"

Her voice carried strong and true as she read the story of when God gave the nation of Israel their day of atonement. She glanced often at her uncle, waiting to see if he dozed off. By the time she reached the end of chapter twenty, his breathing became steady and deep, gentle rumblings confirming that he finally slept. She slipped the journal from under his hand and placed it back on his bedside table. Pulling the covers up over his shoulders, she kissed his forehead. "Good night, Uncle Nikko. May your dreams be sweet."

Salt air filled Holly's lungs and lifted her hair as she pushed open the thick glass doors and emerged from Hibiscus House. A stunning day greeted her. She turned her face to the ocean breeze and inhaled the tang from the bay, pausing for a moment to enjoy the bay below her. The moored boats all pointed north, their bows facing the incoming tide, like pigeons on a phone line with their beaks to the wind. In the distance, a sailboat glided past Morro Rock. She was familiar with most of the boats in the harbor and didn't recognize the large cutter rig. She paused to watch its crew hoist the sails. As each of the white triangles reached toward the sky, it snapped before catching the wind. With all three sails deployed, the big, dark-hulled boat heeled over, shouldered into the building swell, and surged toward the deep blue Pacific.

Holly felt the temptation to abandon the rest of the day and take out her own nineteen-foot West Wight Potter. The challenges of sailing a small boat in a good stiff breeze for a few hours would provide her with the brief illusion that she hadn't lost control of her destiny. That somehow she could hold Uncle Nikko here with her, just a bit longer, just until she was ready to be alone.

Turning away from the sea, Holly headed for her car, parked, by intent, two blocks down the street from the senior residence. The distance allowed her time to transition from the concerns about her Uncle

Nikko to those of her real estate business. Her Honda Accord glistened in the sun, even from this far away. She admired its sleek lines and pristine condition. She had worked hard to pay it off, another goal achieved. All this success should be enough, but it wasn't. Tendrils of loneliness clutched her heart. Her pace slowed, and the car's gleam blurred in her tears. Soon her precious Uncle Nikko would be gone. She could see him fading with every visit she made. When he passed, then ...

She allowed the tears to run free, destroying her makeup, but she didn't care.

It's not fair! Her emotions exploded. His body was healthy for his age, but his mind was succumbing to a slow, agonizing death. She wanted to fight back, but against what?

A trash truck rumbled down the street toward her. She squared her shoulders and turned her face away, pretending to enjoy the view of the harbor. When it passed, she sniffed, dabbed her eyes with a tissue from her skirt pocket, and shook her head in anger. "I'm tougher than this," she mumbled into the tissue as she blew her nose.

Forcing her mind away from her emotions, she turned her thoughts to the distractions of business. Tomorrow she had an appointment to show property to a new pastor in town, and she had a few details left to take care of. Although they had corresponded by e-mail for two weeks, she had yet to meet him. His pre-approval letter sat on her desk, ready to accompany the offer she expected to write for him this week. But how could a pastor of such a small church in Morro Bay afford a six-hundred-and-fifty-thousand-dollar house? She looked forward to meeting him and finding out where all that money came from.

Reaching her car, Holly plucked an errant leaf from the windshield before climbing in. She scooped up yesterday's unopened mail from the passenger seat and flipped over the first envelope. The return address told her it contained a letter from her attorney. Not what she wanted to read right now. She sighed and moved it to the back of the stack. The next envelope was larger than the rest. She slipped a painted nail beneath the flap and drew a heavily embossed greeting card from the envelope.

Inside, in concise block print, it read:

Dear Holly,

I just wanted to let you know how much I enjoyed our dinner together. Looking forward to many more.

A.J.

As her fingers traced the embossed rose on the front of the card, the memory of her dinner date last week gradually lifted her spirits. A.J.'s precise note told her he intended to turn up the heat on their relationship.   Did she mind? Was this the next chapter in her life? He made her feel like a sleek and sexy sports car. All curves and shimmer. Instead of the carefully crafted professional she presented to the world. She tucked the card in her purse and turned her attention to the rest of the mail. Glancing through the various advertisements and assorted bills, her hand stopped at a white envelope with no return address. She turned it over. The back was also blank. Curious, she slit it open and removed a single sheet of paper.

One typed line sprung from the page:

Bring your checkbook Wednesday.

The sheet trembled in her fingers. She dropped the note and set her hands on the steering wheel to steady them. Were the stakes truly that high? Blinking, she picked up the note and without looking at it again, slipped it back into the envelope. The court date for the Mitchell's lawsuit crept closer with each passing day, and her dread increased every moment she thought about it. Now this. Next Wednesday all the parties met for the mediation, and someone wanted to play hardball. Holly picked up the envelope from her lap and ripped it in two.

Chapter Two

Across town, seagulls circled the steeple of Mariner's Chapel. The aging church perched on a low hill overlooking the Morro Bay. The sun was just breaking through the morning fog as the congregation trickled out the door and down the steps to the parking lot beyond.

"Great sermon, Pastor." The old man's hand clutched the head of his cane as he stepped into the sun.

"Thanks, Charlie." Brady McGregor patted Charlie's shoulder, where his blue flannel shirt draped over what had once been a strong, broad back. The cancer was slowly taking its toll.

Folks like Charlie made this Sunday ritual bearable. He didn't require much personal interaction, and that's how Brady liked it. For the last three months, he had played his role as pastor, guiding the small flock in the little white church with a practiced hand. Everyone had been thrilled when he agreed to take the position. For them, he was a dream come true. For him, Mariners Chapel was simply a place to land, regroup, and recover.

Today, though, something seemed off. Two people had left without shaking his hand, not bothering with the after church meet-and-greet. Somehow, folks were a bit less friendly. Disconnected. Maybe the honeymoon had come to an end.

Makes my job just that much easier, he lied to himself. Deep down, this unaccustomed rebuff from his flock stung at a level he didn't think was alive anymore.

Charlie winked and Brady grinned. "Now Charlie, I know I saw you nodding off before I finished my first point."

"Never did such a thing." Charlie enjoyed the weekly joke. He steadied himself and shuffled over to the steps leading down toward the parking lot. The railing wiggled as it took his weight. Brady's pulse quickened for a moment, making a mental note to reinforce the railing— again. Dry rot, another kind of cancer, slowly ate away at the ancient building. He hoped there would be some good wood left to tie into.

Watching to be sure Charlie could negotiate the stairs, he reached out automatically for the next person to his right.

"Pastor Brady?"

Brady turned to greet one of his elders, giving a firm clasp to his rugged, tanned hand. "Hello, Arlen, going sailing this afternoon? Seems we have the wind for it."

Arlen glanced toward the ocean in the distance and shook his head. "Not today, Pastor. I have other plans."

"I can't believe you are going to pass up such a fine sailing day."

"Business before pleasure, Pastor, it's the story of my life. When do I get the chance to take you out? You've missed some fine sailing since you've been here."

"All in good time, Arlen. All in good time.

"If I didn't know better, I'd think you were afraid of the water." Arlen laughed and slapped Brady's shoulder before trotting down the steps. He strode into the small knot of people on the lawn, his head rising above the crowd, his Hollywood smile flashing.

A gloved hand slipped into Brady's. He turned to greet the church's prim, petite bookkeeper, Evelyn Davenport, her turquoise and burgundy scarf tucked in around the collar of her overcoat. "Evelyn, good to see you today." Then, "Cheri," he said, nodding to acknowledge the younger woman at Evelyn's elbow.

"Quite a blustery day we seem to be having." The comment followed the pattern of those before and after with mind-numbing regularity.

Don't these people have anything better to talk about than the weather?

Brady maintained his plastic grin and endured, turning his attention to Evelyn's daughter. "Are we still on for our meeting this afternoon, Cheri?"

Evelyn turned to face her daughter, eyebrows arched under stiffly-sprayed bangs. "What meeting?"

Cheri's eyes darted from one to the other. "Yes... yes, Pastor, this afternoon at two." Her eyes darted in her mother's direction and then back at Brady again. The wind whipped her long auburn hair across her face, a look in her eyes holding his. As her mother pulled her around toward the stairs, Cheri glanced back over her shoulder at Brady. A gesture speaking volumes that Brady couldn't translate. He lifted a hand. Cheri responded with the slightest of nods, and then they slipped around the corner and out of sight.

Brady paused briefly outside the door as the last of his congregation filtered through the parking lot and climbed into their cars. A couple held hands as their children darted up the sidewalk. For a heartbeat of time, his own loss surfaced, stinging his eyes before he forced the feelings back into the little dark place where they lurked.

Running a hand through his thick black hair, he turned back into the church. Pulling the double wooden doors shut, he locked them with a big, ancient key, the metal cool in his palm. He hefted it, weighing its legacy. This key had locked these doors for almost one hundred years. The salt air from the Pacific Ocean had played havoc with the mechanism over time, but skilled members of the little church had fought back, repairing the damage again and again. Men of the sea had established the church many years ago, and men of the sea still worshiped here each Sunday. But that legacy was passing. The church needed new blood and it was now his job to infuse it with new life.

Brady's steps clicked on the worn hardwood floor. Sunlight streamed in the eastern windows bathing the aging church in a mantle of gold. The wooden pews gleamed beneath their new application of lemon oil, lovingly applied by the women's guild. Brady had forgotten to thank Evelyn and Cheri for their hard work in completing the process in time for church today. He made a mental note to thank Cheri at their meeting this afternoon.

He gathered his sermon notes from the simple pine pulpit. Pausing, he looked out at the empty pews. He drew a breath from deep within himself as unwelcome memories flitted at the edge of his thoughts. He lifted his chin and relaxed. For a moment this stage was larger, the lights were brighter and the congregation entranced. Then his jaw tightened. He tapped the papers once on the pulpit and slowly headed to his office.

Brady glanced at the clock again, two-twenty. Cheri was late. He rubbed his face with both hands. The frustration building, he had to keep the lid on. He remembered as a boy waiting with his folks for Old Faithful to blow, feeling the ground rumble and then the release as thousands of gallons of scalding water shot into the air. He could identify. In the not-too-distant past, an appointment with him would have been scheduled days if not weeks in advance. He wasn't accustomed to being stood up.

Get a grip. That was then, this is now.

The subtle snubbing he received this morning still grated. He deserved it. His heart wasn't in the sermon and the church knew it. They had cut him some slack over the past three months, but he was running out of rope. They deserved better.

So did Karen and Jeremy. *You let them down, too.*

The harsh words stung—needle sharp and accusing. The pain jolted him. He acknowledged the possibility that his ministry here was over before it began. Or had it ever truly begun? His lack of personal conviction left his Sunday messages flat as a popped balloon, full of spit but no bounce. When the pastoral search committee interviewed him, Brady had chosen not to share his inability to come up with any new material for sermons since his wife's death. He hardly admitted it to himself. In a pinch he knew he could still deliver, maybe. He had years of material to draw from. What was the rush?

No rush, just a commitment you made. Another broken promise.

How easy it would be to grab his coat, and go … where? He looked over at his windbreaker hanging on the back of the door. Go where, do what? That was the kicker. He didn't know any other life, and he hated the one he was living.

Brady glanced at the clock again. Five more minutes had passed. The church secretary, Vera Shankston, sat in the outer office, counting the offering and preparing the deposit.

"Vera, have you heard from Cheri?" He called through the doorway.

"Not a word, Pastor McGregor." Vera responded from the next room. "No surprise, though. She's always been a bit on the unreliable side, if you ask me."

The fact that Brady hadn't, and never would have asked didn't seem to bother her. He went to the door, his nails digging into his palm. Forcing the edge from his voice, he said. "Would you mind calling her house to see if she's been delayed somehow?" Turning, he resisted slamming the door as he returned to his desk.

Twenty minutes later Brady again poked his head from his office to find no evidence of Cheri. "Vera, did you call Cheri's house to check on her?" The young woman's haunted look this morning was slowly melting his anger, revealing a building concern for her welfare.

"No, Pastor," Vera replied. "I don't have her new number."

That would have been nice to know half an hour ago. Brady set his jaw, vowing to hold his temper.

Five minutes later Brady heard the side door open and glanced one more time at the clock, two fifty. His anger rose again like fire in his throat. He dialed it back to a simmer and went to greet Cheri.

Dressed in an oversized sweatshirt and jeans, she appeared younger than her twenty-four years. Brady reached out a hand in greeting. She hesitated, meeting Brady's eyes before accepting his handshake. He escorted her into his office, leaving the door open a few inches for propriety's sake, and took a seat. Cheri perched on the edge of the chair, her clasped hands wedged down between her thighs.

"So, Cheri, how can I help you today?"

She hesitated, looking around the room before her eyes came to rest on Brady. "Um, I'm not sure this is such a good idea." She started to rise.

Brady raised a hand to calm her. "I'm just here to listen, Cheri. What is said in this room stays in this room." He settled back in his chair to give her the illusion of more space.

Her eyes flicked to the open doorway. "How much do you know about me, Pastor Brady?"

"Very little, really. You're Evelyn's daughter, and I believe you are just back from college. Do I have that right?"

"In a nutshell."

The clock on Brady's desk ticked off the seconds. He forced himself to relax, slowing his breathing and smiling encouragement. Waiting for her to continue.

She didn't.

"So, did something happen at college that you want to talk about?"

She shook her head and looked down, her small hands now twisting a knot in her sweatshirt.

"Something since you got home?"

She nodded and sniffed, wiping her nose on her sleeve.

Brady resisted the urge to push. He shifted in his seat and uncrossed his legs, then leaned forward, clasping his hands over his knees. "Cheri, I can't help you if you don't talk to me." A slight edge crept into his voice in spite of his efforts. He heard it and winced.

She looked up then. Her eyes red, but no tears dampened her cheeks.

"I'm not sure now that I should." She didn't look away this time, her eyes telling him she wanted to talk, desperately.

"How about giving it a try?"

Another few seconds of silence passed.

"Okay. So, do you believe there is an unforgivable sin?"

Brady leaned back again, relieved that some kind of dialog had begun. "Yes, I do."

"What is it?"

"I've heard several approaches to that question." He crossed his legs, finally getting comfortable with the direction of the conversation. "Although lots of people have put forth theories, it is a hard concept to nail down. Unrepented sin is, some say, the unforgivable sin. If you confess a sin and don't do it again, then you are forgiven. God has said it, and His word is good. Having said that, one thing seems clear— for all intents and purposes, the sin is unforgivable because—

"Don't patronize me," she whispered, her voice tear-laden, the knot on her sweatshirt getting tighter.

The words whipped him. Karen had said the same thing that fateful night two years ago. She strode across their living room in Wyoming telling him he had lost his way, lost his ministry. The topic, a recurring theme in their marriage, had escalated during those last few weeks. He had tried to explain how the ministry had evolved. The church was growing at an unprecedented rate, and he was keeping up with that growth.

"Karen, I'm sorry."

"My name is Cheri."

He startled, his internal eyes coming back to the present.

"Of course, Cheri." He shook himself away from his last argument with Karen and refocused. "I'm trying to explain the theology behind—"

"Just talk to me." She snatched a tissue from the box beside her chair and dabbed her nose. "Theological discussion is for seminary. This is my life." She blew her nose, and wadded the tissue into her fist.

Brady was at a loss—a familiar feeling. His discussions with Karen had taken a similar path. He tried to begin again. "The concept of unforgivable sin has been discussed at length—"

"I'm not interested in discussing it *at length*. Just tell me what it is."

"Most people hold the position that..."

She bolted to her feet, hands clenched in tight little balls at her waist. "You just don't get it! I don't want high-brow theology. I want the bottom line." She grabbed her keys and her purse from the back of the chair.

"Cheri, don't go. Give me a chance."

"You've had your chance, now I'm going to take mine." The tears finally broke free and ran in sheets down her cheeks.

Brady stood, his palm up and open. "Cheri, let me . . ."

But she was gone.

Chapter Three

"Ahem."

Startled, Brady turned to see Arlen Parkfield standing in his office doorway. Forty-five minutes had passed since Cheri stormed out.

Dressed casually in an animal-emblazoned shirt and shorts, a pair of sunglasses rested in his thick brown hair, he looked every bit the successful contractor that he was.

"Hello, Arlen, good to see you again." Brady stood and thrust out his hand in welcome, trying to force the irritation from his voice. Vera had apparently forgotten to lock the door behind her when she left.

"Sorry to barge in this way, Pastor Brady, but I saw your Lexus in the parking lot and hoped you would have a moment to talk."

"Of course I have time, Arlen. Have a seat." He motioned toward the chair where Cheri had been sitting.

Arlen sat forward, then leaned back in his chair and pulled the sunglasses from his head, twirling them in his fingers. "I'm not real sure how to go about this, Pastor, so I'll just jump in. Some of the folks in the church had some concerns today, and they asked me to come and talk to you." The sunglasses stopped twirling. "I probably should have made an appointment."

"Not at all, Arlen. My door's always open. You know that."

"Well, that's the thing, Pastor Brady. Folks are feeling a bit put off."

"Put off, how so...?"

Arlen ran his fingers through his hair and then replaced the sunglasses. "You and I get on all right, Brady, but some folks feel like you are hard to talk to. We all know you came from a big church, with lots of money and—"

"We went through all that when I took the job, Arlen." Brady sank back in his chair and steepled his fingers.

"You and I talked about it and so did the other elders. But some folks still don't understand why you left that big church in Wyoming for our little church here in Morro Bay. They aren't sure you are comfortable with our small congregation."

"Comfortable?"

"Well, perhaps *connecting* would be a better word."

"Okay . . . " Brady shifted forward. "Then what do you suggest I do?"

Arlen stood and walked to the one small double hung window in the office. He twitched back the curtain and peered into the afternoon light. Then he turned to Brady and rested a hip on the windowsill. "One of the issues that came up was that you never accept lunch invitations after service. It hurts feelings, Brady."

Lunch? I don't think so...

Arlen sat back. "I can see by your face that the idea doesn't sit well. Lunch with the pastor is a big deal for us, and such a small thing for you to do. Spending some one-on-one time with folks would go a long way toward breaking down some barriers."

Brady started to drum his fingers on his desk then stopped himself. "I hadn't realized." He eyed his windbreaker again, and glanced out the window at the waning afternoon sun.

"I know you didn't, Brady. But you have to remember that you intimidate some people. Maybe you could start a men's breakfast or maybe a Wednesday night Bible study. Kinda get to know folks."

Just the thought of doing that exhausted Brady. Making nice and discussing all the same old questions. Been there, done that. Not interested.

"Now I know that we don't pay you a whole lot—"

"Money isn't the issue, Arlen. I made that clear when we first started talking about my coming here. As I told you before, I left Wyoming for Morro Bay to get my feet back under me after the ... the accident. I'm fully prepared to pastor this church, and I'm open to any and all suggestions."

"You know all about pastoring, Brady. Lord knows you've had great success before. I don't mean to tell you how to do your job."

Even though you are. Brady forced himself to take a deep breath and lean back into his chair. "No, no, your advice is well taken, Arlen. How about we meet again after church next Sunday—for lunch." He winked, hoping to ease the tension.

Brady liked Arlen. The two men had instantly connected when they met. Unfortunately, the whole issue with Cheri had left him edgy today. "We'll talk about some programs. If you want to invite some of the other men along, it will be on me."

Arlen stood, and the two men shook hands. "I knew you would see where I was coming from, Pastor Brady. Thanks for taking time with me."

Brady shut the door behind Arlen and sat in silence, processing the conversation. A heavy mantle settled over him, pressing down on his soul and making him weary beyond words. He knew exactly what Arlen was talking about. Out of habit, he started to pray, but the words evaporated before they left his heart.

Coming to Morro Bay had been an easy decision. He knew the church was a small, struggling congregation. They needed his skills, and he needed a place to heal from his loss. Guiding Mariners Chapel should have been simple—preach on Sunday, be nice to the old ladies, visit the sick, and bury the dead. Simple.

But there was nothing simple about it. He was back among the people, not shielded by assistant pastors of this and that. This little congregation expected their pastor to be led by the Holy Spirit, his sermons prayerfully considered, and not rehashed from another church, another time.

Brady's Bible lay untouched at his elbow—the cover cracked and the pages curled from years of use. Today, a layer of dust frosted its surface, stark witness to his broken relationship with its Author. Karen had given it to him on the anniversary of their first date. He opened the cover to read her inscription on the inside, tracing her words with his finger as he read.

"To my dearest Brady. May God continue to work great things in your life through His Word." Those words from God had once given him a purpose, a direction in life. Now he couldn't read them. He couldn't even open the book. His life had become a shadow thing, thin and insubstantial. He should feel something but all he felt was ashes.

He wiped away the dust so no one would suspect the truth, realizing as he did that the truth might already be out.

There had been a time when he would pray through the week as he prepared his sermon, following the Spirit's prompting, and lifting hearts with the words he had been given. He had been closely connected with the people back then, feeling their pulse as clearly as he felt his own. The church had exploded. On the advice of his staff, he was gradually removed from the day-to-day needs of the congregation so he could focus on his Sunday sermons. His world had become a cocoon of staff and the most important people.

Brady looked out the window at a cloudless blue sky. In the distance, fragrant eucalyptus trees danced on the ocean breeze. The walls of his small office seemed to be leaning in, crowding the already confined space. He grabbed his jacket, locked the door, and headed out into the brisk late afternoon sun.

Chapter Four

Brady's stomach burned from the aspirin he had taken for a headache—brought on from a night of pacing the confines of his cramped bungalow. This morning, his frustrating conversation with Arlen mixed with Cheri's outrage still spun together in a swirling tangle of thoughts. He knew what he needed to do. He knew his job. But something deep within him resisted. His jaw tightened at the thought of lunch with a bunch of men next Sunday. Arlen had deftly maneuvered him into that. But did he really? Or did he only point out the truth? Brady knew he had done the right thing by making the offer, but now he felt trapped. And angry.

He checked the time on his Rolex wristwatch. The realtor he'd been corresponding with was due any minute. Vera and Yosef Shankston's backyard rental had been a simple solution when he first arrived, but Brady needed his own space.

As he entered the narrow hallway leading from the sanctuary to his office, he saw Vera chatting with an attractive woman, her cinnamon hair catching the sun. He paused for a moment and observed her, struck by her simple beauty. Abundant curls tumbled to her shoulders, errant wisps framing her face. He didn't know what he had expected Holly Fain to look like, but her simple beauty caught him by surprise. He gathered himself and entered the church office, smiling at Holly as he reached out his hand.

"Pastor, this is Holly Fain. She says she has an appointment with you?" Vera raised an eyebrow.

Brady didn't hear her. His world had closed in on the small cool hand in his.

"I didn't have this appointment on your schedule, Pastor Brady." Vera liked knowing his schedule down to the smallest detail—an aspect of her personality Brady was determined to help her overcome.

"Hello, Holly. Nice to meet you in person." His large hand had engulfed her smaller one, their brief touch leaving a warm tingle in his palm. He closed his fist, trying to hold the feeling a moment longer and knowing at the same time that he should let it go.

"Please to meet you, ah, Pastor." Holly glanced between Vera and Brady, her green eyes twinkling.

20

"Brady is fine." Maybe this wouldn't be as tedious as he first thought. A little humor would go a long way in his life right now.

Holly pulled a folder from under her arm. Extracting a stack of stapled papers, she handed them to him. "I've arranged for us to see six of the homes you selected from those I sent over the past week. Four are short sales and two are owner occupied." She closed the folder and tucked it back under her arm. "One of the homes you selected went into escrow yesterday, but another came on the market, so I added it to the list. I think you will like it."

"I appreciate that, Holly. Shall we?" He motioned her to the door, his hand gently at the small of her back as he escorted her out. "I look forward to finding something. Vera and her husband have provided their guest bungalow behind their house." He held the door for her to pass through. "But I'm ready for something of my own. And they're probably ready for me to move on, too." As she stepped past, he caught the slightest whiff of her fragrance, island spices with a hint of gardenia.

"To be frank, I don't like this process much. I'd like to wrap this up as soon as I can so I can focus on my work here." Their shoes crunched on the graveled path leading to the parking lot.

"I'll make it as painless as possible, Brady." The top of her head barely rose to his shoulder. She moved with confidence, her tailored beige suit lending professionalism to her petite frame. Holly looked up at the little white church and Brady followed her gaze. The whitewashed walls, peeling here and there, rose three stories to the steeple, bright against the blue sky. "This is a lovely old church. I've admired it for years,"

"Some of the families have worshiped here for generations. I'm honored that they invited me to be their pastor."

Liar.

Holly punched her key fob, unlocking the doors to the Honda. "How many people attend?"

"Oh, I'd say we have about twenty-five active families. They're a very close-knit bunch. Where do you worship, Holly?" Brady slid into his seat, moving it back to accommodate his long frame.

"That's a very pastor-like question." She laughed, rolling her eyes as she started the car. "How long have you been in Morro Bay?"

She had dodged the question; he was intrigued. "I've been here for three months."

"And you came from…?"

"I came from a church in Wyoming. I pastored there for twelve years."

"What prompted the change?"

Brady didn't respond. The question hung in the air.

Holly drove toward the ocean. In the distance, Morro Rock wore a mantle of fog that shrouded its craggy back. Beyond it, the ocean was brilliant blue. Puffy clouds hung in the bright sky.

Brady rolled down his window, enjoying the fresh air and searching for a safe topic. "That rock is amazing. Is it volcanic?"

"Yes, it is. Juan Rodriquez Cabrillo named it in the sixteenth century. The rock and the whole bay looked quite a bit different back then. I've seen early pictures of it. Morro Rock itself was much larger and symmetrical. And the causeway leading out to the rock wasn't there at all. Quarrying did a lot of damage in the nineteen hundreds."

He turned to her, surprised. "Someone was actually allowed to quarry it?"

"I know. It's hard to believe. Back then, California wasn't as protective of the coastline. They used some of the stone to build houses, and quite a bit was used in building the breakwater here and in Avila Bay."

Brady smiled at her. "You sound like a practiced tour guide."

"I show quite a few homes to people from out of the area. I guess I'm rather proud of Morro Bay. It's been a great place to grow up." She guided her car to the curb. "Here's our first house."

They got out and followed the cement entryway up to the house. Holly checked both sides of the front door and then leaned down into a large bush, coming up with the key to the house. A leaf clung to her hair as she emerged. Brady chuckled. She looked puzzled, missing the joke. He pointed at her hair, and Holly felt around until her hand touched the leaf.

"Eeek!" She brushed the leaf away with both hands, dropping her folder, and her keys. Her thick mane of hair flashed in the sunlight.

"Easy, it's just a leaf." He laid a hand on her shoulder to settle her, and then carefully removed the rest of the leaf from her hair.

"I thought it was a spider. I hate spiders. I just know that one day when I have to dive into the bushes to retrieve a key, I'm going to get one right down my back." She shuddered. "I don't know why agents have to put lock boxes in such ridiculous places." She brushed off her arms and shoulders one more time as Brady retrieved her folder and keys from the ground.

She stepped past him to the front door, her cheeks flushed and her breathing a bit labored. Brady thought she looked stunning.

Holly knocked, inserted the key, stepped aside, and invited Brady in with a wave of her hand.

Brady immediately hated the floor plan. As he entered, a long flight of stairs ahead of him led to the second story, with the garage and two bedrooms downstairs. Upstairs had just a peek of the ocean from the deck through telephone wires. The kitchen was simple, with composite granite countertops and stainless steel low-end appliances. The master bedroom looked out over the neighbors' rooftops.

Brady crossed the small living room and looked out the window toward the ocean.

"I was hoping for a bit more view."

"We're just starting," she cocked her head and winked at him with a grin tugging the corner of her lips. "Your feedback is helpful. The more houses we see, the more I will understand what it is you're looking for. Let's head to the next one." Holly scribbled a note in the file and then led the way downstairs.

The next home they visited was farther up the hill, away from the ocean. Tenants occupied it, and the word tidy was apparently not in their vocabulary. One room, a teenager's nest, reeked of marijuana. Holly and Brady both rolled their eyes and left without seeing anything more there.

On the way to the third house, Holly filled Brady in on the colorful politics of the town. "Everyone has an opinion in Morro Bay. If the council wants to put in a stop sign, you have twenty people for it and twenty people against it. Keeps things interesting." She flashed a practiced smile over at him.

Her easygoing manner made this tedious task a bit easier. He wasn't looking for a home, he was looking for a place with an address that provided privacy and a place to work. He had left his real home in Wyoming, that chapter of his life was closed—permanently.

The third house was north of Morro Rock and didn't have a view. However, being across the street from the beach was in its favor. The ocean's constant murmur provided a soothing melody as they stood on the back patio. Terra-cotta pots filled with lush palms and blooming hibiscus gave the little yard a tropical feel. Brady liked it, but Holly pointed out that the roof shingles curled and termite damage had shredded the rafter tails and extended up into the attic. They rapidly moved through the interior of the house. The owners had closed all the blinds, and cigarette smoke permeated every room.

Brady breathed in the fresh salt air as they emerged. "Money sure doesn't go very far in this market, even in these times."

Holly replaced the house key in the lock box, brushing more leaves from her jacket. "The closer you are to the ocean the higher the price."

He stood in the street, looking up and down for any more real estate signs. He liked the neighborhood. "And if you can actually see it, the price is double, I'd guess."

"You're getting the picture."

With his bank account flush from the sale of his house in Wyoming and the settlement from the accident, Brady thought he could find something comfortable near the ocean. Their home in Wyoming had been palatial compared to what he was seeing today. Karen had kept it welcoming and comfortable, ready for guests to drop in at any moment. His private office looked out over the Medicine Bow Range. Watching the seasons settle onto the mountains had inspired him over the years. He had hoped for a similar setting here in Morro Bay. So far, he was disappointed.

"I feel like I'm being a bit pickier than I led you to believe, Holly."

Her green eyes twinkled. "Don't worry; homes are coming on the market every day. If we don't find the home you want today, we'll just keep looking."

Back in the car, Brady noticed again the light fragrance Holly wore. The floral tones helped clear the rest of the acrid cigarette smoke from his nose, but it also resurrected unwanted memories of happier times. House hunting was proving to be a painful process. Memories haunted him today, memories best left buried. Perhaps he should have chosen a man as his agent. But of all the e-mails he had sent out, Holly had been the only agent who had responded consistently. She obviously was professional and took her work seriously.

The fourth and fifth houses were on a busy street. The traffic noise was a distraction from otherwise wonderful ocean views. Finally, they headed to the last house on the tour. The single-story structure was located at the south end of Morro Bay on a quiet road that wound up through a stand of eucalyptus trees. Holly made a left into a short cul-de-sac where several boys shot baskets into a portable hoop. Pulling up to the house, Brady's interest was piqued.

He could tell that the rear of the cedar-shingled house had an unobstructed view of the bay framed by huge eucalyptus trees. As he walked in the entry, a sense of calm settled on him. Someone obviously loved this house. Looking through into the living room, he could see a bank of windows offered a spectacular view of the sand spit to the south and Morro Rock to the north. In the distant haze, the coastline wound north toward Cayucos. The home was small and older than the others, but he could see that attention to detail was evident in every room. The ceilings were coffered, with progressively darker shades of color making them seem high and spacious. He strolled out the French doors that led to a back yard. Lush and fragrant blooms greeted him. It would be a wonderful place to sit and watch the sunsets. Back inside, terrazzo tiles, accented by dark woods and rattan touches gave a Mediterranean feel. Curtains at the open windows danced in the gentle breeze. The kitchen had recently been updated without losing its charm. Old world ambiance mixed with modern functionality. Perfect.

Chapter Five

Bingo. Holly told herself as she watched a transformation take place in Brady. He hadn't lingered in any of the other homes, moving through each of them quickly and decisively. This one he savored, a little twinkle dancing in his deep brown eyes. She allowed him to go through the process without her intervention, having learned over the years to read her clients. When she detected buying signals, she got out of the way and allowed the buyers to realize that they had found their new home.

Holly dropped her business card on the kitchen counter. *Time to ask the big question.*

"You seem to like this one, Brady."

"I do. This house seems to have everything I'm looking for. The kitchen is a bit small . . . but I really don't need much." He opened the French doors leading to the back yard but didn't step out.

"Do you like it enough to make an offer?" *The most important question of the day.*

He took one more long look at the back yard then closed the double doors and locked them. "No, I'd like to see what else comes on the market this week before I decide."

Big mistake, Pastor.

"You're aware that it may be gone by then." She kept her voice casual, as if she didn't care, one finger slowly organizing the realtor's cards strewn across the kitchen counter. They told the story. The house had been on the market for twenty-four hours and had already been shown, seven times.

"I'll take that chance."

"I'm sorry to seem pushy, Brady. I just want you to keep in mind that the best homes sell very fast, even in this market. I'd hate to see you miss the right house for you." Her years in the business told her they stood in that house.

"I understand the risk. I just want to give it some time. I like the house well enough, but I have always been cautious with money, and this is a lot of money." His eyes held just a heartbeat longer than necessary.

Holly's heart gave a little jump. *Stay on task.*

She watched as he turned a full circle again, taking in the view, the kitchen, the living room, and finally back to her. "This house does have everything I want. I'll give it some serious thought."

"I understand." *Think all you want. This house probably won't be available tomorrow.* "I'll keep an eye on this one for you, and we'll see what else comes up this week."

After dropping off Brady at the church, Holly headed back to her office, frustrated, of course, but not really surprised. She had a sixth sense when it came to buyers. Brady was cautious, unlikely to make a quick decision. She suspected it was going to bite him this time. That last house had been priced to sell, and even in a depressed market, the best houses sold the quickest because they were the best houses.

Inside the office, she picked up her messages from the receptionist and sorted through them on her way to her private cubicle.

"Oh, great!" She slapped the message she just read against her thigh.

"What?" Roy Simpson, the new guy in the office, called from the next cubicle.

"My escrow on Sienna Street just tanked." Holly slumped down into her chair and took a long drink from her water bottle.

"That was the only thing you had going, wasn't it?" Roy strolled around the corner munching on a Snickers bar, his shirt untucked as usual.

"You're so right. This month is going to kill me. That's the second escrow I've lost in as many weeks. I'm going to have to apply for food stamps if this keeps up." She reached for a hard candy in the bowl on her desk. Holly had been living on her savings for the past three months. She would have to close an escrow, soon.

"Didn't you just get back from a showing?"

"Yes, a new pastor in town. I showed him the house on Cerrito Place. I think it's the right house for him, but he's not ready to make an offer. I saw tons of cards on the counter."

"I know that house; I showed it yesterday. The price is right for the market. I don't think it will last the week."

"I told him that, but you know how it is. Nobody trusts realtors or used car salesmen."

"He'll find out. Some people have to lose the one they really want before they believe you."

"True. But in the meantime, I have to figure out how to make my *own* mortgage. By the way, have you seen Cheri? The pastor was a referral from her, and I want to thank her."

"She should be in tomorrow to pick up the accounting books and write checks. I'll tell her you're looking for her."

"Thanks, Roy."

Holly dropped her purse on the floor and settled in front of her computer screen with a sigh. Real estate could be a brutal business. Customers gave their trust sparingly and their loyalty rarely. She never calculated what she made an hour. The amount would be too discouraging when sales slowed and too self-serving when the market turned hot.

Uncle Nikko had frowned on her pursuing such a capricious career, but for Holly it was a perfect fit. Now, four years into it, she had three top producer awards on her wall and a promise of a corner office. But when the market shifted, the buyers evaporated and her savings along with them. Having Brady in the car today had encouraged her. But more than that, she had enjoyed his company. She hadn't expected him to be … what? Good looking? Charming? Fun to be with? Their email exchanges had been businesslike, and she had pictured an older man, more fatherly. Brady seemed anything but fatherly. The word *hunk* fit him better. She chuckled. *That's so high school.*

The following morning, Holly stopped by Hibiscus House to visit her uncle. She took a deep breath before pushing the heavy doors that opened into the sun-bathed reception area. She paused to let the soft music drifting up from speakers in the atrium sooth her. The care facility maintained a tranquil atmosphere, dotted with lush ferns and bird of paradise. Signature hibiscus overflowed from massive clay pots. The receptionist greeted her as Holly turned down the hallway in search of her uncle. Not finding him in his usual location by the window, she made a quick check of his room. The bed was freshly made and the room tidy, and empty. Puzzled, she looked up and down the hallway for one of the nurse's aides. Spying one she recognized, she approached the counter.

"Looking for your Uncle Nikko?" The aide pulled latex gloves off her plump hands with a pop.

"Have you seen him?"

"Try the recreation room."

"How has he been doing?"

"We started putting his medication in a cup of hot chocolate. Seems to be doing the trick." Her eyes softened. "He's been sleeping through the night."

The kindness the young aid displayed was a signature feature of this facility. It was more expensive than some others she had visited but the kindness her uncle received was well worth it. Relieved, Holly thanked her and headed for the recreation room at far end of the hallway.

Uncle Nikko sat in his wheelchair, writing in his ever-present journal. The reading light over his head made a soft halo of his thinning hair. Hearing her approach, he straightened and snapped the journal shut, tucking it next to his hip.

"There you are, Uncle Nikko." Her voice was gentle as she kissed the top of his head. "You're not sitting in the sunshine today."

He looked up at her, his heavy brows drawing down. "Who are you?" Suspicion hardened his face.

"I'm Holly, Uncle Nikko, Irma's daughter." She waited while the puzzle pieces dropped into place.

"Holly?"

"Yes, Holly."

"Good, it's good you are here. Come and sit." He jabbed a finger at the floral print couch in front of him. "I have to talk to you."

Holly sat and studied her uncle's damp, red-rimmed eyes. "Are you wearing your glasses, Uncle Nikko? Your eyes look tired."

"Never mind that." He brushed the words with a flick of his hand. "We have to talk."

"All right, let's talk."

"The nurses are trying to poison me. I'm writing it all down in my journal." He patted the red cover next to him. "They are putting something in my hot chocolate that makes it taste funny. I dump it out when they leave."

"Did you sleep last night, Uncle Nikko?"

He didn't like the question. "No, they find me when I sleep."

"Who finds you, Uncle Nikko?"

He glanced into the shadowed recesses of the large room. "They know what I did, Holly. I never should have done it, taken the money. I should have told someone."

"What money? You can tell me, Uncle Nikko."

"No, then they would find you, too." He shook his head. "I can't have them after you."

"Are you having bad dreams?"

He studied her, his breath rattling in his chest. "If I don't sleep, I don't dream."

"What did you do?" she pressed...

"What the eye doesn't see, the heart won't grieve over." His eyes locked with hers, willing her to understand.

Leaning forward, she rested a hand on his knee, feeling his bones through the afghan. "Did you do something you shouldn't have?"

"Yes."

"What?"

He pulled his red leather journal from beside him and laid it on his lap. His old hand, once strong and skilled, caressed its soft cover. "You'll know in time. By then, it won't matter."

Chapter Six

The drill was awkward in Brady's hand. He had spent most of the morning trying to strengthen the loose handrail at the front of the church. Carpentry was way down his list of skill sets. "Strictly ornamental," he would tell Karen, wiggling his fingers, when she asked him to perform a repair job around the house. But his circumstances had changed. The repair needed to be done, church funds were limited, and the work fell to him.

He set the last screw just as Evelyn marched down the sidewalk toward him. *What could she want?* He stood and wiped his hands on his jeans. "Hi, Evelyn. Beautiful day, isn't it?"

"Have you seen Cheri?" Her tone sharp, her face hard.

Brady felt his defenses rising. "Not since Sunday afternoon, why?"

She took a step closer. "You had a meeting with her, didn't you?"

Brady stood his ground, resisting the urge to take a step back. "Yes, I did."

"No one has seen her since. What did you say to her?"

"Our conversation is confidential, Evelyn. You know—"

"You must have said something that drove her away." Evelyn's insistent voice raised a level.

"We didn't get that far. Cheri seemed upset when she came in and didn't stay all that long." Brady ran through the conversation in his head. He knew their talk hadn't gone well. Could he somehow be responsible for her leaving town?

"You were the last person to see her. I've been all over town." She wrapped her arms around herself, looking up into the sanctuary and then back to Brady.

"Honestly, Evelyn, nothing transpired in our conversation that would drive Cheri away."

I hope.

"Did she tell you anything?"

"We had a very brief visit. She...well. Evelyn, I can't tell you what we said, I'm sorry. I'm sure you understand my position."

"No, I don't understand." She started to reach for his arm, but pulled back. The anger turning to fear. "My daughter is missing and you were the last person to talk to her. I want to know what you said to her."

"Again, I can't tell you. I'm sorry." He reached out to take her elbow, to comfort her.

She snatched her arm away and stepped back. "I don't think you are!" Her hands dropped to her sides and clenched into fists. "You know something. You're part of it. If something happens to Cheri you *will* be sorry, I'll see to it."

An hour later, the electronic doors of Sav-On Drug opened to admit Brady. Jessica looked up from behind the photo counter and smiled in acknowledgement. But before Brady could make his way over to her, he was waylaid by Sylvia Thorndyke, a tanker-sized woman in a voluminous muumuu resplendent with yellow orchids on a purple background. She swept up to him. "Pastor Brady, what a wonderful coincidence."

A pungent floral perfume made his eyes water as it enveloped him. "Hi, Sylvia." Brady extended his hand in greeting. Sylvia was one of the few parishioners he thoroughly enjoyed. Life was never boring in Sylvia's world.

She sandwiched his hand in her two smaller ones, her sausage fingers collared by several large rings. Then letting go and stepping back, she cleared her throat as she patted her hair, tucking a gray strand up into her tight chignon. "Well, Pastor Brady, it's a blessing I ran into you today. Do you have a moment?"

"Of course," Brady replied.

Sylvia visibly gathered herself and began. "The ladies at the Monday night Bible study have asked me to mention some things to you and seek your guidance."

"I'll help if I can." His eyes stung from her perfume as he tried to look attentive.

"Well, Pastor, well… this is a bit awkward you see. As a matter of fact, it's about Cheri."

Brady groaned inwardly. Cheri again.

"What about her?"

"I'll try to explain, Pastor. You see, we have been meeting as a group for almost twenty years. There is a flow to the study, you see. We have

tried to help Cheri blend into our group but, well, she . . . has issues."
These last words made her lips pucker.

"Issues? Can you give me a specific example?"

Silvia paused. "Well, just the other day we were working through a passage in James, and Mrs. Popney started to share an inspiration. We were all deeply interested in what she was saying. Cheri spoiled the moment by suggesting she was gossiping. Her uppity attitude killed the whole conversation. Mrs. Popney was very embarrassed, of course."

Of course. "I can see how that would kill the conversation. Is it possible that Cheri was correct?" Brady raised one eyebrow, trying to keep a grin from tugging at the corner of his mouth. The Monday women's study was a favorite topic for Sylvia. Brady saw the group differently. The women were closely woven together, and in Brady's opinion, as inward facing and stagnant as the shallow end of a summer pond.

"But, Pastor, we have been meeting together as a group for almost twenty years!" Sylvia repeated, her face beginning to mottle.

"Sylvia, Cheri doesn't have your years of camaraderie, but she does bring a fresh face to your study. She also needs the guidance of women of deep faith such as are in your group. Do you think perhaps Cheri was picking up something the rest of you might have been missing?"

"We don't need such comments from a young, unmarried slip of a girl, Pastor Brady." She drew a long breath. "After all, twenty years of meeting together, you would think we would be able to manage our study by now."

"You would think." He tapped his fingers against his leg.

Sylvia's hand shook slightly as she raised it again to her hair. "Pastor Brady—"

"Sylvia, it was kind of your group to ask Cheri to join the study. May I suggest you give it some time? I think you will find that Cheri is just a young woman trying to figure out how to fit in. I suspect she is seeking guidance, and your group is a wonderful vehicle for that. By any chance, did this incident happen last night?"

"No, Cheri didn't show up Monday night. That was another thing. It was her night to fix the tea, and she didn't even call so we could find a replacement. I tell you there is no helping the girl. All the same, I suppose the Christian thing to do is offer to come alongside her." She let out a long sigh. "Well, thank you for your time, Pastor Brady." With a weak smile of farewell, she navigated out of the drugstore, leaving a trail of pungent fragrance in her wake.

He continued over to the photo counter. Cheri seemed to have dropped out of sight since their conversation on Sunday. How had a question that theologians had been struggling with for centuries have sent her running? She had been upset when she left but not any more upset than when she arrived. He fingered his car keys. These people needed a pastor who really cared for them, not one who didn't much care about anything or anybody any more. Back in Wyoming, he thought a small church experience would be rejuvenating. Return him to his roots. But did he really want to go back there?

When Brady arrived at the photo counter, Jessica slid two envelopes containing Brady's latest wildflower pictures across the counter. "Nice to see you, Pastor Brady," she began ringing them up.

Brady reached for his wallet as he ran through his meeting with Cheri again in his mind. What would unforgivable sin have to do with gossip? He regretted that Cheri had gotten off to a rough start with the women's study. He had hoped that encouraging the ladies to invite Cheri into their group would have freshened things up. Maybe it had, but not the way he expected.

Karen would have known how to deal with this. She would have gotten involved with the women, joined the women's study, and managed the "issues" without much need to confer with him. He, on the other hand, couldn't bring himself to care that much.

Brady opened his wallet and waited while Jessica's fingers flew efficiently over the keys of the cash register, her long red nails beating a rhythmic tattoo. "Afternoon, Jessica. Say, have you seen Cheri around?"

"Uh, nope. She didn't come in to work this morning. And didn't call either. It's kinda weird. She's like, usually really good about that. Frank had to call me in to cover." She reached for Brady's twenty-dollar bill. .

"I hope everything is all right. She was at church with her mother on Sunday."

"Oh yeah? Do you want me to, like, check her apartment? I know where the key is. She has me feed her cat when she's out of town."

"Is it close by?"

"Not far. Just down on Monterey. I'm off in ten minutes. We could meet there, if you want."

Brady hesitated, weighing the decision. Perhaps it would be better to call the police. But Evelyn and Cheri were already upset with him. Calling the police could further erode their relationship if all this worry was for nothing.

"Yes, let's do that. I'll wait for you out front." He gathered his change and slipped the pictures in his inside coat pocket.

A few minutes later, Jessica joined Brady in the Sav-On parking lot. An early afternoon fog was sneaking up the hill into town, deadening traffic noise and slipping chilly fingers down Brady's collar. Wyoming had been colder in the winter, but the dampness here on the oceanfront went to the bone. He zipped his windbreaker and got into his Lexus.

Brady followed Jessica to Cheri's place, one block off Morro Bay Blvd. The pale yellow, two-story building was shaded by huge cypress and had just a peek of the ocean. Jessica led Brady up the wooden staircase to the front apartment door. Brady waited while Jessica knocked and called Cheri's name. She tried the door. Finding it locked, she ran her fingers along the top of the blue doorframe, bringing down a rusted key, which opened the door to the tiny apartment.

The stench emanating from inside caused them both to take a step back and turn their heads.

Chapter Seven

Holly had been waiting for twenty minutes when the receptionist finally escorted her back to her attorney's office in San Luis Obispo. Oscar Reynolds' name was boldly displayed on a new brass plaque beside his door. Holly felt her shoulders cinch up one more notch.

Nice plaque, Oscar. Putting my fees to good purpose, I see.

Her checkbook felt the pinch of several appointments behind this door. She needed good representation, but the cost was staggering and she hadn't seen much return for her money.

Oscar stood as Holly came in. The room smelled of leather and furniture polish, the thick carpet and shelves of books sucking the sound from the room.

"Hello, Holly, have a seat." He motioned to a chair at the front of his desk. "I'm glad you had time to come into the office one more time before the mediation. I've been going over my files, and I wanted to chat for just a few minutes about what you knew and when you knew it, so to speak." He smiled reassuringly as he returned to his seat and turned to a filing cabinet behind his desk. He pulled a large file from the cabinet and twisted back to face her. "How's the real estate biz these days?"

"Slow to none right now." She wasn't here to talk real estate on her dime.

"Okie dokie. Let's get started." Opening the folder, he scanned some notes then looked up. "How long have you lived on the Central Coast?"

"I was born in Morro Bay." He had asked this question before. Didn't he remember?

"So you are familiar with the area where the house was built?"

"Yes." She bit the word.

"Holly, I'm just running through some of the questions you may have at the mediation. This is sort of a dress rehearsal, okay?"

No, it wasn't okay. Her checking account balance said as much. "Oscar, we already went through all this. I thought you had something new to discuss."

"I want you to be clear on the facts when you attend the mediation. A stumble can make all the difference." Oscar leaned back in his chair, considering her. "Holly, I know this is an expensive process and your insurance covers only a fraction of the cost. I'm trying to save you a jury trial, which could drive the cost through the roof. Do you want to cooperate with me, or shall we call it a day?

Holly mulled over his words, holding his gaze. It seemed beyond absurd that she was defending herself from these ludicrous charges. But such was the price of her industry. The stakes were high and Oscar was one of the best. She sighed and slid back into the comfort of the leather chair. "Okay, Oscar. I'm all yours."

"Alright, back to business. When the house was under construction, did you ever go to the construction site?"

"No, I wasn't even in the area at the time. I was away at college."

"So you never had any knowledge of any archeological finds in the area?"

"Not until I received the phone call from the Mitchells after they started the demolition of the old house."

"Have you ever had any dealings with Morro Bay Construction?"

"No."

"When the home inspection was done, did you see anything that wasn't mentioned on the report?"

"No, nothing at all. I did the customary visual inspection."

"You didn't see anything around the property that raised your suspicions?"

"Nothing. The property was covered in landscaping. I walked the property when I did my visual inspection, but I didn't tromp through the landscaping."

"Well, you should know that the Mitchells are looking for forty-five thousand dollars in repairs and damages. They say you missed the problem and should have known it was there."

Holly was stunned. How could they blame her? Did he say forty-five thousand dollars?

"They claim that you didn't perform your due diligence in finding or disclosing the potential burial site. Since the State of California protects such sites, the Mitchells won't be able to build their home for months, maybe years, while the area is studied."

"That's beyond crazy. How can I disclose something I didn't know or see?" Holly fought to remain professional and keep her rising anger under control. Beneath the coat on her lap, she balled her hands in frustration, nails digging into her palms.

"I understand your position, Holly, but I suspect you will be expected to pitch in some of your commission to make this go away."

"You mean I will have to pay them off, even if I didn't do anything wrong." Her face flushed with irritation and dismay. She thought again about the cryptic envelope resting in her purse. Should she tell Oscar about it? Probably. But she was afraid it would escalate the issue. Better to settle in mediation and get on with her life. She just wanted the whole thing to be over.

"That's the way the game is played. You have Errors and Omissions insurance for issues like this. If it goes to a jury trial, the jury may find you negligent, and it could be even more expensive. I'm going to try one more time to negotiate a settlement this afternoon before we try the mediation."

"What happens if we can't come to an agreement in mediation?"

"Then we go to court. The mediator will be handling things tomorrow. I won't be there. We discussed that. Bring your checkbook." He smiled at her and stood to signal that their meeting was over. "If things change, I'll give you a call."

Bring your checkbook. The same phrase. The words slapped her.

She pulled the heavy door closed behind her and paused for a moment in the hushed hallway. It was so hard to know what to do. In the past, she would have called Uncle Nikko. A lump rose in her throat and tears threatened.

Holly avoided the receptionist's eyes as she passed through the plush lobby and out into the glorious afternoon sun. College students littered the grass at Mitchell Park. A shirtless young man played Frisbee fetch with a black lab whose tongue lolled and tail wagged furiously as he waited for the next toss. On another day, she would have basked in the warm San Luis Obispo sunshine. So different from the coastal chill of Morro Bay just twenty minutes up the coast.

She watched for a moment as the big lab leapt and caught the mangled yellow Frisbee. He streaked back to his owner and dropped it at the boy's feet. Oh, that life were so simple again. She knew it was a matter of when, not if, she would be sued. Lawsuits were an occupational hazard of being a realtor. Her shoulders slumped and her throat ached with the effort not to cry. Quick tears were a legacy of her mother. Joy, stress, anger, all misted her eyes from time to time. She hated it, but there it was.

She bounced the cell phone in her hand, wondering if she should call A.J. A tempting thought. She would really like someone to talk to. He liked her, she was well aware of that and enjoyed his company. Calling him would move their relationship forward. That wasn't necessarily a bad thing, but still she hesitated.

With a shake of her shoulders, she turned her face to the breeze and strode down the sidewalk to her car.

Chapter Eight

Brady and Jessica stood on the wooden landing outside Cheri's apartment. Jessica held her nose and stabbed her finger toward the apartment door. Brady stood rooted to the ground. The last thing he wanted to do was go into that apartment.

"Jessica, I'm not sure this is such a good idea."

"What if Cheri's in there and nobody knows?"

Brady peered into the dark interior, breathing through his mouth.

"I think we should call the police."

"And tell them what? That Cheri missed an appointment today, and her apartment smells. That will bring them for sure," she scoffed. "What are you afraid of?"

Brady's pulse built a staccato in his ears. He didn't like this at all, but if he stopped now he would look like a coward. He glanced at Jessica. She expected him to know what to do. Everything within him told him not to go in.

"Alright, you stay here, Jessica. I'll have a quick look."

Taking a deep breath, he covered his nose with his jacket sleeve and stepped into the dim interior. His stomach lurched as he was forced to take another breath of the putrid air. One window, open just an inch or so, allowed the damp ocean breeze to bump the bottom of bright red curtains against the sill in a rhythmic tapping that amplified the silence. Colorful ceramic pots full of silk flowers highlighted the simple utility of the small room. A doorway to the left led to the bedroom. The corner of a saffron-colored bedspread caught the fading light.

In two steps, Brady was in the bedroom when a scream from his left took his breath. He turned his head and braced himself.

A large tabby hissed its annoyance at his intrusion. Brady scowled at the cat, his heart thundering. He looked around the room quickly and found it undisturbed.

Back in the living room, Brady headed for the kitchen. The source of the stench evident on the kitchen counter. A pound or so of spoiled hamburger provided an enthusiastic meal for a dozen large, iridescent-blue flies.

Jessica peered in the doorway a few moments later. "Is she here?" Her voice wavered just a bit.

"No, just a cat that scared the wits out of me and some rotten hamburger. Any ideas where she might be?" He began disposing of the offending meat, resisting the gag that threatened to bring up his lunch.

Jessica stepped into the apartment. "Let me look at something." She headed for Cheri's laptop sitting open next to the living room sofa. When she moved the mouse, the screen came to life and illuminated her face. "She's got an e-mail open on her computer. Someone doesn't like you much. Told her not to meet with you. I'll check the bedroom. Maybe she took a trip." Jessica shot through the door. He could hear her sliding open the closet, then rummaging through the dresser drawers.

Brady felt awkward in the apartment, but he was curious about the e-mail. He moved over to the computer, glanced quickly at the bedroom door for Jessica and then focused on the illuminated screen.

Cheri:

Pastor Preachy Britches doesn't need to be involved in this. Let's talk in person...

Pastor preachy britches? Where did that come from? Ironically, Brady tended to agree with whomever the sender was. Although he didn't need to know every detail of his small flock's lives, he was painfully curious about what he didn't need to be involved in. He was tempted to check her e-mail account for previous messages. As he reached for the mouse, Cheri's right to privacy warred against his desire to know. Brady paused for a moment, then removed his hand from the mouse and the temptation it offered. If Cheri wanted him to know her business, they could meet again. He had said as much in the voice mail he left her this morning.

Jessica's return from the bedroom sealed his resolve. "I don't think she's taken a trip. Her suitcase is on the top shelf and her toothbrush is in its holder. I just don't know what to think." She slumped against the doorjamb, her arms crossed in concern.

"Do you know Cheri very well, Jessica? Does this seem unusual to you?"

"Cheri is like clockwork, Pastor Bracy. She shows up on time every day she's scheduled. Her cash drawer is always right. Everyone likes her. She's even picking up some accounting jobs around town. She studied that in college."

"Well, we definitely have something to pray about, don't you think? Something is wrong here."

"Well, you go right ahead and do your praying, Pastor. Might as well be talking to the ceiling, if you ask me." Jessica lifted her chin and waited for Brady's reply.

"Not into praying, Jessica?" Her defiant look told Brady that this was not a new position for her.

"God's never done nothin' for me. And I used to ask plenty."

Brady could identify with that. "We don't always like his answers, but he does know what's best for us."

Liar.

"Yeah, right. I've been to the church. Prayed and all. Nothin' ever happened."

"What did you pray about?"

Jessica shot Brady a "MYOB" look. "This is crazy. I don't need to explain anything to you." She flipped up her hand, dismissing the conversation. "We need to figure out what happened to Cheri." She headed for the door.

"That went well," Brady muttered as Jessica jogged down the stairs.

Brady closed up the apartment after putting down a fresh can of food for Cheri's unsociable cat. He tossed the rotting hamburger in the building's dumpster that sat catawampus in the parking lot. The three-block drive home gave Brady a few minutes to rehash events of the past few days. His stomach knotted as he revisited his conversation with Arlen. He was between the proverbial rock and a hard place. He had once had a reputation as a charismatic church builder, but the reality of who he was today was very different.

He knew if he stayed here, he needed to break out of the protective shell he had been encased in since the accident. Maybe he could start a new sermon series for this church, something that touched the hearts and minds of these people. In years past, the inspiration had flowed. He had only to ask and the ideas were there. "Father God," he prayed awkwardly, the words strange in his mouth. "I know your Word. I've studied and written about it for fifteen years. But...." The next words stopped before they left his heart.

Trusting a God, who had taken his wife and child was out of his reach. He felt betrayed. He had trusted God for everything since he was in high school, and his career had flown on the wings of the Holy Spirit's inspiration. Then, on that awful night, his trust in his God and Savior was ripped away. How could God have condoned such a thing? He had given his life for God, and God had let him down. The question returned often and was unanswerable. Oh, he knew what the books said—lots of them. Too bad his heart couldn't read.

Brady arrived at Vera and Yosef Shankston's tidy home and drove down the driveway to his small bungalow in the back. Aromas of pot roast and fresh bread carried on the slight breeze, making Brady's stomach growl. Vera, a transplant from Wisconsin, was an excellent cook and invited him over often for dinner. His loosening belt buckle already showing the evidence of her skill and Midwestern hospitality.

Enthusiastic barking greeted Brady as he got out of his Lexus and strode down a cobbled path to his front door. Daisy, his miniature red dachshund pranced about his feet as he entered.

"Hey there, Daisy, how did your day go, huh?" He picked up the wiggling bit of joy and went over to the message machine while Daisy attempted to clean his chin. The light blinked insistently. Brady dropped his coat on the couch and settled into his office chair. He tucked Daisy up next to him and punched the button.

"Brady, this is Holly. I received word today that an offer is coming in on that house you liked up on the hill. If you are interested in the home, we need to move quickly. I'll be in the office till five-thirty, and you can catch me after that on my cell phone." She left the number.

Well, did he want the house or not? Maybe something better would come on the market this week. Maybe he didn't want to stay in Morro Bay at all. Holly wanted an answer tonight. He looked at his watch. Five forty-five. He should call her before dinner with Vera and Yosef at six. He reached for the phone when a knock on the door startled him. Daisy wiggled from his lap, and dashed to the door, barking furiously. "Daisy, hush, that's enough."

When he opened the door, Vera stepped in from the early evening chill. Her face was red, her body shaking. "I . . . just received a call . . ." She paused for a breath, hand on her heart. "They found Cheri Davenport's body at Spooners Cove this afternoon. She..." Vera swallowed. "The sheriff's at Evelyn's right now. I thought you should know."

Brady stared at Vera, stunned to inaction for a moment. *Dead? She can't be dead.* Karen. No, Cheri. She's talking about Cheri.

"Pastor?"

Vera's voice brought him back to the moment. He exchanged looks with her for a long second before he grabbed his coat and was out the door.

Yosef and Vera followed Brady over to Evelyn's home. As he drove the darkened streets, his mind struggled to process the horrible news. Could he have done or said something differently on Sunday?

Don't patronize me! Cheri's words screamed in his mind, ringing with condemnation. Then another. *Don't patronize me, Brady.* This time, it was Karen's words, Karen's voice. Why had he made them both so angry? Driving to Evelyn's was like a nightmare rerun. Anger and death again. He had been unable to foresee them or stop them.

He fought the illusion that he was back in Wyoming. The similarities between what happened to his wife and the circumstances leading up to Cheri's death made it almost impossible for him to function. The last thing he wanted to do right now was go to Evelyn's house. He wanted to run. Anywhere. Just to be free from being trapped in a pastor's job.

Because he was no pastor.

All the lights were on in Evelyn Davenport's stately Craftsman-style home when Brady, Vera, and Yosef arrived. Cars lined both sides of the street, forcing them to park over a block away. The fog had moved in so thick it was more like a light rain. Sylvia Thorndyke opened the front door and stepped silently aside for them to enter.

Evelyn was standing in the formal living room with two sheriff's officers. Her eyes were pink and puffy. In her hand, a lace-trimmed handkerchief hung damp and limp. "Thank you, gentlemen, for coming personally. I'll be down tomorrow morning to make the arrangements." Evelyn's voice cracked at the end. She shook both their hands, and Sylvia saw them out.

Evelyn dabbed her nose and looked up to see Brady and the Shankstons in the entry. She returned to her chair by the fireplace.

Brady went over to sit with her. "Evelyn, I'm so very sorry. Do they know what happened?"

She studied him for a moment and then glanced at Vera, Yosef, and Sylvia. Her eyes finally returning to Brady, her voice hushed and hoarse. "They don't know how it happened. Some folks found her at Spooners Cove this afternoon." She took a breath and blew her nose. "She had her checkbook in her back pocket along with her driver's license. That's how they knew . . . it was her." She shivered and dabbed her nose again.

"Are you cold, Evelyn? Brady, why don't you make a fire?" Vera moved to stand by Sylvia Thorndyke. "I have a pot roast just finished at my house. I'll go get it. Maybe we should make a pot of tea as well. I suspect more people will be here soon."

"You're right, Vera. I'll start the tea water." Sylvia headed for the kitchen. Brady breathed a small sigh of relief to see the women of the church springing into action.

Brady struggled with getting the fire going. His fireplace in Wyoming had been gas. You just turned it on at the wall switch. From behind him, Yosef reached down, picked up a fire starter stick and handed it to Brady. He pointed to the bucket of kindling to the left of the old fireplace. Brady smiled his thanks.

When Vera returned with the roast, Brady had a nice fire going, which slowly drove out the chill. More than a dozen people gathered in groups in the kitchen and living room. Mrs. Thorndyke and Vera were serving up the pot roast to those who wanted some. Deli trays, bags of salad, and two roast chickens brought by church members completed the meal. Evelyn sat near the fire with a plate of food untouched on her lap. Her wet eyes now thick and red, she occasionally brought the hankie to her nose and dabbed. The room was quiet except for the occasional touch of a fork to a plate.

Brady's mind continued traveling back to two-and-a-half years ago— to a mirrored scene in own his living room. Grief welled up bitter in the back of his throat. The officers had been courteous that night also, when they brought the news of the death of his wife and young son--hit by a drunk driver. The emotions swirled up and near y overwhelmed him. He fought against the memories again. Rage, disbelief and grief all vied for prominence, choking him till he could hardly breathe.

Chapter Nine

Holly sat on her balcony sipping hot tea and watching the sun settle into the fog over Morro Bay. The view had cost her a bundle, but she reveled in every sunset. A file folder sat open on her lap; several passages marked in yellow highlighter. Holly looked down at the documents. She pored over the file, trying to draw any new information from its pages. From what she could determine, the sellers of 4753 Highline Drive had hired a local general contractor to demo the old home and build a new one. During the demolition, bones were discovered under the old foundation. Upon investigation, local archeologists determined that the home had been built on an unregistered Indian burial mound. Work was immediately halted while archeologists and representatives of the local Chumash tribe were brought in. Because of the artifacts found, the building permit was suspended, and the owners had sued anybody who had been even remotely connected to the real estate transaction.

So tonight, she once again sifted through the details as she knew them, because tomorrow was the mediation. Oscar had told her to expect it to take most of the day.

"Oh, Father, help," she sighed. "Help me to rest in you, Lord. This lawsuit, my business, Uncle Nikko, there is just so much going on right now." Brady flitted across her mind. He hadn't called her today. Maybe he wasn't a ripe buyer after all, but he was the only good prospect she had right now. She rubbed her eyes, money issues crowding into her thoughts. She felt an urge to call A.J. and discuss it all with him. She glanced at the phone on the kitchen counter. Just do it, she told herself.

A.J. picked up on the second ring.

"Hello A.J., its Holly. Am I interrupting anything?"

"Holly!" His obvious pleasure at hearing her voice wrapped her in a warm hug. "You're never an interruption. What are you up to tonight?"

"I'm fretting about this case, A.J.. The mediation is tomorrow. I'm so angry to have gotten caught up in all of this. How could I have known there was an Indian burial site under that house? How can they find me liable for something I couldn't have know about?"

"Welcome to my world, Holly, the world of courts and lawyers."

"I know being a realtor paints a big target on my back, but it's just so wrong." She fiddled with a pencil on the counter.

"Doesn't matter if it's wrong. You have insurance so you have a deep pocket. That's what they are looking for."

"Thanks loads."

"I'm just speaking the truth. Those lawyers, they can actually smell fear, you know. I hear they teach that in law school."

Holly laughed. "Oh, A.J., honestly, you are too much sometimes." She stifled a yawn. "This whole thing has me worn out." She could hear voices around him. He must still be at work.

"How's your uncle?"

"I think he's slipping further away every day. He keeps talking about someone finding him when he goes to sleep. I can't make sense of it. Listen, you sound busy. We can talk later."

"Sorry, Holly, I'm starting a new investigation, and I'm afraid it has my attention. Get a good night's sleep, and take it as it comes tomorrow. Call me when you're done, promise?"

"Promise. Good night, A.J."

Not that long ago, she would have called Uncle Nikko for advice. The photo he had taken of her two years ago hung just above the telephone. It had been a great day, filled with fresh wind, mild swells, and good company. Uncle Nikko had taken the picture of her doing something she loved above all things, sailing her boat. She fingered the telephone receiver as a tear slipped down her cheek. Her life was taking a heart-wrenching turn. It was time to recognize that Uncle Nikko's cheerful voice would never again be on the other end of that phone.

Thursday morning, Brady headed south down Hwy 1 to the San Luis Obispo County Sheriff's Department. He had spent most of the night staring at the ceiling in his bedroom, longing for sleep to release him from the guilt. Was Cheri dead because he hadn't been available to her when she reached out? If he had been able to listen to Karen, would she be alive today? What part of him was missing? The thoughts circled round and round, nipping at the heels of his conscience, pestering, bothering, driving him toward a sick desperation. As morning approached, he had decided to drive over to the sheriff's department. Perhaps he could provide some bit of information that would help in the investigation.

Brady arrived at the Sheriff's Department at nine a.m. and gave the receptionist his name through the thick glass. "I think I may have some information regarding the body that was found at Spooners Cove yesterday."

She directed him across the parking lot to building that appeared to be a relic from earlier times. Once inside, a friendly woman at the counter asked him to have a seat. Brady had only a few minutes to wait before a door opened up the hallway and a uniformed deputy poked his head out. "Brady McGregor?" he asked.

"Yes, I'm Brady."

"Come this way, sir."

Brady followed the officer through a rabbit warren of doors, hallways, a locker room and yet another hall. Finally the officer opened a nondescript white door and motioned Brady to have a seat beside a small metal desk in the bare room. A square one-way glass window was the only thing that relieved the otherwise austere interior. He wondered briefly if anyone was on the other side of the glass.

Brady didn't have long to wait before a detective in a western style suit and tie came in. Without a word, he took a seat across from Brady and opened his notebook.

"Brady McGregor?"

Brady nodded.

The plain-clothed officer was a big man. His ruddy face and rough hands alluded to hard work in the outdoors. He made a note on his pad, checked the time, and made another notation. "I'm Detective Walker. What can I do for you, Mr. McGregor?" He settled his arms on the table across from Brady and locked him in a steady stare.

"I thought perhaps I might have some information for you that would be helpful regarding the finding of Cheri Davenport at Spooners Cove yesterday."

One eyebrow lifted. "And how did you know Miss Davenport?"

Brady glanced at the door, at the clock, and back at the detective. He started to tap his fingertips on the tabletop and then stopped himself; perhaps coming had been a bad idea. No, he knew that coming was a bad idea. "Well, I had an appointment with her on Sunday afternoon." He finally replied.

"You didn't answer my question."

"I'm the new pastor at Mariners Chapel. I was called over to Evelyn Davenport's home last night."

The detective made a quick note. "And what kind of appointment did you have with Ms. Davenport?"

"I'm her pastor. She said she had something to discuss with me."

"A padre, huh? So what did she discuss, Padre?"

Brady felt the blood rise to his face. He forced himself to stay calm.

The detective sat back in his chair, relaxed and confident. "Well, Detective Walker, since she is deceased, I'm not held to privacy ethics. She asked me to explain what the unforgivable sin was."

"Unforgivable sin?" The detective set down his pen and leaned farther back in his chair, rocking it up on two legs.

"In a nutshell, the common definition has to do with unrepentant sin."

"Any idea why she'd want to talk about this?"

"Not a clue. We never got that far. I tried to answer her question but, well, she didn't really give me a chance."

"What do you mean?"

"She got up and left before I could finish."

"You been at this long, Padre?"

"At what?"

"Doing what you do. You know, being a padre?"

Where does this guy get off? "Almost thirteen years."

"Did you have any meetings with Ms. Davenport before this?"

"No, that was the first one."

Detective Walker looked at his watch and then at Brady, studying him. Seeming to come to a decision, he stood and offered his hand. "I have an appointment I can't miss. I think I have enough for now, Padre. Do you have a card? I might have more questions for you."

Brady fished out a business card. "If you want to get in touch with me directly, here's my card." Detective Walker handed Brady his card and escorted him out of the interrogation room.

As the two men walked back down the hall, Brady reviewed what just happened. Had his coming been the right thing to do? Perhaps he had injected himself into something that really was not his concern now. After all, he had tried his best with Cheri, hadn't he? A man can only do so much.

A light rain was falling as Brady returned to his car. He glanced at the card in his hand. *Detective A.J. Walker* was printed on one side along with the Sheriff's Department phone number. On the other side was a handwritten cell phone number. He tucked it in his jacket pocket, settled into his Lexus and started the engine. As he drove the short distance up

Hwy 1 to Morro Bay, the rain increased to a thundering roar. Brady struggled to see the road just as a car came flying by from behind. Suddenly, the speeding car spun sideways and slid into his lane. Brady braked and turned to the right to avoid it. His tires began to break loose. The skills learned from driving in the snows of Wyoming kicked in, he corrected delicately, bringing his car to a stop on the shoulder with a lurch, one tire off the pavement.

Brady sat for several minutes to allow his heart to settle back to a more normal rhythm. He peered through the rain, expecting to see the spinning car off the road in front of him, but it was gone. He leaned his head back and shut his eyes. "Thank you, Lord, for keeping me safe." He prayed out of habit, without thinking about or questioning if God was listening.

Tap tap tap.

Brady's eyes flew open. He looked out his window into the concerned face of a highway patrolman. His Smoky Bear hat had a rain cover and he was clothed in foul- weather gear.

Brady rolled down the window. Rainwater dripped onto his leg and arm. "Yes, officer?"

"You okay, sir? I saw you avoid that spinout. Your right rear tire is pretty deep in the mud. Do you need some help?"

"Yes, I'm fine. I was just praying. I wanted to settle down a bit before I headed back to the church."

"Well, God bless you, sir. Shall I stay till we're sure you're not stuck?"

"Thanks, officer. I'd appreciate it."

The burly, bundled patrolman started for his cruiser, then stopped for a moment. He turned and came back to Brady's window. Brady rolled down the window again. "Yes, officer?"

"Are you a pastor?"

"Yes, I am. I have a church in Morro Bay."

"Well, since you're praying, Pastor, would you keep my daughter Heather in mind? She's in that rebellious teenage stage, you know what I mean? She's making bad decisions and all."

"I'm happy to, officer. Do you attend church locally?"

"No, haven't been since before high school. My wife doesn't see the point."

"Well, you're always welcome at Mariners Chapel. I'm the pastor there." Brady reached out into the rain and shook the officer's wet hand.

The officer returned to his cruiser as Brady started his car and gently put pressure on the accelerator. He felt his right rear tire slip a bit so he stopped. He tried again and the tire slipped, grabbed, slipped again, and his right front tire dropped down into the soft shoulder.

The officer came back to his window. "I'm going to give you just a bit of a push. Turn your tires to the left and give it a little gas." The rain pounded down on the officer's back. He touched his hat and went back to his cruiser.

A moment later, Brady felt the large cruiser make contact with his bumper. Brady cranked the wheel to the left and gently gave it gas. The car lurched. The back end slid a bit to the right, and then he was up on the pavement and down the road. Brady opened his window for a moment, lifted his hand into the rain, and waved his thanks. The officer blinked his headlights and continued past him down the road.

He knew he shouldn't have agreed to pray for the officer's daughter. He wouldn't pray for himself, let alone someone else. His life was a farce, and people were getting hurt. Something had to change. Brady took the next freeway off ramp and headed toward home.

Inside his bungalow, Daisy's usual enthusiasm was muted. She didn't like the rain, so she simply begged to be picked up. Brady slung her under his arm and went to check the message machine. The rain thundered onto the roof, so Brady turned up the volume in order to hear. "Hello, Pastor Brady." Vera's voice addressed him. "I thought you should know, the roof in the sanctuary is leaking. Yosef is on his way."

"Oh, man. Where are we going to get money to fix the roof? Unbelievable," he muttered.

He punched the button for the second message. "Hello, Brady, this is Holly. Would you give me a call when you can? Thanks."

The house. Brady had totally forgotten about the house. He'd have to deal with that later. In the meantime, he had a leaking roof to address.

When Brady arrived at the church, Yosef stood in the little office alongside Vera. He shook out his coat, wiped his shoes, and joined them.

"Did you get my message?" Vera asked.

"Yes, the roof is leaking. Let's take a look."

Yosef met them in the sanctuary. The plink plink of drops hitting buckets greeted them. Trash bags covered the adjoining pews and floor. Brady looked up into the gloom of the dark vaulted ceiling. Light caught the drops as they fell in a steady patter.

"Has this happened before?"

"Hmm, let me think." Yosef rubbed the side of his nose. "Not since the new roof twenty years ago." He looked up. "I think some shingles must have blown off in the wind this morning."

Brady let out a sigh. "Okay. Vera, do you know where we stand money wise? At the last elder meeting, funds were a bit thin."

"Evelyn has the books at her house. I hate to bother her today."

"Can you just go and pick them up? I'm sure she'll understand."

"I'll give her a call." Vera went back into the office. Brady and Yosef stayed behind to empty the buckets and put down fresh towels.

Vera was just placing the phone back on the receiver when Brady and Yosef entered. "Ah, there you are. I spoke to Evelyn. She sounded fine until I asked for the books. I didn't even have a chance to tell her about the leak. She just said, 'Not today,' and hung up. She must be very distressed, don't you think?"

Brady wiped a drip from his forehead. "Well, I can go down to the bank and get a copy of our statement. Let's not bother her again today. The statement will at least give us an idea of where we stand."

Yosef picked up the office phone. "Arlen Parkfield owns a construction company. His father put on the last roof. I'll give him a call to get an idea of how much it will cost." While Yosef made the call to Arlen, Brady stepped into his office to call Holly.

Brady smiled when he heard her voice answer the phone. "Holly, this is Brady. Sorry I didn't get back to you yesterday. Things got a bit crazy last night."

"Because of Cheri? I'm still in shock. We all are." Brady could hear the sincerity in her voice. It crackled with emotion.

"How did you hear?"

"Morro Bay is a small town, Brady. Word travels fast. And she did the books for our agency. How is her mother doing?"

"I went straight to Evelyn's when I heard. She is pretty devastated. I keep wondering what could have happened. I never got a chance to know Cheri." His stomach gave a sick jolt, guilt washing through him. He closed his eyes, reflecting on the thought that he might somehow be responsible.

"She was a sweet girl. I got to know her—not well, of course. But she always had a smile for me when she stopped in. Such a shame."

"Yes, yes it is."

"Sorry to jump to business, but that house you liked went into escrow last night. However, a similar one just came on the market. Would you have time to see it this afternoon?"

Brady glanced at his watch and then his calendar. All clear. "That will work for me, Holly. You don't mind going out in this weather?"

"I don't want you to miss another great house, Brady."

"What time?"

"How about I pick you up at your office at four?"
"Great, that gives me time to tie up some loose ends here."

Chapter Ten

Holly clicked her cell phone shut and repositioned herself on the chair in the mediator's office. She was miserable from head to toe. Six inches behind her, through a plate glass window, rain lashed the bushes. She wiggled her toes, feeling moisture ooze into her stocking from a misstep into a puddle getting out of her car.

The two pieces of the threatening letter rested safely in her purse. She had tossed it away yesterday, and then later went down to the dumpster to retrieve it. It felt like a *thing* that had invaded her life. An evil influence she didn't want in her possession. Then reason returned and she retrieved it. It was possible it would be her ace in the hole today.

The front door opened suddenly, causing her to jump. Arlen Parkfield came in, shaking the rain from his hat and raincoat. After he hung them both on a hall tree, he came across the room, offering his hand with an amused look dancing behind his eyes.

"You're Holly Fain, aren't you? Your uncle used to work for me. I understand he is back in town. What's he up to?"

"He's living at Hibiscus House."

"Oh." He said as he dropped onto the couch across from Holly, one arm thrown up along the back. "They run a wonderful facility. My aunt was there at the end."

A flicker of something crossed his face and then was gone. Sadness? No, something deeper.

Holly wasn't sure where to take the conversation. Arlen owned the company that had built the house they were here to discuss. She probably shouldn't even be talking to him. She looked over at the conference room door, hoping it would open and rescue her from this awkward conversation, but it remained shut.

"How long ago was your aunt there?" *What a lame question.*

Arlen had been looking past her at the picture that hung above her head, his eyes distant and unfocused. He visibly pulled himself back into the now.

"She passed two years ago." He paused and looked around the room. Then his eyes returned to Holly. "So, you seem to be successful in your real estate business, Holly. I see your ads all over town. How's the market?"

"It's a mess." She said simply. "People are taking longer to make decisions. Hoping prices will go down some more. The banks aren't lending, and money is tight. Nothing new there. Fortunately, I stay pretty busy. No complaints." Holly lifted her purse and dug around for nothing in particular. Surely, the other parties would arrive soon. She glanced at her watch. Five minutes to go before their mediation started. She needed an out sooner than that.

"I seem to have left something in my car. I'll be right back," Holly lied. She pulled her damp raincoat from the hall tree and ducked back into the rainstorm. The roar of traffic, amplified by the rain, met her as she pulled the heavy office door shut behind her. Putting her head down, she followed the covered porch around the side of the building to the parking lot and climbed back into her car, this time carefully avoiding the puddle on the driver's side.

What a chicken I am. She made a show of looking around inside the car, aware that Arlen could see her if he looked out the window behind him. She could see the back of his head through the glass. As she watched, a tall man in a dark suit approached Arlen. He rose and the two shook hands, Arlen clapping the other man on the shoulder. They laughed together and after an exchange, Arlen pulled his wallet out and handed the other man something.

A car pulling into the spot next to her drew Holly's attention away. The sellers had arrived for the mediation. When Holly looked up again at the law office window, Arlen was looking down on her. Their eyes met briefly, before Arlen turned and sat back on the couch.

A chill ran down her and it wasn't from the cold and rain. Something in Arlen's look made her think of the letter again. He had sent it. She knew it like she knew her own name.

Holly returned to the waiting room and within minutes, the other parties finally arrived. The receptionist escorted everyone into an oak-paneled meeting room. They found seats around a polished wood table. Both the buyers and sellers had been pleasant and happy when escrow closed last year. Now they spaced themselves as far apart as possible and avoided eye contact. Holly pulled out a yellow note pad and pen, and focused on writing the date, time, and who was present. The pen shook as she wrote, making her writing jagged.

Steady girl. This is awkward but not the end of the world.

She scribbled it out and wrote it again, forcing her hand to slow down.

The mediator cleared his throat to signal he was ready to start. He was the man that had greeted Arlen in the waiting room. He tugged at his shirt cuffs and turned to address the buyers.

"You have received the documents pertaining to today's mediation. Are there any pertinent facts that you wish to elaborate upon or wish to add?" His eyes moved from party to party. Each shaking their heads until he stopped at the buyers, Jarred and Vivian Llovera, seated at the far end of the long table.

"I do have something to add." The portly man tugged a kerchief from his coat pocket and wiped sweat from his forehead. "I would like to emphasize the ongoing health issue suffered by my wife since purchasing the house. Our lives have been turned upside down, completely upside down. The stress has been unbelievable."

Other than gaining a few more pounds, Jerred Llovera hadn't changed much in the last twelve months. His ever-present handkerchief still dabbed his face, even in the relative comfort of the mediator's office. She recognized his cologne as it drifted down the table, mixed with the underlying scent of his body odor. Her nose wrinkled. She rubbed it, forcing back a sneeze. The words pompous ass didn't do him justice. Vulgar seemed more fitting.

He patted his wife's hand. "My dear Vivian's health has deteriorated and our medical expenses have mounted, not to mention the financial loss we have suffered."

Holly looked at Arlen Parkfield for a response. He was sitting back, fiddling with his cell phone.

The mediator continued the circuit of the table. "Mr. Parkfield, any thoughts from you?" The mediator asked.

Arlen looked up. "No, Jim. I've made my position clear."

He looked to his right. "Miss Fain, any thoughts?"

Holly's chest tightened. The speech that had been tumbling around in her mind for a week had disappeared. She glanced at the sellers, Bill and Margaret Gallager, but they avoided her eyes.

She looked down at her yellow note pad. Blank. No help there. She wrote her name to give her something to do for just a moment so she could gather her thoughts. Finally, she looked around the table and focused on the mediator. "I just want to emphasize that the only information I had was what my sellers, the Gallagers, told me in the disclosure, along with the property information available from the county.

I'm not sure how I could have known this home was built on an Indian burial mound. Quite frankly, I'm not sure why I'm here."

"What!" Jerred Llovera stood and slapped his hand on the table. "How can you sit there and...!"

"Mr. Llovera!" The mediator interrupted, forcing him to silence with a stern look.

Holly understood what a rabbit must feel like, cornered by a slathering dog. She shook off the fear and squared her shoulders, preparing to continue her statement.

"I..."

The mediator lifted his hand. "No, Miss Fain. I think we will move from here to separate negotiations."

"But she needs to know what she's done." Llovera sputtered, slamming his hand on the table.

"Mr. Llovera, please be seated."

Llovera stood his ground, glaring at Holly who returned his look, unflinching.

"Mr. Llovera!"

"Sweetheart, please." His wife tugged his sleeve. "Your heart, remember?"

Holly's heartbeat thundered in her ears.

Jerred Llovera snatched a file from the table and stomped from the room.

Holly realized she was holding her breath. She let it out gradually and then drew another long breath in through her nose and out. Her anxiety turning to anger. Although Jerred Llovera was a bully, she wasn't afraid of him, physically. It was the yelling that unnerved her. When the bones were discovered a year ago, he had stormed into her office, demanding she do something, menacing her with his bulk and bluster. But there was nothing to be done. The soils engineer had been on site when the discovery had occurred and promptly reported it to the county. From there, it was out of her hands. The site then swarmed with archeologists from the state university and the local representatives of the Chumash Indian tribe. The Llovera's had eventually been able to start the construction of their home, but the delay had been costly.

Three hours later, Holly still sat in the conference room, alone. She had passed the time reading two fishing magazines from cover to cover and a six-month-old *Time* magazine. After reading through those, even the classified ads in the back, she pulled random books from the law library shelves. She had never read a law book and now knew she never wanted to read another. The mediator had been in to talk to her five times, asking her how much money she would be willing to pay to make her part in this go away, each time coming in with a different offer. She had refused every time.

Their last discussion had been almost forty-five minutes ago. She could hear him moving from the buyers to the sellers to Arlen, doing his version of shuttle diplomacy as doors opened and closed down the hallway, and the rain tapped its counterpoint on the window behind her head.

An hour later, Holly opened the door of the church office. It felt good to move around after sitting all day. At three thirty, the mediator had informed her he had cut a deal between the parties. Holly didn't know who had paid what, all she knew was she had held her ground, and what was left of her bank account. Relief and exhaustion had almost made her cancel this appointment. But she needed the sale. So a quick stop by her condo to check for any new listings and change into slacks, and she was ready for Brady.

He stepped from his office just as she entered. "Hi there. I'm all ready to go. I'll just get my coat and be right with you."

"Dress for weather, it's still raining. I have four more houses that just popped up this morning. If you're game, we can go see those as well." She followed him into the reception area. The two of them fought the rain and wind for an hour and a half, in and out of house after house. None of the four houses worked for Brady as well as the one that was now in escrow. She knew he was disappointed. He had been silent for the past twenty minutes.

The sun was setting as they finished the last house. Holly paused before starting the car, turning in her seat to face him. "How about we go back to my office and regroup?"

"Oh, I don't know. I'm pretty disappointed right now." He turned away and looked out the passenger window toward the house they had just visited--another two story with a view of rooftops, power lines and a glimpse of the sea.

If you had listened to me, we'd be in escrow right now. In spite of her thoughts, Holly determined to be kind.

"That's understandable, Brady." She kept her voice light. "This can be a very frustrating process, and doing it in these miserable conditions only makes it worse." She started the car and pulled away from the curb. She could go left to her office or straight and head back to the church.

"Which way?" she asked as she pulled up to a stop sign.

"Let's go back to your office. Maybe we could look in another town."

"Los Osos and Cayucos are both close and offer ocean views."

He nodded and she turned left.

The office was dark when they arrived. Holly unlocked the door, her head tucked in her collar, trying to avoid another raindrop down her neck. She was frustrated. Brady had lost the house he wanted, and she was going to have a hard time finding something that suited him as well.

She flipped on lights to half the office space. "My desk is this way." She led him down the office hallway past half-a-dozen deserted desks.

"I'm keeping you after hours. Are you sure you want to do this tonight?"

"It's not a problem--unless *you* have something else pressing. Let's look at some nearby communities and see what's available. Then maybe tomorrow we can start fresh."

Holly stepped around the partition and into her corner cubicle. A large bouquet of red roses sat in the center of her blotter. Her eyebrows lifted in surprise. She shifted them to a side table and settled into her chair.

"Aren't you going to see who they are from?"

"I can look later." She glanced at the velvet loveliness of the roses, their fragrance filling the air, driving away the memory of Jarred Llovera. They had to be from A.J.

Seven homes came up on Holly's computer screen in Brady's price range. She brought them up individually so he could take a look, but none sparked his interest. When they had finished with the list, she turned away from the computer and mulled over her options briefly before meeting his gaze.

"What would you say to making a backup offer on the house you liked? That way, if it falls out of escrow, you're right there to pick it up before somebody else does." She raised her eyebrows, questioning.

"What are the chances of my getting the house?"

"In our market, about sixty-five percent of homes fall out of escrow for one reason or another. It's worth a shot, and we can keep looking in the meantime."

Holly watched emotions play across his face as he mulled the option.

Finally, he returned her look. "Works for me. Let's do it."

He picked up a picture sitting on Holly's desk then turned the photo around toward her. "Seems we have a mutual acquaintance." He tapped the top of the frame with his finger.

"Jessica?" Holly turned from her computer screen back to Brady. Her face softened with good memories "I was involved in a mentoring program through the Realtors Association. We worked with at-risk teens to help them get jobs and turn their lives around."

"She seems to be doing well. I see her at the drug store where I get my photographs developed."

"She's held that job for almost a year. That's her at high school graduation." She nodded at the picture on her desk. "Helping her graduate was my first order of business."

"Looks like you did a great job. I bet it was rewarding to see her succeed."

"We had some tough times. She was a hard nut to crack."

"Somehow that doesn't surprise me."

Forty-five minutes later Brady signed the last page just as Holly's stomach growled. She blushed and touched her stomach. "I'm so sorry. My uncle used to tease me about that."

"I'm hungry too; can I interest you in a bite to eat?"

She hesitated.

"As a thank you for all your hard work, of course."

She looked at her watch and then back at Brady. "All right."

At the front door, he helped her on with her raincoat. "I haven't a clue where to go. I've only eaten out once since I've been here. Any suggestions?"

"I know just the place."

Chapter Eleven

Holly drove them to Morro Bay State Park. Rain had given way to broken clouds. Wisps of heavy fog filled the low spots on the golf course to their left, and up the hill, a yellow glow from the clubhouse filled the night. Pulling into the State Park Marina, Holly parked facing the boats to avoid the drippy eucalyptus that lined the parking area. Here and there, lights on the marina boats sparkled through the mist. The rhythmic clang of a halyard against the mast of a boat was the only sound they heard as they headed down the parking lot to The Bayside Café. Large outdoor heaters glowed orange, fighting back the chill for diners waiting for a seat inside the restaurant. Holly wrote her name on the clipboard next to the front door, and turned to join Brady on a rustic bench under the low roar of one of the heaters. A limp cat luxuriated on a wooden fence behind the bench, basking in a pulsing heater's glow. Holly gave it a gentle pat before taking her seat.

"This won't take long; we're the only name on the list." Holly rubbed her arms vigorously. "Glad the rain stopped."

Brady stood. "Here, scoot over under the heater."

She slid closer to the heater, grateful for the warmth. Brady took her place at the end of the bench glancing around at the eclectic patio. "I would never have found this place."

"You'll love the food." She tried to relax and enjoy the heater's embrace and the welcoming ambience of the patio. Potted plants tumbled from their containers and tangled through scattered shipyard artifacts. The outdoor dining area behind them was empty tonight, it's tall space heaters cold and quiet. On less inclement nights, however, it was a prime spot to watch the sun set and enjoy a crisp Chardonnay.

They sat silently for an awkward few moments until Holly's name was called. Brady held the door as they entered. Heady fragrances enticed them as they moved through the dining area cluttered with bits of quiet conversations and the clink of dishes. The hostess escorted them to a table in the corner, overlooking the north end of the marina and the kayak rental. Holly looked around, enjoying the feel of the eclectic decorations and simple atmosphere. An old wooden rowing shell hung along the ceiling on one wall and warm wood, muted tones, and other nautical trappings provided a rustic touch.

The waitress stopped by with water and menus. After running his eye over the menu, Brady looked up. "I usually order fish and chips, but I think I may change my mind this time."

"Everything is great here." Holly had set her menu aside without opening it.

"You already know what you want?"

"Bayside is one of my favorite restaurants. My Uncle Nikko and I used to come here a couple of times a year."

When the waitress returned, they listened to the specials and made their selections. Holly ordered the scallops on fried green tomatoes with aioli sauce, a Bayside classic. Brady confessed to playing it safe with grilled wild king salmon served with artichoke tapenade and red mashed potatoes. The waitress hurried off to the kitchen and again they lapsed into another uncomfortable silence. Holly searched her memory for a conversation opener. Relying on a real estate training seminar she took as a rookie, she reviewed the acronym F.O.R.D: family, occupation, recreation, dreams. Family? For some reason, she steered away from that one. Occupation? Definitely not. Recreation? That would work.

"So, Brady, what do you do for fun?" She fiddled with her water glass and wished for a glass of wine. He hadn't ordered wine, so neither did she.

"Wildflower photography, actually, I took a class in high school years ago and have been playing around with it ever since. My dad was an avid photographer. He taught me quite a bit."

"You must have tons of pictures."

"Yes, I do, notebooks full." He gazed out the window at the slowly receding day. "I am finding there are lots of new flowers here that I've never seen."

Holly sensed some uneasiness. She ran her finger along the top of her water glass and then turned it slowly, searching for her next question. Brady beat her to the punch.

"What about you? Do you have a hobby?"

She smiled. "Sure, if you call work a hobby. Real estate is a full-time, seven-day-a-week proposition."

"All work and no play?"

"That pretty much sums it up. I love my job, so I guess it's a hobby as well."

Their salads came, providing a convenient diversion from the painful lack of meaningful dialogue. Holly played around with her salad, and then decided to dive in deeper. Why not?

She speared an olive. "So, what brought you to our little section of the coast?"

"I needed a change." A flat statement, not inviting further questions. *Apparently, she had landed on the wrong question.*

The waitress stopped by. "How is everything?"

Holly looked up from her salad. "I would like a glass of your house white, please."

Brady sat back with a grin. "So would I."

After the waitress left, Holly chuckled. "I wasn't sure if you drank or not, Brady. I didn't want to make you uncomfortable, but my dinner will be much better paired with a nice local wine."

"Drinking wine is something I wouldn't normally do in public. However, nobody knows me here yet. My family had a vineyard up in Napa for many years. I come from a long line of wine aficionados where dinner wasn't complete without a perfectly-paired wine."

"I couldn't agree more." When they touched their newly arrived glasses, their eyes held for just a beat. Holly's pulse quickened. *What was that about?*

She sat back, forcing the moment to pass. Looking around the room to kill the tension she felt, she turned back to Brady. "So you're worried someone might object to your drinking a glass of wine with dinner?"

"Some folks would. If my having a glass of wine causes someone else to stumble, then I shouldn't have the wine. It's that simple."

"If I buy a new car and it makes my neighbor fall into jealousy, did I make him stumble by buying the car?"

His left eyebrow twitched up and a twinkle glinted in coco brown eyes. He rolled the wine in his glass, studying the amber liquid. "In First Corinthians, chapter eight, the Apostle Paul talks about doing and not doing things that would cause his fellow Christians to fall into sin." He continued to swirl his wine, dropping his nose into the wine glass to test the fragrance it gave off. "He thought it was better for him to refrain from doing something rather than cause someone else to stumble."

"But wasn't Paul talking about eating food sacrificed to idols and being seen in the temple? Paul even urged Timothy to have a little wine for his stomach's sake."

A little grin tugged at the corner of Brady's mouth. "True. I personally don't think having a glass of wine is a sin, but some folks do."

"But don't you think that scripture should dictate what is and isn't sin? Adding man's law to scripture was the unbearable yoke, wasn't it?" *Stop it, Holly. This is the wrong thing to discuss with a client.*

The waitress came to retrieve their salad plates giving Holly some time to think. She hadn't expected the conversation to take this direction tonight. She would have to steer the conversation back to safer territory in a hurry in order to keep her relationship with Brady from becoming strained.

"When I asked you where you were going to church on Sunday, you dodged my answer. Why? You obviously know the Word."

"Brady, it was stupid of me to even bring it up. Mixing politics or religion with business is never a good idea. I shouldn't have brought it up. I'm sorry."

"Well, you've already broken that policy tonight, so are you going to answer my question?" His dark brown eyes invited an answer.

Holly broke her eyes away and studied the other diners around her, not seeing any of them. She was on professionally shaky ground. But it wasn't in her nature to back away from a direct question. Politics and religion had come up in nightly conversations while living with her uncle and mother. She had been challenged by them both to know what she believed and why she believed it.

She brought her attention back to Brady. . "Okay, since you asked." She reached for her wineglass, holding his gaze. "I was raised in the church and was involved in youth group, and camps and the whole thing."

"And now?"

"When my parents divorced, it was stunning how many of those good Christian folks turned their backs on us—on me. No one ever asked what happened or why my parents divorced. They just labeled my mom with this big "D" on her forehead, and that was that."

"So why *did* your folks divorce?"

"Not for any of the 'good' reasons." She made quote signs with her fingers. "My dad beat my mom. When he hit me, she decided it was time to leave." The words were out before she could stop them, challenging him to condemn her, too.

All the old memories flooded her. Accusing, questioning, insulting questions.

"Why didn't your mom seek counseling?"

"She should have spoken with the pastor."

She folded her arms and waited for his predictable response.

"Didn't your parents get any counseling from the church?"

There it was.

"Oh, sure. Dad was an elder, so we had lots of people calling Mom to tell her she was sinning by leaving him. The women in her Bible study did a tag-team lunch thing for a while. Every one of them told her the same thing. No one wanted to hear what was actually going on in our home." Holly pulled her hands into her lap as the waitress brought their main course. Everything looked wonderful but her appetite had evaporated. She pushed the food around on her plate, not looking up. She was glad it was out. His knowing her feelings about the church would keep things less complicated between them. Strictly business.

"How bad was it?" Brady's voice was soft.

She looked up into his face. His eyes were kind, inviting more from her. His compassion surprised her. But that was his job, right? He was doing what he had been trained to do. She wondered how far she could go before the condemnation started or he changed the subject. It wasn't nice, but she wasn't feeling very nice at the moment. Bringing up the old hurts brought the anger with it.

"The night before we left," she continued, "I remember hearing them argue and then a loud bang. Mom didn't ever scream. I could hear her crying through the door. I would go and listen sometimes. That night Dad opened the door and caught me standing there. He lifted me up by my hair and threw me down the hall into the kitchen. Then he started kicking me. I got up and ran. He chased me all the way back to my bedroom. Mom threw herself in front of him to stop him from coming in. Dad lifted Mom by the neck and hauled her back to the bedroom. That was the only time he hit me."

Brady sat back, his expression hard to read.

Taking a slow sip of her Chardonnay, Holly held his look.

"Did your mother ever tell anyone that story?"

That wasn't the question she expected. She twirled her wine glass, taking a moment to answer. This conversation had tugged a scab off her heart, the wound now as fresh as when it was first inflicted. "Mom felt that she was accountable to God, not the women's ministry," she started slowly. "She knew that getting a divorce would cause Dad to lose his position as an elder. That was enough for her."

"So you left the church?"

"I haven't been back since I was sixteen. The kids in the youth group helped me out the door when they asked me to step down from leadership. They told me that the sin in my family had to be resolved before I could return."

Brady shook his head. "I am constantly amazed by how much pain Christians inflict upon each other in God's name."

Holly took a few bites of her meal, focusing on how the delicate flavors blended on her tongue. She had bared her soul, something she hadn't intended to do. She waited for the usual response. They would finish their meal, shifting to mundane small talk, and tomorrow they would be back to business as usual. This dinner was a mistake. He was a pastor and she was a, well, what was she? She was an unchurched Christian woman who loved God with every ounce of her being, and in spite of herself, she was more than a little attracted to this God-loving pastor.

Brady took a full, deep breath. His shoulders dropping as he took another bite of his salmon. Then he placed his fork down, wiped his mouth with the cloth napkin and settled back in his chair. "Holly, I'm just a man. I don't have any mystical powers or deep insight. I struggle just like you."

"Really?"

"Yes, really."

"Like how?"

"Like how life seems to throw us a curve ball from time to time."

"Life? Not God?"

"Call it what you like."

"You're dodging, Brady. I opened up to you."

Silence. Holly didn't break the moment, refusing to give him an out. She waited to see if he would take the leap.

"Fair enough, you want the whole ugly story?"

"I have nothing better to do tonight." She watched him over the top of her glass.

Brady toyed with his napkin then settled and looked up.

"I was married to a wonderful woman." He looked away, out the window and over the marina, his eyes growing distant. "Karen was her name. We met when I was in seminary. She loved God and God's Word. We spent hours just talking about Him. We married when I graduated, and five years later, we had a beautiful son, Jeremy. I was pastoring a small church in Wyoming. The congregation was growing fast. 'First mega church in Wyoming,' people were saying. We were thrilled at first. Then the fighting started. Nothing I did, nothing I said, stopped it. I felt like I was married to a completely different woman." He paused to take a sip of his wine, avoiding Holly's attentive gaze.

Holly remained silent, allowing him to reflect. Then he continued.

"One night, we were fighting as usual. When the tension became unbearable, Karen took Jeremy and went for a drive. That usually cooled her off. But this time a drunk driver ended the fighting."

Holly gasped and leaned forward. "And your son?"

Brady stared at his plate. "Death was instantaneous according to the report. They never knew what hit them."

"Oh, Brady, I'm so sorry." Her face reddened at her intrusion into his obvious pain.

"I couldn't stay in Wyoming." He pulled a piece of bread from the basket and tore it a bit too hard. "I tried. Everyone was wonderful, but in the end, I knew I had to move on. That was three years ago." He raised his knife and reached for a pat of butter. The knife blade chattered on the plate.

"So now you are at Mariners Chapel, a far cry from Mega-church Wyoming."

"Yes, here I am. Thank you for asking." He offered a forced smile. .

"Really? I feel like I've intruded."

"Yes, really."

Silence hung between them once again. Holly finally spoke. "How old was your son?"

"Two and a half."

"I think I'd die."

"I almost did. There were times I wish I had."

Chapter Twelve

By the time dinner was over, the rest of the rain clouds had cleared away and stars blazed across the sky. Brady was trying to figure out a way to prolong their date when Holly suggested they take a stroll down the parking lot to the south end of the marina. Brady agreed, folding up the collar of his jacket against the damp, chill evening. As they passed the rows of boats in silence, Brady reviewed their conversation and wondered what direction the evening was taking. The impromptu dinner had been awkward at times, but they had made it through. She was easy to talk to, Holly could tolerate the silence between them. Some people had to fill the void with small talk, but Holly seemed different.

Holly paused next to her car. "Would you like to see my boat?" Her eyes shone in the moonlight. He marveled at her beauty, aglow in the soft moonlight. Could God have brought her into his life? He hadn't been looking for companionship. Did he want to take this step? Their conversation tonight had already brought up old pain. For both of them if he guessed right. He paused for a moment before answering. Knowing that moving beyond just dinner would take this casual relationship one step deeper.

You have a boat?" he finally answered, pulling himself back to the question.

"A sail boat. It's right there. "She pointed to a yellow vessel tied to the dock near the shore, bobbing in the mirrored water, gently illuminated by the lights from the restaurant.

"I thought you didn't have a hobby. All work and all that."

Holly pulled her keys from her purse with a grin and unlocked the gate that led down to the dock. Brady followed.

She deftly undid the elastic cords that held the cover. Rainwater dribbled into the bay as she folded the cover back, exposing the white cockpit. As she stepped down into the boat, she placed her hand on the sail over the boom for support. Brady eyed how the boat tipped under her weight, resolving to stay right where he was. The dock beneath him moved enough to make him nervous. He didn't swim well. His parents had insisted on his taking swim lessons as a child. At the end of that summer session, he was barely considered "water safe." As an adult, he didn't even own a pair of swim trunks.

Holly undid the companionway cover and removed it, then slid back the hatch and stepped down into the boat. In a moment, the interior flooded with light. Holly pulled two cushions from below and placed them on the outside bench seats.

"Come have a seat in the cockpit, Brady." She patted one of the seats. "Would you like a cup of tea?"

"I . . . um. Tea?"

"Sure, I have a stove and all the makings. I love to come down here at night. It's so peaceful. Give it a try." She patted the seat farthest from the dock.

"I'm not much of a boat person, Holly."

"You don't have to be a boat person to sit on a boat."

How on earth did he get into this? Better yet, how was he going to get out? Holly disappeared into the small cabin while Brady examined the boat. It seemed sturdy enough, but he didn't like the way it moved as Holly shifted her weight. What would happen when he put all his weight on the seat below him?

Holly poked her head out again. "Come on down, Brady. It's dry and really very comfortable." Brady looked for a convenient handhold, but there wasn't much to grab. Holly had placed her hand on the sail as she stepped in. He reached out his hand but the sail was several inches from his fingertips. He would have to step first.

Brady looked for another option. Finding none, he took a breath, stepped onto the cockpit seat, and grabbed onto the sail. The boom moved, providing minimal support. He dropped both feet to the sole of the cockpit with a loud thump and sat, clutching tight to a low chrome railing with one hand.

"Great, you're in. Have you ever been on a sailboat before?" Holly sat below him inside the small cabin. He could see a sink at her shoulder. Across from her, a teapot sat on a butane one-burner stove. Two plastic mugs with tea bags were nestled in her lap. "Do you like it?" she pressed.

"I really don't know much about boats. What kind is it?"

"West Wight Potter. My uncle helped me pick it out five years ago. He taught me to sail when I was in high school. Sailing helped me through some tough times over the years. Have you ever sailed?"

"Never tried it to be honest. I'm from Wyoming, remember?" By this time, the boat had quit rocking from his descent, and Brady felt comfortable enough to release his grip on the metal railing. He forced himself to look relaxed, leaning back slowly, testing the stability of the little craft.

The teapot whistled and Holly leaned forward to stand, causing the boat to teeter. Brady sat up, shifting his weight to counterbalance. Holly poured hot water into the mugs and climbed up a short wooden ladder into the cockpit. The boat rocked again, sending Brady's hand back to the railing. He attempted to appear casual as he reached out for his tea. Holly sat on the opposite cockpit seat, leaning back against the bulkhead and stretching her legs out before her. Her face, heavily shadowed now, took on a mysterious tone. Brady drank in her beauty then averted his eyes when she turned to look at him.

"Isn't this just lovely?"

Brady turned to take in the view before them. The marina opened into Morro Bay, its surface tranquil in the still evening. Sand dunes across the bay were lighter gray against the darkness of the night. Above them, shreds of clouds hung across the moon. But nothing compared to the loveliness of the woman who sat across from him.

"Yes, Holly, everything is lovely."

The following morning, Brady waited outside Heritage Oaks Bank for the doors to open so he could pick up a copy of the church's last bank statement. He stood in the sun, savoring the memory of the night before. After their tea on the boat, he and Holly had followed the path around the point to the entrance of the marina. The night sky had cleared and the bay undulated gently, like liquid mercury in the moonlight. Holly had shivered and Brady had started to lift his arm to her slender shoulders, then stopped himself. He clenched his hand now at the thought. It had seemed the thing to do for a brief moment. Why was he drawn to her? She was lovely; there was no denying that. She was bright and obviously had a working knowledge of the Word. But he held himself back. *A man in my position.* The words were hollow now. At one time, he *was* considered a man of some position. Now, he was just a small-town pastor of a sleepy neighborhood church. What position was he protecting? He was doing the job he had been trained and hired to do. He could do it in his sleep, almost. Nevertheless, his little congregation was beginning to take notice of his lack of connection. Did he care? At some level yes. But at a deeper level, he wasn't so sure.

Losing Karen and Jeremy had closed a door within him. In the past, his relationship with God had been as natural as breathing, but he didn't trust God anymore, or maybe he didn't trust himself.

At ten, a smartly dressed woman unlocked the bank doors and welcomed him in. The sunny interior of the small-town bank was tastefully decorated with pictures of sailboats and paintings of Morro Bay.

A teller looked up, her expression welcoming him. She motioned him over. "Good morning, how can I help you?"

"I'm Brady McGregor, pastor over at Mariners Chapel. I was wondering if I could get a copy of our last bank statement.

"Of course, may I see your ID?" The teller turned to her computer screen and started typing. After glancing at Brady's driver's license, she handed it back.

When she gave him the statement, he glanced at the name at the top and then folded it and placed it in his coat pocket. Thanking the teller, he went back out into the sunshine. Seagulls shouted at each other overhead, and the surf boomed on the breakwater. A large swell was predicted for today, and it sounded like it had arrived. The waves would be rolling in from the south, which meant the harbor mouth would be closed, shutting down the local fishing and recreational boats for at least a day.

Back at the church, Brady settled into his office and turned on the ancient electric heater. Then he pulled out the two-page bank statement and glanced at the bottom line: $350,468.23!

What? Brady double checked the name on the statement then pulled out the last recap Evelyn had given the elder board at the beginning of the month. Evelyn's statement showed an income last month of $2,327.61 and disbursements of $1,268 for a net income of $1,059. 61 and a bank balance of $10,287. 53.

Brady ran his eye over the bank statement more closely. Large sums of money moved in and out of the account every Thursday with the last deposit being $156,293. Evelyn's small weekly deposits were also identifiable every Monday. Something was terribly wrong with the bank accounting. Evelyn's trim, well-groomed image came to Brady's mind.

Out in the reception area, Vera was just getting off the phone. Brady got up from his desk to speak with her.

"Vera, how long has Evelyn been doing the accounting?"

Vera's brows dropped in concentration. "I don't remember when she didn't. Probably been twenty years anyway, as ong as I've been in the office, why? "

Brady hesitated. "I was just hoping there was someone else I could talk to. Evelyn is so distraught right now. I don't want to bother her."

A deepening sense of foreboding crept up his spine as he reached around the door for his jacket. "I'll be back in a little while, Vera. I have my cell phone if you need me.

In the car, Brady paused and closed his eyes.

Think, think, think! There had to be a simple explanation.

He returned to the bank and waited for the same teller. "Hi, I have another question for you. Can you tell me who else can sign on this account?"

The teller went into another room and came back a few moments later with the signature card for the Mariners Chapel account. Four names were on the card, Brady McGregor, Evelyn Davenport, Yosef Shankston, and Arlen Parkfield, just as he remembered. "Would you mind printing out the last six months' statements?"

Back in his car, Brady checked the statements quickly. The pattern was the same, steady large deposits and withdrawals every week. He needed time to think. His mind raced with possibilities he didn't want to consider. He needed to talk this out with someone. But who?

Holly had just sat down at her computer when the phone rang.

"Holly, this is Elizabeth Hollingsworth at Hibiscus House. Could you please come down here right away?"

"Of course. Is something wrong? Is my uncle all right?"

Elizabeth hesitated, sending off warning bells in Holly's head.

"It will be best if we speak face to face. I hope you understand."

"I'm on my way."

Holly forced herself not to rush. Her hands trembled as she inserted the keys in the ignition, fearing the worst. Fortunately, there were no traffic lights along the two-mile route to Hibiscus House.

Three police cars were in the parking lot when Holly pulled in. Dread quickened her stride up the sidewalk. She struggled for composure as she entered the bright atrium. Elizabeth Hollingsworth, the director, met her and escorted Holly to her office, closing the door behind them both.

A. J. stood to greet her. *What was he doing here?* Holly's palms started to burn, then sweat. Her heart thumped audibly and her lips trembled as she turned questioning eyes toward Elizabeth Hollingsworth.

"I'm sorry, Holly. Your uncle passed today. About three hours ago."

"Three hours? *Three hours!* Why didn't you call me sooner?" She took a step toward Elizabeth, hands clenched. She had been chatting on the phone and sending off emails while her uncle lay dead. She could have been with him—holding his hand. How could they ...

Elizabeth looked at A.J.

"Well, that was my doing, Holly."

Holly's stomach lurched and she turned toward A.J., baffled by his presence. His eyes gave nothing away. "*Your* doing, A.J.? You don't even...didn't even know my uncle."

A.J. shifted his weight and took a deep breath. "Well . . . you see . . . your uncle didn't die of natural causes."

Holly's thought processes flipped from raging irritation into slow motion—her brain fogging over, thick, like a summer morning on the coast. "I'm . . . I'm not sure what you are saying," she whispered, then teetered as the room spun.

A.J. reached out to steady her. She tried to brush him off.

"Holly, please sit down. This isn't an easy situation," Elizabeth soothed.

A.J. took her elbow and led her to a couch, then sat facing her. "When the nurse found your uncle, he was in the cafeteria. By himself. Holly. I'm sorry to have to tell you this. He was strangled." A.J.'s usual tough guy demeanor was overshadowed by compassion in his eyes. "I'll find out who did it, Holly, I promise." He placed his hand on her knee, his eyes holding hers.

Stunned, Holly broke his gaze and looked around the room. She should go to Uncle Nikko. "Where is he?" She began to rise, but A.J. put a restraining hand on her arm.

"He was just taken to the morgue. You don't want to see him Holly, trust me on this."

This couldn't be true. Uncle Nikko was such a good man—a sweetheart. He never met a stranger—never had an enemy. Now he was gone, and she hadn't said good-bye! Just like her mother, he had been snatched from her without warning. Holly crumpled into a ball, lowering her face into her lap and sobbed.

A.J.'s warm hand rested on her arm, and Elizabeth tucked a tissue into her hand. The pain was too great, and their compassion made her cry harder. Her life was a desert. No one in it but her. She tried to stop crying, to compose herself, but the tears wouldn't stop. Where had the God

Uncle Nikko had trusted been? Had God watched as his life was squeezed from him? Anger pounded her from within, leaving her limp and sore.

A.J. and Elizabeth stayed with her, comforting her, until her tears finally subsided. She sat up, dabbing at her eyes. The black smudges on the tissue told her that her makeup was a mess. She didn't care.

"This is so wrong! Uncle Nikko didn't have an enemy in the world."

"I know, Holly. I never met him, but I felt like I had."

"Do you think it was someone from Hibiscus House? The doors are all alarmed. How could a murderer get in?"

"We're looking into that. In the meantime, I'd like to drive you home. I can have an officer bring your car later. What do you say? "

She dabbed her eyes and nodded. "Can I at least go to his room first?"

"I'm afraid not right now. It's a crime scene. We have to have a look around before you disturb anything."

Her lips trembled again. She fought for control. "I can't even see his room? I won't touch anything. Please, A. J." She laid her small hand on his.

Chapter Thirteen

The boards squeaked under his feet as Brady made his way down the gangway of Bayfront marina to the dock, and from the dock to the slip where Yosef kept his Compac 23 sailboat. Brady had ventured down to this private marina at the base of an old fish-processing plant a couple of times, but Yosef had not been able to convince him to go sailing. And Brady wasn't planning to sail today, either. He needed to talk.

When Yosef saw Brady approaching, he stood and waved a greasy hand, then wiped it on a terry towel. "Welcome aboard, Pastor! Here, give me your hand."

Yosef's boat was larger than Holly's little West Wight Potter. The broad, deep cockpit didn't dip they way the Potter had when he stepped on board. The smell of diesel oil lingered around Yosef like an old friend.

"What brings you down this way, Pastor Brady? Ready to go for that sail? "

"I don't think so today," Brady looked about for the best place to sit. "Do you have a moment to chat?"

"Sure, let me get something to wet my whistle first." Yosef ducked down into the cabin and emerged in a moment with two icy sodas. "Pastor?" he offered Brady one of the sodas.

"Yes, thanks." Brady ran his fingers along the gleaming teak trim of the boat. Bristol was the word he had heard to describe a boat in this condition. The smooth wood exuded warmth under his hand.

Brady pondered where to begin. Yosef and Vera had provided Brady with a roof over his head for the past few months, and they had become close. But he still wasn't sure how far to take this conversation. The boat bobbed gently beneath him, and the crisp salt air filled his senses. The cabin blocked the wind, and the sun felt warm and comforting. Brady relaxed a bit and leaned forward, resting his elbows on his knees.

"Yosef, I'm confused about the finances of the church. I thought you might be able to enlighten me."

Yosef settled himself on the seat across from Brady and took a swig of soda. "If I can, what's your question?"

"I went down to the bank and got a copy of last month's statement. According to the bank, we have well over three-hundred-thousand dollars in our account. Does that make sense to you?"

Brady watched Yosef's response carefully but couldn't read the emotions hidden behind his soft gray eyes. He knew he was taking a chance by being so open in his discovery, but his instincts told him he could trust Yosef. He had to trust somebody.

Yosef sat back and rested his elbows on the combing. His sharp, blue eyes held Brady's from beneath bushy brows.

"Three hundred thousand? You sure they gave you the right statement?"

"Here it is. See for yourself." Brady produced the most recent statement from his jacket pocket.

Yosef took the paper and studied it for a few moments, folded it and handed it back to Brady. "I don't quite know what to make of that. Only four of us have access to that account."

"I know. You, me, Evelyn, and Arlen."

"Do you think we could be the victims of that identity theft thing they talk about—where people get into your account?"

"I don't think so, Yosef. Those types tend to take money, not give it to you." Brady kept a smile from tugging at his mouth. Yosef wasn't exactly a financial wizard, but he was wise in the ways of the world. That was what Brady needed right now, wisdom.

"Well, maybe somebody is just storing it there for a bit."

Brady tried to mask his surprise at Yosef's odd thought.

"I know that sounds crazy, but what else is there?" Yosef spread his large hands and hunched his shoulders. "So, let's spend it quick on the roof before it disappears!" He chuckled and rubbed his hands together; mock greed glinted in his eyes.

Brady grinned and shook his head. Yosef always had a way of lightening things. "Has anything like this happened before, Yosef?"

The old fisherman grew serious again. "We've always been a small congregation. I've seen finances so thin, that at times folks took turns paying the utility bills. I can't for the life of me think of where such a large chunk of money would have come from. Vera usually knows everything that goes on at the church, and she's been friends with Evelyn since they were girls. Something is wrong. No doubt about it."

Yosef finished off his soda in two long pulls. "I need to try out this motor, Pastor Brady. Want to come along? I think better with water moving under my keel." Yosef swept his arm to encompass the beauty of the estuary, sand dunes and Morro Rock. "We can talk this out enjoying God's creation."

Brady's eyes flicked to the dock and then back to Yosef.

"Just around the harbor, I promise." Yosef put his right hand over his heart and raised the left in a solemn oath.

Brady started to refuse and then remembered his conversation with Arlen. His job was to connect with these people, but he thoroughly disliked the idea of sailing. "All right, Yosef. I have a little time. Tell me what to do."

Yosef tossed Brady a life jacket and donned one himself. Then he flipped a switch on the stern, and the engine coughed, sputtered, and ignited. Yosef told Brady how to cast them off from the slip, as Yosef gently eased the classic sailboat out into the channel. The tide was running hard this time of the day and Yosef used the momentum to swing the heavy shoal keel around and head the boat north toward the harbor mouth. The putt, putt, putt of the little motor pushed them steadily along against the tide.

A fresh breeze lifted Brady's hair and lightened his mood for a moment. His hand clutched the nearby winch, telegraphing his nervousness. He glanced at Yosef who winked encouragement. Brady rotated his shoulders several times in an attempt to loosen them and drew in a few deep breaths. He forced his eyes away from the water and toward the shore in an effort to distract himself.

The bright afternoon sunshine caused the colors around him to pop. Kayakers in red plastic, cigar-shaped boats maneuvered around the larger vessels moored in the harbor. A family of six paddled by. One of the older boys splashed his little sister, and the salt air filled with her squeals.

Seagulls perched here and there on boats in various stages of disrepair. Some were obviously derelict, others well-used, and a few gleamed with pride of ownership. Laundry hung from the lifelines of a blue-hulled sloop, its occupant waving happily to Brady as he tended a barbeque hung from the railing.

Farther along, they came to what was left of the Morro Bay fishing fleet, huge, no-nonsense crafts built to withstand heavy labor with minimal care. The sky held a raucous swirl of seagulls hunting scraps of fish. The boats had been out for a couple of days and looked to have made a haul.

Nearing Morro Rock, Yosef brought the little cruiser about and winked at Brady. "Now you just sit quiet for a moment, Pastor, and I'm gonna treat you to a special experience." Yosef pulled on a line to his right and the big jib sail that was wrapped around the forestay unfurled and snapped as it filled on the breeze. When Yosef cut the motor, the silence was profound. They glided along to the whisper and gurgle of the water as it caressed the hull. Pelicans squawked and mumbled to their right along the mud flats, a sound that would otherwise go unheard over the din of a motor.

Brady looked to Yosef for reassurance at the loss of engine power. The older man just smiled and leaned back, enjoying the quiet pleasure that was sailing. Brady decided to try to do the same, and closed his eyes, letting the breeze soothe his anxiety.

After a while, Yosef broke the reverie. "What does Evelyn have to say about this mysterious windfall?"

Brady opened his eyes and squinted into the sudden brightness. "I haven't heard anything from her since Vera called her yesterday from the church. She didn't seem to be in a place, emotionally, to talk about it."

"Don't let that prim and proper exterior fool you. Evelyn is one tough old bird. Raised Cheri herself after her husband died in a car accident. No life insurance, nothing. He had worked for old man Parkfield, Arlen's father. Parkfield did the right thing. He gave Evelyn a job in the back office. Eventually she became the bookkeeper and kind of an overall back-office manager. She can go nose to nose with the toughest contractors. I swear that woman could squeeze blood from a turnip. If anyone knows what's going on, it's Evelyn."

The door to Holly's uncle's room was slightly ajar. Yellow police tape barred their entrance. A.J. pushed the door the rest of the way open and the two of them peered in over the tape. A man in a suit but no tie was taking pictures of her uncle's nightstand.

"Don't touch anything, Holly," A.J. instructed. "Just stand here and look around. Do you see anything that looks different? Anything out of place or missing?"

Holly slowly scanned the room. Uncle Nikko's bed was made, and his Bible was where she had left it on Sunday. Something was wrong though. She scanned the room again; turning her head slowly she studied each detail. There. The bookcase. The five red leather journals were gone, the space they had occupied now filled with books from the shelf below.

"Uncle Nikko's journals are missing." She turned in a slow half-circle again, checking every surface. They were definitely gone.

The man taking the pictures stopped and looked up. "What did they look like?"

"They were worn, red leather covers, nine by twelve." She indicated the size with her hands.

"When did you last see them?"

"I don't really know. They always sat on that shelf." She pointed to one end of the bookcase.

"He also always had one with him. It was never out of reach. Did he have it with him when you found him?"

The two men exchanged glances and then looked at Holly. "We didn't find a journal with him, Holly."

Tears welled up. Another desecration to her uncle's memory. Someone had stolen the journals, but why?

A.J. spoke softly to her. "Do you know what's in them?"

"I only saw inside one once when I was a teenager." She dabbed at her nose with a soggy tissue. "I was curious. But they were written in Hebrew."

"Hebrew?"

"Uncle Nikko was a Messianic Jew. His parents were very devout and taught him Hebrew. He could read and write it as well as speak it."

"So you weren't able to read them."

"No. Uncle Nikko tried to teach me Hebrew, but I was a miserable student when it came to languages."

"Did he ever tell you what was in them?"

"No, I always assumed they were his personal memories."

"Someone apparently thought they were important."

Chapter Fourteen

Brady followed Yosef's mustard-colored Chevy pick-up over to Evelyn's. The two men had talked at length, and Yosef finally convinced Brady that the best course was to pay Evelyn a visit and see what they could discover. The front door was ajar so Brady and Yosef stepped in after knocking. The drapes were drawn. The only light came from a window in the kitchen. Brady's eyes took a moment to adjust.

"Hello, Evelyn, may we come in?" he asked.

"Hello, Pastor Brady, Yosef, please come in. Vera was just here. She left a lemon bundt cake on the counter. Help yourself." Evelyn sat stiffly in her chair, her hands clenched in her lap. In the parlor, several of the women from the Monday night Bible study sat with a cup of tea, their interrupted conversation hanging awkwardly in the air.

Yosef pulled his hat from his head and held it in front of him like a fig leaf. "We just wanted to stop by and make sure you didn't need anything, Evelyn."

"I'm doing quite well. Thank you, Yosef." Her tone had an edge. The women that surrounded her were still, eyes averted. The message was clear. *Please leave.*

Yosef sniffed, scratched his nose, and gave Brady a sideways glance.

Brady took a step into the room. "Have you had many visitors today, Evelyn?"

Evelyn took a sip of her tea and didn't look up. "Not many."

Silence.

"Since we're here, Evelyn, I was wondering if I could take the books back to the church. We have to repair the roof, and I want to see where we stand before ordering the work done."

Yosef's fuzzy eyebrows rose for a moment. Then he looked down, sniffed, and scratched his nose again.

"I told Vera I would bring them in the first of next week." She looked up and pinned Brady with a direct stare.

"I appreciate that, Evelyn, but the roof is leaking today, and something needs to be done before the rains come again. So if it's not too much trouble—"

"Well, at the moment, it *is* too much trouble, Pastor. Thank you for visiting. Yosef, please thank Vera for the cake." She held Brady's eyes, daring him to challenge her.

The air grew thick as Brady held her stare. This was a showdown, but was it the right hill to die on? No, he decided. She was grieving and needed space. If necessary, he would fix the roof with his own funds and figure all the details out later.

Out on the sidewalk, Yosef turned to Brady. "Phew! That was like visiting a den of vipers." He looked back over his shoulder. "I thought we agreed not to mention the books—to wait until after the funeral."

"Yes, we did. And I feel for Evelyn's position, and understand her pain. But I went with a hunch. I wanted to *see* what she would do when she was asked for the books."

Brady kicked at a small weed that was forcing its way up through the asphalt. Evelyn's reaction was definitely odd. The hairs on the back of his neck had prickled. Something was going on, and whatever it was, it definitely wasn't good for the church.

"Have I ever mentioned, Pastor Brady, that Vera and I think you are doing a great job?"

Brady smiled down at the hardy old fisherman. "Thanks, Yosef. Sometimes it's hard to tell. I've heard that some folks don't like the sermons I have been giving. Have you heard anything about that?"

"You just keep doing what you're doing, Pastor. God will take care of the rest."

"I hope you're right. I spend the week in prayer and watchfulness. The Holy Spirit prompts me, and that's what I speak on. It's a pretty basic approach that's worked for me over the years."

Liar.

His conscience slammed him. Perhaps he could dig back into his old sermons and find something fresh.

"Keep it up. You're moving hearts. The folks that complain are probably the ones you are touching the most."

"If that's so, it's not me. I just speak the words. The Holy Spirit does the rest. See you soon."

Brady cringed as he fished for his car keys and headed up the street.

Chapter Fifteen

Holly spent two more hours at Hibiscus House answering A.J.'s questions, especially about her uncle's state of mind in the days leading up to his death. She tried to recall anything at all that would help in the investigation, but other than his strange ramblings and fear of sleeping, there wasn't much to tell.

Exhausted, Holly declined A.J.'s offer of a ride home. Once on the road, she automatically drove back to her office. But when the driveway came up on her right, she passed it and continued to Hwy 1. She chose the onramp south for no reason. Home held no comfort for her. She took the next off ramp and drove along South Bay Blvd until it split to the right, wove along the estuary, and back to the State Park Marina. Pulling into the parking lot she stopped, turned off the engine, and looked down at her little West Wight Potter. Glancing at the wind vane and a flag at the top of the mast on a boat down the marina, she made her decision.

She pulled a duffle from her trunk, slung it over her shoulder, and headed down the gangway to the dock. A young couple was ferrying boxes from their truck to their boat and had left the gate propped open. Holly didn't lift her eyes as they passed on the narrow gangway. Pulling the damp tarp off the Potter, she nearly fell as she scrambled down inside. Unzipping her duffle, she reached in and pulled out an old green jacket. Uncle Nikko's jacket. Holly buried her face in it, inhaling his scent.

Fresh sobs wrenched her. She could see his smiling eyes as he sat across the kitchen table from her all those years ago. Then her thoughts shifted to his frail body, bent and weak, resting in his wheelchair as someone incredibly evil crept up behind him, intent upon snuffing out his precious life. She unwillingly imagined his pitiful struggle, like a kitten in the grip of a wolf. She screamed into the jacket until finally, in exhaustion, no sound came at all.

Spent, she wiped her face on a towel dipped in water from the faucet and pulled her hair into a ponytail. At her shoulder was a marine radio. She turned it on and pressed the weather channel button. A mechanical voice droned through the weather up and down the coast as Holly slowly changed her clothes. There was no hurry. She had all afternoon. Looking around the small cabin, she automatically checked to be sure the centerboard was locked down and all the cabinets were secured. She yanked a ball cap snug on her head and went up on deck, turning back to pull the cockpit cushions up from below.

"Mind some company?"

Holly jumped, hitting the back of her head on the companionway hatch. She pulled her head out and looked up to see Brady standing on the dock.

Yes, I do mind. But she couldn't answer. She knew if she spoke, she would cry. She simply nodded, placed the cushions in the cockpit, stood, and began to remove the blue sail cover.

"Are you going out?"

She nodded again, not looking at him.

"By yourself?"

Holly finally met his eyes and the tears burst forth. She wiped them on her sweatshirt sleeve and began untying the sail in short, violent jerks.

"Holly, what's wrong?" Brady gingerly stepped into the boat and stood across from her. The sail, lashed to the boom, separated them. "Holly, talk to me."

"My uncle," she whispered, the ache in her throat choking out the words. Her eyes pleaded with him, begging him not to make her say the words.

"What about your uncle?"

She buried her face in her arms, leaned on the sail and sobbed.

Brady set his hand on her shoulder gently and squeezed. The pressure brought a fresh shudder of grief.

"He died today. Somebody ... murdered him, Brady!" She lifted her wet face. "How could somebody kill sweet Uncle Nikko? He was a good man. A kind man." She snatched the last sail tie and whipped it the rest of the way off, balling it and tossing it into the cabin. Then she turned and levered the outboard motor attached to the back of the boat down into the water. With two quick pulls, it started.

"You coming or not?" Her words came out fierce.

"You're going out? Holly, you can't go out alone."

"Get on or get off. Make a decision." She brushed past him, climbed onto the dock, and released the bow line. Then she returned to the cockpit and released the stern lines.

"Make a decision."

"I can't let you go out alone."

"Suit yourself." She bent over the stern and put the outboard into reverse. The sailboat backed slowly out of the slip. When they were clear, Holly put the motor into gear and guided the boat out into the marina channel.

In five minutes, they were in the main channel of the harbor. "Here, take the tiller. I'll get you a vest." Holly stood and waited for Brady to take the smooth wooden tiller in his hand.

"But I don't know ..."

She didn't wait to hear what he was going to say. Brady needed a vest if he was going out with her. She didn't want the company, but here he was. She was too numb to care. Holly went below and grabbed a life vest from the v-berth in the bow of the boat, then snagged a tissue, blew her nose, and climbed back out into the sunshine.

When Holly emerged, Brady was rigid, his right hand clutching the tiller, and his eyes glued straight ahead. A small skiff passed in front of them, sending a wake under the boat. As the Potter rose and fell, Brady's eyes widened in terror.

Holly glanced forward and saw they were headed for a large sailboat. "Push the tiller to the right, Brady."

He obediently moved his hand to the right and the bow of the Potter moved to the left, passing the anchored sailboat by a wide margin and bringing them back into the middle of the channel.

"Now pull it back to the center," she said as she climbed out into the cockpit and took the tiller, handing him the life vest. "If you're going out with me, you need to put this on. Otherwise, I'll drop you at the launch ramp. Your choice." Her words barren of color or emotion.

Brady pulled on the vest, snapped together the buckles, and pulled the straps snug.

"I'm staying. But I want you to reconsider what you're doing." He looked around the boat then back at Holly. "I don't know a thing about sailing, but I'm not going to let you go out alone—not today."

Holly stood in the cockpit, feet splayed and her hand on the tiller. She was heading out, and if he wanted to come, it was up to him. The only place she wanted to be right now was on the water, away from the pain, with nothing to think about but the wind and the waves.

As they approached the north end of the harbor, Holly attached the line for the tiller tamer and secured it. The mechanism would keep the tiller locked in whatever position Holly placed it. Brady obviously couldn't be trusted at the helm until she had the time to show him what to do. And she was in no mood to show anybody anything. She pointed the sailboat straight ahead, into the wind and locked it down. Moving forward, she released a lever on the cabin top and pulled the main halyard, lifting the mainsail up the mast until its leading edge was taught. The big white sail snapped and filled, heeling the little boat over to the right. Holly reached back and released the main sheet that controlled the back of the boom, dumping the air out of the sail, and the boat popped up on its feet.

She glanced down to see Brady staring at her. His hands locked on the stainless steel cockpit rail. "Why did it do that?"

"The wind filled the sail, Brady. That's what's supposed to happen." Her voice had an angry edge. No surprise. She was angry with him for coming. Angry at Uncle Nikko for dying. Angry at the heartless coward that killed him. Impotence tightened in her gut. She glanced at the flags along the waterfront, ruffling and popping in the stiff breeze. This would be a good sail. She wanted a good sail, a hard sail. Something that would take her to the edge of her skills, cleanse her of the toxic fury that burned and twisted in her heart.

Returning to the tiller, Holly released it and turned the Potter west toward the mouth of the harbor. The wind filled the main sail, tilting the sailboat to the left.

"Stay on the same side of the boat as I do. When I change sides, you change sides."

Brady nodded, white lines of grim determination showing along his cheekbones.

Holly scanned the harbor entrance. The silhouette of the swell could be seen against the horizon, heaving and rolling. Nice long rollers. She glanced at the main sail, eased it out a foot, and locked down the tiller again. Then, going forward, she reached past Brady and pulled the jib sheet hand over hand, slowly unfurling the big white sail at the bow. When it was fully extended, she locked the sheet down and returned to the tiller. Adjusting her course to keep the Potter in the center of the channel, she shut down the outboard and tilted it up out of the water.

Over the next hour, as they headed north up the coast, Holly stayed silent. Brady was wise enough not to break into her privacy. She watched him slowly relax first one hand and then the other. He finally took a deep breath and, bracing his feet on the opposite cockpit seat, he turned his face to the wind. The slow rhythm of the swells was the tonic she needed, the cool wind soothing the searing pain a little. The Potter plowed valiantly ahead, rising up one side of the swell and falling happily down its back, the steady wind driving it northward.

She would never sail with Uncle Nikko again. The thought came suddenly and her eyes stung for a moment. The grieving, in quick, unexpected jabs, was like the phantom pain from a severed limb. They would eventually grow further and further apart, as they had when her mother died. She would survive this, too. She knew she would. She had to.

Holly eyed Brady from under the brim of her ball cap. His death grip on the combing had relaxed and the fear that had hardened his face earlier had fallen away. She had to admire the courage he displayed in staying with her this afternoon.

"You're relaxing a bit, Brady. Want to try taking the helm?"

Brady turned to her, a bit of sun reddening his cheekbones and his dark hair whipped and tumbled. He eyed the tiller. "It doesn't look that hard. We're just going straight, right?"

"No turning, nothing to run into. Want to try?"

"Sure. Tell me what to do."

They changed places and Brady grasped the tiller in his left hand. Holly instructed him to move it gently to the left and then to the right, getting the feel of how the boat behaved. She showed him how to pick a spot up the coast where it curved out to sea and keep the bow pointed at that spot to maintain their course.

After about five minutes, a smile spread across Brady's face. "I'm beginning to see what you and Yosef find so wonderful about sailing."

"In a way it's like golf. You never master it." She checked her watch and eyed the fog bank building off the coast. "The weather is changing. We should probably turn around. Want to bring her around yourself?"

Brady nodded. "Tell me what to do."

Holly took a few minutes to explain to Brady what to expect as the boat came across the wind and settled in onto a new course. She was a good teacher and he accomplished the maneuver well. Holly gave Brady another point of reference down the coast from Morro Rock, and then she allowed herself to relax. The wind was now at their back and the sun on their faces. Perfect conditions.

When they were within two miles of Morro Rock, a clanging jerked Holly upright. At the bow of the boat, the forestay had come loose and swung wildly. She brushed Brady's hand off the tiller and turned the Potter directly downwind.

"Holly, what happened?"

"I don't know, but I have to get that forestay reattached or the mast will come down on our heads." She looked up at the main sail, which was

86

pushed up against the shrouds by the wind now coming from behind them. The pressure from the wind would hold the mast up. "Hold this course. I'm going forward."

Holly scrambled up the right side of the boat, around the shrouds, and onto the foredeck. She grabbed at the stainless steel reel at the base of the flopping jib, missing it twice before catching it on the third try. The bow of the boat came up just a bit, taking pressure off the mast and filling the jib. The sudden change of wind direction jerked the big reel from her hands, sending it back over the side in a crazy swinging dance. "Brady! Hold your course. Keep the wind directly at your back!"

Brady nodded, his face grim, as he pulled the tiller toward himself, bringing the boat back on course.

With another quick grab, Holly once again had the reel in her hands. She examined it and then the bracket on the bow where it should have been attached. The stainless steel pin that joined the two was missing. She ran through her head all the bits and pieces of equipment she had below that could hold the two pieces together long enough for her to get the jib rolled up and the main sail down. She tied the reel onto the foredeck with the bowline and returned to the cockpit.

"I have to somehow reattach the forestay." Holly looked ahead and realized her time was short. Morro Bay breakwater laid dead ahead, great waves crashing on its granite back.

In her haste to go below, her foot skittered down the companionway ladder bringing her shin up hard against the centerboard trunk. She barely acknowledged the pain as she pulled the wooden steps aside and retrieved a bin full of hardware. Clawing through the jumble, she hoped to find another stainless steel pin. Finding none, she considered some thick line and then discarded it, opting instead for some rigging wire and a pair of wire cutters.

Back up on deck, she glanced quickly at the breakwater. The Potter was now rising higher and falling farther with the building swell. As the seabed rose beneath them, the water piled up into large waves that rushed toward their final crashing death on the rocks ahead.

She forced herself to move slowly as she went forward. Now was not the time to lose her grip and fall in the water. Once back on the foredeck, Holly threaded the wire through the stem fitting, shoved the pliers in her hip pocket and untied the reel. The Potter lurched beneath her, knocking her feet out from under her. Her tennis shoes skidded across the bow and she straddled the stainless steel bow pulpit, clutching the reel in one hand and grabbing the bow pulpit with the other.

"Holly!" she heard Brady scream. She prayed he wouldn't lose his nerve.

Her weight was pulling the Potter over further. She leaned back and grabbed the other side of the bow pulpit, levering her legs up on deck.

Holly paused. Think! She commanded herself. What will work to reattach the reel to the stem fitting? A quick glance at the fast approaching breakwater told her she had no time to think, she had to make this happen.

Holly tied the bow line around the base of the jib, above the reel, and then passed the line under the anchor hanging from the front of the boat. If she pulled hard, the bottom of the reel clinked against the stem fitting. Close enough. If she could hold the reel there, she could wire them together. The Potter plunged down a steep swell and Holly nearly slipped off the deck again. She wrapped her arm around the flapping jib and went to work, threading the wire through the bottom of the jib, back through the stem fitting and back through the jib. Over and over she worked until there was a thick band of wire connecting the two.

She turned toward Brady. "Pull the thin white line on your right." She lifted the white line off the deck to show him. Brady nodded, his eyes set with determination. Keeping one hand on the tiller, he began to pull on the furling line.

The reel twisted, binding the line. Holly grabbed the reel with both hands, holding it in place.

"Try it again!"

This time the big jib slowly wrapped around the forestay and into a neat bundle. Holly examined her connection. If she could get the main down quickly, it should hold.

A quick glance at the breakwater told her she was out of time. The swells in front of them were beginning to crest and break in a headlong dash to the rocks.

Holly scrambled back into the cockpit, quickly levering the outboard down into the water. The motor started on the first pull and she took in a brief breath of relief. She shifted it into gear and opened the throttle. The boat surged ahead. Holly grabbed the tiller and threw it over, pointing the Potter away from the breakwater.

"Take the helm." She handed off the tiller to Brady and eased the main sheet so the big sail could easily be lowered. "Point the boat that way!" she shouted, nodding west. Rushing forward, she quickly released the main halyard and tugged at the flapping white sail until it filled the cockpit. The Potter rolled heavily back and forth, as the swells now came from the side. Holly sat across from Brady and took the tiller, guiding the boat father out to sea and away from the menacing rocks. Fifteen minutes later, they were again passing under the shadow of Morro Rock. The water was calm and the heavy granite wall of the breakwater blocked the wind and waves "You did a great job out there, Brady."

"Thanks, but I was terrified." He chuckled nervously. Shaking his arms as if to shake off the fear. Then he sobered. "If you had fallen in the water, we would have hit those rocks for sure."

"But we didn't. We're safe."

Holly's gaze traveled up to the top of Morro Rock just in time to see a Peregrine falcon land on an outcropping near the top. It was a rare sighting of the endangered bird. The nesting pair that lived on the rock would have another chick this year if nothing disturbed them. A new life, a step forward for the species. If these beautiful birds could fight their way back from the brink of extinction, she could overcome as well.

Chapter Sixteen

Two hours later, Holly pulled up in front of the Morro Bay Post Office. She had received a notice the day before that a package was waiting for her. The small parking lot in front of the low stucco building was empty. She pulled into one of the three available parking spots and walked up the wheelchair ramp into the building. No other customers in the lobby. Good, it shouldn't take long. Holly handed the signed yellow slip to a petite postal clerk Holly recognized from Top Dog Coffee Bar. Holly drummed her nails on the counter while the clerk retrieved the package from the back room.

The clerk returned and set a large box on the counter. Holly tugged it toward herself. Heavy.

Spinning it, she glanced at the upper left and corner. No return address. Odd. Lifting it onto her chest, she carried it to a workstation just inside the big glass entry. Maybe there was some mistake. She wanted to check the contents before getting all the way home. She glanced up as two more people came in and walked behind her.

An uneasy feeling rose in her chest; better to open it in the car.

Popping the trunk with her key fob, she placed the box inside and slit the tape with her penknife. From inside, wrapped in the local newspaper, she pulled one of Uncle Nikko's journals into the light.

She clasped the precious worn book to her chest. "How on earth?" A tear escaped and trickled down her cheek. Opening it, she thumbed through page after page of neat Hebrew script. Even the dates were indecipherable. How had Uncle Nikko managed to mail them to her? He had been nearly incapacitated the last time she had seen him. Her hand caressed the worn red cover. Should she tell A.J.? He would probably confiscate them. But if they moved the investigation forward, then why not? She hesitated, not wanting to let the journals out of her hands just yet. Perhaps she could dig out her old Hebrew language books and take a stab at deciphering them. In spite of what she had told A.J., she still remembered some of what she had been taught. What harm could a day or two make?

She replaced the journal, closed the trunk, and headed home.

Vera was hanging bright orange towels out to dry in the side yard when Brady drove down the driveway. She waved, her lips full of clothespins.

Yosef came out of the house and followed Brady into the bungalow. Daisy flew in the dog door from the back yard and greeted Brady with wiggling enthusiasm. Then she parked on Yoesf's lap while Brady pushed back the white cotton curtains and went to the kitchen for something to drink.

His temporary home reflected his internal conflict. Unopened boxes lay stacked in the corners, but a few favorite pictures had found their way to the walls. Brady had always liked Monet, and Karen had purchased two reprints for him during their ten-year marriage. "Soleil Levant" hung on one wall; the impressionistic sunset of mottled blues and golds was his favorite. Yosef liked it because it had boats in it.

A plate of cookies was wrapped and waiting on the kitchen table. Vera dropped off these little treats now and then. His waistline didn't need it, but she said they were good for his soul. He chose to believe her and indulged.

"These cookies are still warm. Want to share, Yosef?"

"I'd love one, but don't tell Vera. She hounds me about my sweet tooth." Yosef took two of the chocolate chip cookies from the proffered plate. Then Brady settled into the only other chair in the living room.

"I had an adventure today, Yosef. I went sailing with Holly, my realtor."

Yosef's fuzzy eyebrows rose. "Did you go out of the harbor?"

"We did. I even sailed a bit. I liked it." Brady enjoyed watching the smile spread across Yosef's face. "But that's not everything. As we were coming back in, the jib came loose and Holly had to go up and reattach it while I steered." Brady continued to tell the story as the two of them finished off the cookies.

Finally, Brady had answered as many of Yosef's questions as he could. "So, did you talk to Arlen about the roof?"

Yosef roused himself. "Yes, as a matter of fact, I did." He sat up straighter in his chair, readjusting Daisy in the process. "He actually remembers when his dad put on the new roof twenty years ago. He said he'd replace the missing shingles himself as soon as he can. A couple of his men came over and put a tarp on the ridgeline. We're not supposed to have any rain again till next week, so that should work out well. He asked if you'd like to help, actually. Ever patch a roof, Pastor?"

Brady cringed. After boats, heights ran a close second for places he didn't want to be, and he was useless with his hands. Books had been his realm since childhood. While his friends built forts and dug caves, Brady stayed in and read.

"I don't know that I would be much good helping, Yosef. I haven't much practice with a hammer and nails."

"That's no problem, Pastor Brady. You're never too old to learn." Yosef saluted with his cookie and took another bite.

Brady never imagined that roofing the church would be part of his ministry, but then he had found himself doing all sorts of odd things back in Wyoming in the early days. Herding cattle, fighting fires, you never knew where God would use you next. Sometimes God asked some surprising things.

He visualized the church. The west-side wall was shorter. Falling from the roof there, he would hit the grass and probably survive. The side with the missing shingles was twice that high, and he would land on the asphalt. Brady shook his head. This was crazy thinking. Why did he envision the worst? He looked up to see Yosef across from him with his eyes closed. His chest moved rhythmically with a gurgling muffled snore, one hand on Daisy who was curled on his lap, asleep as well.

Brady smiled at the tender scene. It was nice to have a few quiet minutes to sit and think. Back in seminary, he had envisioned leading a church to a deeper understanding of their roots based on the Apostle Paul's letters. Who were the people Paul preached to? What did they deal with, and what was behind Paul's letters? He had labored over this study for years and had volumes of research. He remembered a time when he had enjoyed crafting sermons. The church in Wyoming had grown and thrived under his direction. God had moved in a mighty way back then. He wondered, did he miss those days? Perhaps. It had been an exciting time. A grueling schedule that kept him out late and away from home all too often. But he had been serving the Lord, right?

He finished his last cookie as Yosef stirred and opened one eye. "I think it's time to head home." Brady nodded with a wave as Yosef placed a groggy Daisy on the floor and headed out the door. Brady grinned at the smear of chocolate in the corner of Yosef's mouth.

The next morning Brady retrieved the newspaper from the driveway as the coffee maker hissed and toast baked in the toaster. Coming back down the driveway to the house, he slipped the paper from its plastic sack and unfolded it to the front page. A picture of Cheri Davenport was in the left column. "Suicide Suspected in Death at Spooners Cove," it stated in bold letters beneath her picture. A short article below the picture began: "Coroner says Davenport, 24, was five weeks pregnant." Brady stopped in the middle of the driveway and read the rest. There was no evidence of foul play. Cheri's car was found at the scene, the keys sitting on the floorboard. The Sheriff's Department had no further comments, since the investigation was still ongoing.

Brady stood for a moment in the damp air and looked off into the distance. His mind churned with this new information. Was that the unforgivable sin Cheri wanted to talk to him about? Was it the pregnancy? Had Evelyn known about it? Cheri hadn't struck him as suicidal, but then, many suicidal people never give anyone a clue of their intentions.

The chilly morning fog brought him back to the moment. Returning to the kitchen, he stood and watched the coffee pot fill the glass carafe, but didn't see it.

Suicide.

Cheri had come to *him*, and *he* had been unable to reach her. Was it possible that he …?

He left the thought unfinished, unwilling to look that closely. His thoughts went to Evelyn. How would she take the news? He remembered her behavior yesterday. She was obviously devastated. However, was she devastated about the pregnancy or devastated because people found out? It wasn't a kind thought. But how much did he really know about Evelyn's relationship with her daughter? Brady's heart ached for Karen's wise counsel. He thought about Holly, but she had plenty of grief of her own. A knock on the door ended his musings.

The door opened and Yosef stuck his head in. "You busy?"

"Never too busy for you. What's up?"

"Have you seen this morning's paper?"

"Yes, about Cheri you mean?"

"We just opened it. Vera has breakfast almost ready. You want to talk?"

Perfect. Yosef and Vera could fill him in better than anyone. If only he could ask the right questions. "Sure, be right there."

The smell of fresh coffee and baking waffles filled the kitchen and wafted out the door to welcome Brady. Vera's cooking was legend within the church. The Shankston home always smelled of fresh-baked goods. Their kitchen and breakfast nook took up the entire back corner of the house where banks of windows let in the muted, foggy light. Bright red and white geraniums sat in pots on every available flat surface, their cheerful flowers mirrored in Vera's china collection displayed in glass-fronted cupboards.

The local newspaper lay on the kitchen table. Yosef picked it up and folded its grim news away for the moment. Vera greeted Brady with a wan smile and a steaming cup of coffee. Cream and sugar were already on the table, as were two kinds of syrup and soft butter. Efficient Vera followed the coffee with a pile of waffles and three plates. A platter of bacon completed the breakfast banquet. Vera settled herself into the chair closest to the kitchen.

The three held hands as Brady offered up a blessing.

"Father, I offer up Evelyn today. Only you know, Father, what is in her heart. I pray that your spirit fills her with a comfort only you can provide. Thank you for my good friends, Vera and Yosef, and thank you for this unexpected breakfast blessing, in your Son's name. Amen."

Vera slipped a napkin onto her lap. "Well, Pastor Brady, what do you make of the newspaper today?"

In spite of himself, Brady was growing fond of Vera's blunt manner. She had done her part by making breakfast. Now it was Brady's turn to talk about what was on everyone's mind.

Brady took his time pouring out the thick olallieberry syrup, the product of a fruit stand in nearby Cambria. As the thick, burgundy liquid meandered across his waffle, Brady allowed it to hold his concentration as he formulated an answer.

"I hope Evelyn knew about the conclusions of the Sheriff's Department before the paper came out. I can't imagine getting that kind of information from the newspaper." He took a bite of the syrup-laden waffle and chewed a bit longer than necessary to buy a bit more time to answer. "Being new to the church, I don't know all the ins and outs of the

94

families and their relationships. Sometimes it places me at a disadvantage." Brady hoped this comment would open the door to more insight.

Yosef poured syrup on his waffle. "You don't know anything about Evelyn and Cheri. Is that what you mean?"

"Yes, I suppose. Gossip is always a danger, so getting to know folks can be a delicate process."

They chewed in silence, the clink of silverware on plates and the sipping of coffee filling the nook. Brady concentrated on his plate and waited. He hoped Vera or Yosef would talk—helping him in his desire to understand what was happening with Evelyn and how that related to Cheri's death, and to deal with his rising anger. If something he had or hadn't said caused her death, he wanted to know. He needed to know.

Yosef poked at his waffle, arranging two pieces into different configurations.

Vera filled her coffee cup. "Well, Evelyn and Cheri had a hard time getting along once Cheri hit that rough patch as a teenager. Evelyn is a bit strait-laced as you probably know, and Cheri was a wild oat in high school. This isn't the first time her name has been in the local paper. I think Evelyn had mixed emotions about Cheri coming home."

Vera took a sip of coffee, allowing Yosef to pick up the thread. "Ever since she came back from college in Nebraska and got that little apartment, Evelyn has been on edge."

Vera continued Yosef's thought. "I think she was just waiting for something like this to happen, not that she expected Cheri to die, of course. It's just that Cheri had been an embarrassment to Evelyn for years. When Cheri started coming to the women's study, Evelyn looked as pinched as a prune."

"Vera!" Yosef chided.

"Well, it's true." Vera set her fork down, challenged her husband with a look, and then continued. "When Cheri left for college, life got simpler for Evelyn. Cheri was twelve when Walter died. Right after that Cheri started her shenanigans. If I were Evelyn, I would actually be breathing a sigh of relief that the burden's finally been lifted."

Brady winced at Vera's blunt and unkind words. She rose, lifted the coffee carafe and refilled Yosef and Brady's cups. "We tried to reach her in the Monday night women's study. She was always a stubborn child and was just as stubborn as an adult." Vera slid a small pitcher of milk toward Brady. "So, do you think it was suicide? He poured a dollop of milk in his cup. The picture Vera and Yosef were painting of Cheri puzzled him. So different from what he had heard from Holly and Jessica.

"Well, of course, that's what it was. Either that, or else she was drunk and just fell off the cliff. Back to her old ways." Vera waved her fork in the air for emphasis and then resumed eating.

Yosef shook his head. "Nay, Vera. I think you're too hard on the girl. She mended her ways in college and got her degree. Maybe she just slipped and fell. That would make sense, wouldn't it now?"

Vera lifted her mug, inhaling the nutty aroma that filled the room. "I guess you could be right. I'd rather she slipped than jumped, of course. Who was the father, do you suppose? She's been home for six months, at least." Vera ran one last bite of waffle around her plate to gather the remaining syrup. The question hung in the air, unanswered.

"Evelyn handled Cheri as well as could be expected without Walter. He became an elder in the church two years before he died. That's when Evelyn started doing the church books."

Brady helped himself to another waffle. "She does the books for Arlen Parkfield's company. Isn't that what you said, Yosef?"

"That's right. Back then, she was working for Arlen's father, Hank. He started Santa Rita Construction back in the forties."

Yosef took a sip of orange juice and continued the saga. "Like I told you yesterday, Walter died and Hank Parkfield gave Evelyn a job. Walter was a framer, learned the trade from Hank personally. Hank died suddenly about eight years ago. He got liver cancer. Hank never liked going to the doctor. When he finally did, it was too late. Arlen gave up his college plans and came home to take over the business."

Vera took the last waffle. "I think it was hard for Arlen to give up school. He seemed to lose a bit of the charm he had as a boy. He started building big housing tracks inland and down in Santa Maria, something Hank never wanted to do. He grew the business fast and had to relocate to the outskirts of town to fit all the equipment he bought."

Brady nodded and listened attentively. Vera, and to a lesser extent, Yosef, were like a well-primed pump. After a bit of effort to get them going the information just flowed. His plan was working.

When breakfast was over, Vera announced her intention of heading over to Evelyn's to see how she was doing.

"See if you can pick up the church ledger while you are at it," Brady suggested.

It never hurts to try.

Vera promised she'd ask and then busied herself with cleaning the dishes.

Chapter Seventeen

Back in his bungalow, Brady settled into one of his overstuffed living room chairs to go through the pictures he had picked up on Tuesday. Wildflower photography had become a passion for him when, as a child, his father had taken him on hikes and shown him how to block the wind, bounce the light, and capture their beauty. Moving to the coastal climate of Morro Bay from the more arid environment of his native Wyoming was a shock to his system, but the new and abundant wildflowers kept him busy and his mind occupied. He was even trying his hand at catching the occasional bug or butterfly when the opportunity presented itself.

Brady had a large notebook with plastic pages where he carefully organized each photo and strip of negatives. The digital world held no appeal for him. He liked holding the negatives in his hands, secure in the fact that no electronic glitch would snatch them away. The bookshelves at one end of the living room held several large notebooks of his photos. A life's work carefully stored.

At the other end of the small room, his computer area stood framed by a second set of bookshelves full of references and CD holders. The shelves held years of the sermons he had prepared. Brady had come to Christ as a freshman in high school and thrown himself into Bible study. After his schoolwork was done each evening, he would spend time searching out the mysteries of God's Word. His depth of understanding and rapid maturity in Christ had naturally placed him among the leadership of his church youth group. This deep knowledge combined with his passion for Christ led him into ministry. But that was a long time ago. He had to deal with today and today he faced writing Cheri's eulogy. He had moved the task several times, putting off working on the eulogy because it brought back too many hard memories. Losing a child was beyond devastating. Nothing anyone could say to him two years ago could ease his pain. He didn't look forward to revisiting those emotions.

He worked steadily, organizing the photos for twenty minutes and then realized one roll was missing. "Well, time to work on that talk, I guess," he mumbled to himself. Grabbing his jacket, he headed for the church.

Holly dropped another damp tissue into the wicker wastebasket beside her. The *Tribune* sat open on her lap, her second cup of coffee gone cold in the chill air out on her balcony. The story about Cheri brought fresh, painful tears. Trying to hold back her frayed emotions just made her heart hurt instead. Uncle Nikko's death—his absence—now her friend's suicide; her head already throbbed from crying and a sleepless night. Had God intended *her* to do something for Cheri that she had missed? Had she been so focused on her work that she allowed an important relationship to slip past her unrecognized? The protective wall she had built during her tough teen years made it hard for her to slip easily into friendships. Uncle Nikko often chided her for working long hours and missing all that God had to offer in relationships with others.

Holly had many acquaintances, mostly made through real estate, but few true friends. And one of them, Uncle Nikko, was gone. She wanted to call someone, just to talk. But who?

Brady? No. In spite of their nice dinner and sailing misadventure, she needed to keep him at arm's length—as a client as well as the lifestyle he represented. Nope, not going there.

A.J.? His being on the case made calling him awkward. Who else? So many thoughts swirling through her head made it hard to concentrate. Better to keep her own counsel, and God's. She picked up her Bible and began to read.

"He will judge between the nations and will settle disputes for many peoples."

The words of the prophet Isaiah brought the lawsuit to mind. "Lord, thank you for settling this dispute for me." She spoke quietly, looking out across the bay to Morro Rock. The threatening letter was the only unfinished detail. She had placed it in her safety deposit box, but it still caused her concern. There was anger behind those words. "Grant me peace, Lord," she prayed, eyes closed and right hand open to heaven.

Holly had worked past midnight trying to decipher her uncle's journals. She ached to read what he had written, to hear his voice again in his words. Although his writing was neat and precise, her ability to decipher the words was frustratingly difficult. She had found a few familiar ones here and there, but nothing helpful. She had even tried an

Internet search, which brought up several free translation services, but that would take too much time.

Gathering her things, she went back inside, took her coffee cup to the kitchen, methodically washed it, and returned it to its place in the cupboard. Wiping the counter, her eyes strayed to the phone. What would A.J. do with the journals? She suspected he would confiscate them for evidence, and who knew if, or when, she would get them back. If the journals held a clue to her uncle's killer, she knew she should give them up. But she didn't want to. Not yet. Holly opened the phonebook, looked up a number, and made the call.

At 8:25 a.m., Holly nursed a cup of house blend from Top Dog Coffee Bar in her car while waiting for ASAP Reprographics to open. Over an hour, and a hundred dollars later, she held copies of the journals in her arms. Since she couldn't decipher the Hebrew dates, she color-coded each set of copies and dubbed them volumes one through five.

Back home, she replaced the journals in the cardboard box and took the large stack of copies to her bedroom, stowed them beneath her bed in a suitcase and called A.J.

"Hey, Holly, how are you this morning?" Compassion flowed through the phone to bathe her heart. She forced the tears from her voice.

"I'm okay. But I received a package yesterday afternoon. My uncle's journals."

"All of them?"

"Yes."

"When were they mailed?"

"That's the funny thing, A.J. They were mailed the day he was killed. How could he have mailed them? He could hardly walk and his mind was so confused."

"You should have called me, Holly." A touch of grit lowered his voice.

"I know. I'm sorry."

"Where are they now?"

"Here at my condo. Would you like me to bring them over?"

"No, I'll be there in twenty minutes."

Holly replaced the receiver, her palms sweating like a naughty schoolgirl waiting for a visit from the principal. But that was silly. She hadn't done anything wrong. It had been after five when she returned home last night and she called him before noon today. Why should he be upset?

Because I have his cell phone number.

Because a murder investigation is underway.

She wiped down already-clean surfaces and vacuumed the carpet … twice. Finally, A.J. was at the door.

She greeted him tentatively, wondering how mad he would be. She need not have worried. He gave her a lingering hug and a peck on the cheek. She rested her head against his chest, the smell of his cologne and the warmth of his arms familiar and reassuring.

"You look a bit better this morning. Did you sleep well last night?"

"No, but that's not surprising. I'll sleep tonight." Holly pushed back and gestured to the box of journals next to the couch. A.J. sat and pulled one onto his lap. After quietly scanning several pages, he looked up.

"Are they all like this?"

She nodded.

He whistled softly in amazement. "This is a new one on me. I'm sure the lab boys can get these translated, but I don't know how long it will take."

"Will you let me know what they say when they're done?"

"Eventually. They're evidence. These things take awhile."

"I understand. Any progress on finding who killed my uncle?"

"Nothing substantial. Whoever did it had a key and knew the alarm system." He leaned back into the couch, settling in.

"Key? How on earth could someone get a key?"

"An old employee perhaps. Maybe a wacked out relative of an employee. We're looking into it, but we haven't any leads."

Holly's chest tightened painfully. Once again visualizing Uncle Nikko so vulnerable. At the mercy of such evil. She had to get up, to do something.

"Can I get you a cup of coffee, A.J.?" Her voice sounding high and tight in her ears.

He patted her knee. "That would be great."

The routine of making the coffee settled her. She forced her mind away from the investigation and onto A.J. He had patted her knee. It was a small gesture that brought some warmth into her life. Had she finally found her life companion? She still didn't know exactly where A.J. stood with the Lord, but there would be time for that. He was kind and attentive, and she felt safe when he was around. There was no denying he had a hard side. She had seen that part of him in action over the past two years she had known him. Twice he had been placed on suspension because he pushed a bit too hard, skirting protocol. He would never move up the ranks in the department, but they couldn't argue with success. A.J. was good at what he did.

Returning to the living room, Holly found A.J. looking down into the box of journals without touching them. "One of them seems newer than the rest. I don't want to touch them till the lab has a chance to check for finger prints."

Holly's heart jumped. Fingerprints? She hadn't thought about fingerprints. "How long do you think it will take to translate them?" Holly's hand trembled as she handed him his coffee and perched on the edge of a chair facing him.

"No way to know. Have you thought any more about what your uncle said just before he died? Did he seem afraid or threatened?"

"Only what I told you yesterday. He talked about 'them' finding him when he was asleep." She made quotation marks with her fingers. "He also kept repeating that phrase about what the eye doesn't see the heart won't grieve over. I have no idea what he meant. I just assumed he had some dementia."

A.J. set the journal aside. "Well, somebody did find him. You told me he had been a heavy equipment operator, right? Do you remember some of the projects he worked on?"

"No, I never paid much attention to where he worked. I was busy with school and then away to college."

A.J. leaned forward. "What about friends of his that came over to the house?"

Holly thought for a moment. She remembered that occasionally a friend or two would stop by for a beer after work. The names and faces were faded in her memory and there was no longer anyone to ask.

A.J. reached over and took Holly's hand, rubbing his thumb across her fingers. "Don't fret about it, Holly. See if something comes to you over the next few days."

The gesture should have run thrills up her spine. But Holly was no longer listening. Something *had* come to mind.

Brady got out of his Lexus just as Vera pulled into the parking lot. He preceded her to the little church office and unlocked the door. She bustled in after a moment and, without stopping at her desk, appeared at his office door.

"I just came from Evelyn." Her fists planted on her ample hips.

"How is she today?"

"She just sits in her chair and looks out the window. I can hardly get two words out of her." She dropped her purse to the floor and settled into the chair opposite Brady.

"Did you ask her about the ledger?"

"That's the funniest part of all. I asked her, and she looked right at me and told me to leave, just cold as ice. I've never seen her act that way. Losing Cheri has really rocked her." Vera's gentle eyes were troubled, hurt giving way to anger.

"Did she know Cheri was pregnant?"

"We never got that far. I'm not sure I'll go back for a while. It's as if Evelyn is gone and somebody else is in her body. Very strange, she's usually the most hospitable person you could know."

"You two have been friends a long time, haven't you, Vera?"

She settled back into the chair. "We went to high school together. She's a couple years older, so we didn't really get to be friends till we were both wives and mothers coming to church here. With Cheri coming so late in life for Evelyn, I spent quite a bit of time with her. I had three of my own by then and helped her through those first couple of weeks. We were real close after that."

"Tell me some more about Cheri. Did she go to youth group as a kid? Was she interested, well, did she—?"

"Was she saved? Is that what you want to know?"

"Well, yes. I guess that sums it up. To be honest, Vera, doing a eulogy is a tough assignment, and the more I know, the more I have to work with."

"You lost a child didn't you, Pastor." Vera's tone was quiet and tender.

"Yes, you know I did." He could finally talk about it now without his throat tightening up, but he didn't like to.

"Then you are the perfect one for this *assignment*. And God will give you the words when you need them, Pastor Brady."

Brady shuffled some papers on his desktop. "I suppose He will."

But first, I have to ask

"You are always well-prepared, Pastor. We all know that," Vera finished with a wave of her hand. She picked up her purse and returned to her desk in the reception area, shutting Brady's door behind her.

Brady hit the play button on his answering machine. He had kept Cheri's message, feeling that if he deleted it, he somehow deleted a part of Cheri's memory. "Pastor Brady, this is Cheri." Hearing her voice sent a chill down his spine. "I would like to come and talk to you on Sunday afternoon. Two p.m. works for me if it works for you."

She didn't leave a number, and she didn't sound distressed. Brady's experience with such suicide was limited, but he assumed that someone who was suicidal would sound distressed. He realized that he hadn't thanked her for cleaning the church that day. The thought seared him. It was such a simple thing, and yet …

A knock on the door brought him back. "Yes?"

Vera's head poked in. "Arlen Parkfield is here to see you."

Chapter Eighteen

"Send him in, Vera." Brady cleared the collection of papers off the spare chair next to the door and went to meet Arlen.

"Brady." Arlen offered a hand.

"Arlen, have a seat." Brady motioned to the spare chair.

"I came to talk about the roof." Arlen slipped his sunglasses into his hair as he sat. "I don't have the spare men to put on the job right now. My dad and I roofed the church the last time. I don't mind working on it again. That is, if you will help me."

Brady examined Arlen's face. *This was a joke, right?*

"Well, I've never worked on a roof before, but I can fetch and carry with the best of them."

"Great. As usual, I'll cover the expenses. What do you say we start Tuesday afternoon?"

"Works for me."

"Then it's settled. Look, I have to run. I'll see you Tuesday."

When Arlen had gone, Brady lowered his face to his hands. What had he gotten himself into?

"I can't believe it."

Brady looked up at Vera standing in the doorway. "Can't believe what?"

She clapped her hands on her head. "Arlen talked you into helping him fix the roof."

"Yosef warned me to expect it. Maybe I'll learn something. Besides, I'm immortal till God calls me, right?" He winked.

"Pastor Brady." Her face reddened and her voice rose a full octave. "It's a good three stories down to the parking lot from the roof." Her finger pointed to the roof and then came down, drawing in the air the path his body would take in its descent.

"Well, I'll admit I don't like heights, but Arlen's paying for it, so the least I can do is help." Her overreaction made him smile.

"You think this is funny? I don't see the humor. We finally get a new pastor and the next thing you know, splat." She clapped her hands together. "He's road kill in the parking lot. Unbelievable!" Vera threw up her hands and went back again to her desk.

The phone rang. Brady could hear Vera answer it. "It's for you," she called.

"Padre, this is Detective Walker. I'd like to talk to you some more about the Cheri Davenport case. Can you come down to the Department this afternoon?"

"Yes, Detective, what time?"

"How about three?"

"Works for me, I'll be there."

Brady hung up the phone, stared at it for a few moments, and then looked at his watch. He had just enough time to pick up that roll of film he was missing before heading to the Sheriff's Department.

As Brady approached the photo counter at Sav-On, Jessica looked up, and then turned to the film drawer, extracting an envelope. She began to ring it up. .

"Anything else?" She didn't look at him.

"No, Jessica, just the pictures." Brady fished out his wallet. "How are you today?"

"Fine." Her tone told him she was anything but.

Brady held back his wallet and waited. Silence stretched between them for a moment until Jessica finally looked up, her eyes puffy and red. When she met his gaze, they welled up with fresh tears.

"What?" Her voice cracked as she dabbed her eyes.

"I think I should be asking *you* what." His heart ached for her.

"That should be obvious. Here are your pictures." She slid them across the counter. "That will be seven ninety-five please." She put out her hand, holding his gaze for a moment then she sniffed and dabbed her eyes.

"It's Cheri, isn't it?"

"There is no way she committed suicide. That is just plain wrong." Tears tumbled down her cheeks, but her voice remained steady.

"What makes you think so?"

"She was happy. She had a boyfriend. Life was good for her."

"You were friends, then?"

"Well, not friends really. She worked the check-out part time and helped with the books and payroll. Girls just kinda talk, ya know?"

"Do you know who the boyfriend was?"

"That guy on the e-mail. Remember, in her apartment?"

"Yes, the one who didn't like me."

"That's the one. She was kind of dreamy about him. I guess he had money and took her to Santa Barbara a lot."

"Did you ever meet him?"

"No. I'm not even sure he was local. She would be gone on the weekends with him. That's when I fed the cat."

"Do you think he was the father of her baby?"

"Yah, probably. It's nature, ya know?"

He waited, watching her.

When he didn't respond she swallowed and scratched her head. "Well, maybe you wouldn't know."

"I'm a pastor, Jessica, not a priest. And I'm not blind. I also know that what is popular isn't always right."

"Yah, well, not everybody thinks the way you do."

"Perhaps Cheri's natural tendencies weren't necessarily in her best interest. What do you think?"

"Yah, whatever. Here's your pictures, seven ninety-five please." A wall rose behind her eyes.

Brady handed her a ten and she gave him change with no comment. "Thank you, Jessica."

She nodded without looking up. He slipped a business card onto the counter. "If you want to talk some more, just give me a call." He hoped she would and knew she wouldn't.

Brady announced himself to the receptionist in the detective's building he had visited previously. After she checked his ID, she escorted Brady to the same small room he had met Detective Walker in previously. When she closed the door, Brady felt trapped and vulnerable. He hadn't anything to fear, but he imagined what it must be like for those who did. The stale sweat of the guilty lingered in the room's musty air.

After a brief wait, Detective Walker entered and dropped down into the chair opposite Brady. He flipped open his notepad with practiced ease and raised his eyes to Brady.

"You want to tell me why we found your fingerprints in Cheri Davenport's apartment?"

Brady's body flushed in alarm. He dropped his hands to his lap to mask the sudden trembling. "Well, um, I went to see if she was home after she missed some appointments. She seemed to have disappeared, and I was worried."

"How did you get in?"

"There was a key above the door, on the frame."

"So you had used it in the past?"

Brady felt a trickle of sweat roll down between his shoulder blades. He had made a mistake by going into the apartment. He had sensed it then, and knew it now. But still, he hadn't done anything wrong.

"No. First time I'd been there. I went with Cheri's co-worker, Jessica. She sometimes feeds Cheri's cat, so she knew where the key was hidden. Jessica offered to check the apartment with me to be sure Cheri was all right. Evelyn, Cheri's mother told me earlier in the day that she couldn't locate Cheri." Brady paused for a moment to give Detective Walker time to comment. When he didn't, Brady continued. "I heard she had missed the Monday night Bible study."

"Who told you that?"

"One of the women from the study, Mrs. Thorndyke."

Detective Walker made a note. "What happened next?"

"When Jessica told me Cheri had missed work on Monday, I began to get concerned. I understood from others that Cheri was someone you could rely on. If she said she'd be there, it was out of character for her to not show up."

Well, some people thought that anyway.

"So tell me again why she met with you on Sunday afternoon?"

"Like I told you, I never really found out. She started to tell me and then changed her mind."

"So you don't really know."

"No, I don't know."

Detective Walker took some notes and then began tapping his pencil on the table while he flipped pages back and forth. Brady waited. The tapping annoyed him. A lot.

"Is there anything else, Detective?"

Detective Walker held up a finger for silence and continued the tapping and flipping. Brady determined that he would force himself to relax and wait out this absurd process.

A few agonizing minutes later, the tapping stopped and the detective looked up. "What is your relationship with Jessica Barnes?"

"I don't know that I have a relationship with her. She works at the drugstore where I have my pictures developed. I knew that Cheri worked there, so when I stopped in on Tuesday, I asked about her."

"How long have you had a relationship with these two women?"

"What?" Brady had had enough. He was on his feet, hands flat on the table. "How dare you insinuate that I have an inappropriate relationship with these women!" Brady glared at the detective, breathing heavily.

Detective Walker's eyes were flat, revealing nothing. Like a snake examining its next victim. "Settle down, Padre." He motioned that Brady should take his seat. "I'm just doing my job." Walker closed his notepad and sat back in his chair. His eyes danced with unconcealed amusement. He regarded Brady for a few moments, resuming the slow tap, tap, tap, of his pencil on the table.

"I think that's about it, Padre. Will you be staying in town? Not planning any trips?"

"No, Detective, no trips." Brady's blue eyes glistened with smoldering anger. "Am I being included in the list of suspects, Detective?"

"Everybody is a suspect till I cross them off, Padre. Just stick around town."

Detective Walker stood and left the room without another word.

Chapter Nineteen

Brady heard screaming. Shrill. A glass-shattering squeal. He couldn't move; his feet stuck in glue. Panic, then terror controlled and consumed every breath. He had to run, but he couldn't run, couldn't move at all. The air inside his lungs burned. The bed pitched and rolled, like the sailboat in the breakwater waves. Earthquake!

Daisy's furious barking roused him. Her jumping from one side of the bed to the other rocking him. He opened sleepy eyes as Daisy leapt on his chest and barked again.

The ceiling rippled with thick smoke. His lungs cried for fresh air. The screaming came from the smoke alarm. His house was on fire!

Brady rolled off the bed to the floor. Crouching, he grabbed for Daisy. She slipped through his hands and under the bed, her eyes wide with terror.

"Daisy, come!" The effort to speak drew in a lungful of the acrid smoke. His heart thundered, and his lungs throbbed. Daisy dashed across the bedroom and into the kitchen. Brady started to follow her, but the heat drove him back.

"Daisy!" He coughed and gagged. No more air. No more time.

Dropping to his knees, he began to crawl, feeling grit beneath his hands as he turned and made his way across the hardwood floor toward the window. The roar of the flames vibrated through him. Brady pushed on the ancient, double-hung frame.

Stuck.

Sitting up on his knees, he heaved against the stubborn lower frame. The smoke now engulfed Brady's head. He coughed and gagged again, dropping to the floor.

He had to get out. His eyes watered and his head swam from lack of oxygen.

"God!" his mind screamed. "I can't end this way. Help me!"

Brady folded over until his forehead rested on his knees. He covered his mouth with his t-shirt and drew in a lungful of cleaner air. His head cleared a little. Taking another full breath, he held it.

Break the glass. Break the glass. The mantra repeated. Brady sat up and slid his hand along the wall until he found the windowsill. Pulling himself higher, he swung his fist and shattered the glass.

The fresh air fed the flames, its greedy arms reaching toward him. Brady lunged through the window headfirst and landed on the grass. Sirens sounded in the distance, muted by the fog. Strong hands grabbed his shoulders from behind and dragged him away from the searing heat. Flames reached out from the bedroom window, licking and searching. Something soft landed around his shoulders, and water sprayed onto his smoldering pajama pants.

A huge fire truck rolled into the back yard. Lights, sirens, and running men exploded onto the scene. Stunned and gasping for air, Brady sat in shock as flames broke through the roof of his bungalow and reached for the sky. Blood oozed from his hands and shoulders, seeping through the yellow yarn of the afghan, staining it with growing red splotches. He felt a hand on his back and turned to his left. Vera sat on the grass beside him, watching the destruction.

Two men in heavy fire suits trotted over to where Brady and Vera sat. One of them slipped an oxygen mask over Brady's face, the clean air prompting another coughing spasm.

Each man worked efficiently, assessing Brady's condition. One started treating Brady's burned legs and feet while the other turned his attention to the deep lacerations on Brady's right hand and back where the broken window glass had raked across his shoulders. Somebody handed him a glass of water, which he accepted gratefully.

Gallons of water poured into Brady's bungalow. The vapor rising from the fire hoses captured the light from the red and yellow emergency beacons. Their whirling dance creating an eerie light show.

Brady thought about the damage the water would do to his photography collection, but it was a silly thought. The photos were already gone.

The two paramedics finished with Brady's legs, arms, and back. Then they helped him onto a gurney and placed him in a waiting ambulance. One of the two paramedics climbed in with him while the other closed the big back doors.

As the tumult outside dropped to near silence, a face appeared above Brady. "I'm Roger. Looks like you made it out OK. You have just a few cuts and scratches. Your feet and legs have some burns, nothing to worry about though." Roger gave him a reassuring grin.

Brady attempted to reply, but another coughing spasm erupted instead.

"That will get better soon. Just breathe deeply. You are on oxygen now. We're going to take you to Sierra Vista, just to have the guys in white coats give you a once-over."

Brady pulled the oxygen mask away. "My . . . dog, Daisy. She was in . . . the house. She's a dachshund." Roger nodded and placed the oxygen mask back over Brady's face. "I'll go tell the guys to keep a look out."

Brady was momentarily left alone in the dim interior of the ambulance. He knew he should be feeling something, but he was numb. His mind touched briefly on treasured items. The paintings Karen had given him, again, his photography collection, the years and years of research for sermons. At each touch, his mind recoiled, unwilling to examine the loss.

His training as a pastor told him he had only lost worldly possessions. His true treasures were in heaven, but those words rang hollow. Like the words spoken at the loss of his wife and son, they didn't help. They didn't bind the wounds and salve the burns. Rather, they burned like salt.

The ambulance door opened again and Roger's face appeared above Brady. "They haven't seen your dog, but they will keep a look out." Roger sat on a stool next to Brady's head as the ambulance started down the driveway.

Brady's vision wobbled and the inside of the ambulance swam before him. He closed his eyes. The last thing he needed right now was to get car sick.

The visit to the emergency room was a mixture of relief and pain. Brady's right hand took twenty stitches, and his legs and feet were swathed in burn dressings. The burns were relatively minor according to the doctor, more like a serious sunburn.

Vera, Yosef, Mrs. Thorndyke, and others from church were waiting to greet Brady several hours later when he emerged from the emergency room in a wheelchair. The compassionate reception barely moved him. He was an emotional gaping wound. A shell that resembled the man they thought he was protected him, keeping them at arm's length from the man he knew himself to be. The church members gathered around him but didn't seem to quite know what to do. Because of his injuries, some patted his knee or touched his undamaged left hand. Others just offered encouraging words.

If they really knew me, they wouldn't be here. He tried to thank them, but no words came.

The clock on the dashboard showed six a.m. when the hospital staff loaded Brady into Vera's car for the trip home. With his bungalow gone, Vera and Yosef took Brady into their place. Their older, California Bungalow style home was not wheelchair accessible, so Yosef, and two other churchmen who followed them home, lifted Brady, chair and all, up onto the front porch.

After the good-byes, Yosef rolled Brady into the cozy, front bedroom. With help from Yosef, he managed to crawl onto the crisp white sheets of an ancient oak sleigh bed, wincing with pain every time he had to bear weight on his burns and cuts.

Vera closed the blinds against the sunrise and turned to him. "Go to sleep, Brady. We can deal with all this later." She breathed a weary sigh and closed the door.

Brady stared at the ceiling, losing track of time. The pain medication made his eyelids heavy as his mind again touched on the things he had lost in the fire. Each memory seared him. God had finally stripped away the last vestige of his former life. No one had found Daisy. Her cheerful little face would never again remind him of happier days. She and Jeremy used to play and roll on the carpet, Jeremy all giggles and Daisy all tongue. He and Karen would laugh until they hurt.

"Why, God?" he whispered into the silent room.

Brady awoke to voices outside his bedroom window. He lay on his left side with the sun pouring in on his face, his mouth dry as dust. He remembered Vera placing a glass of water on the bedside table behind him. He started to roll onto his back, but his legs screamed in protest, taking his breath away. Determined, he tried again, but slower this time, gritting his teeth against the pain. After several excruciating minutes, he was on his back, but the mound of bandages from his lacerated shoulder forced him back onto his left side again. He growled in frustration.

Vera's cheerful face appeared around the door. "I thought I heard you. Glad to see you're awake. Ready for a bite to eat?"

"I'd really like a glass of water, but I can't reach it."

She retrieved the glass; then she pushed a pillow under his head and neck so he could lean back enough to drink the water without putting too much pressure on his right shoulder.

The smell of bacon and coffee crept into the room and Brady's stomach growled.

"I'll get you a plate of breakfast, Pastor Brady. Yosef will be right in to help you."

Moments later, Yosef appeared and helped Brady slip into a light cotton bathrobe. Then Brady eased into his wheelchair. As Yoself wheeled him through the door, half a dozen sets of eyes turned to greet him over steaming mugs of coffee.

"Pastor Brady, how are you?" Sylvia Thorndyke asked as Vera handed Brady a mug of coffee.

"I have to be honest. I've felt better many times in my life." He grinned and raised his mug to her before taking a tentative sip.

"I'm sure that's true, Pastor." Charlie, the sleepy parishioner from church, winked at him from a wingchair in the corner. His cancer-ravaged frame made him appear almost transparent in the morning light.

"Thanks, Charlie."

Vera made a space for the wheelchair next to Charlie. "Before I forget, Pastor Brady, the doctor wants to see you this afternoon to check the burns on your legs and feet."

"I have to be at Cheri's service at four."

The room went silent. "Surely, Pastor, you're not planning to speak. No one would expect it." Vera looked from Yosef to Brady.

"Of course I will, Vera. I may not be able to stand, but I can still talk." He grinned at Vera and caught a wink from Yosef. Chuckles circulated the room.

Then Brady remembered that he had finished the eulogy at the church and brought it home. The manuscript that had been sitting on his computer desk was gone. The coffee cup in his left hand began to tremble. He steadied it with his injured right hand and brought the mug down into his lap. He was totally unprepared to speak. His worst nightmare was coming true today. Brady's eyes went to the mantle. Eight o'clock. He had seven hours to recreate a eulogy that had taken him most of yesterday to prepare.

The room felt very small and confined. Yosef stood behind him, blocking his path of retreat. Everyone was looking at him, assessing his reaction. He knew they could see the panic building in his face. The room began to spin. His mind raced out of control, his chest became heavy, pressure building. Was he having a heart attack, right here in front of everyone?

Rivulets of perspiration ran down his sides. "Yosef, I need to go back to my room." He heard his voice as if through a fog. Yosef came around the chair to face him, and he allowed Yosef to see the terror in his eyes for just a moment.

Yosef spun into action as if caring for burn victims was second nature. He made a deft, three-point turn in the close quarters of the living room and rolled Brady back to the safety of his room.

Once away from prying eyes, Brady's breathing labored even more. He shrugged off the bathrobe and rolled from the wheelchair onto his bed, holding back his moans of pain. He lay there; eyes squeezed shut as the room spun and his injuries screamed. The bedroom door clicked closed.

"Brady, what's wrong? What's the matter with you?" Yosef's voice seemed small and far away. When Brady didn't answer, Yosef placed one hand on Brady's shoulder and began to pray.

"Father, what's happening to Brady right now? Father, I know you are aware of what has happened these past twenty-four hours. I know you say you will never leave us or forsake us. So I ask you in your most precious Son's name, to fill this room with your presence and love. Brady needs your help right now."

As Yosef prayed, his voice filtered into the maelstrom of Brady's mind. The old man's deep resonance rumbled on until the warmth spreading from Yosef's hands began to envelop Brady in peace. His breathing steadied as Yosef prayed on. Finally, his eyes fluttered open. He placed his hand over Yosef's and squeezed.

"Thank you, Lord Jesus, for hearing my prayers," Yosef finished and looked up at Brady.

"Thanks, Yosef."

"Brady, what happened?"

"I don't know. I thought I was going to have a heart attack or something. Maybe the pain medication is wearing off. What I do know is I need to get over to the church. My eulogy for Cheri burned up in the fire, but there might be some rough drafts in my trash can."

"You can't remember what you wanted to say?"

"Not a chance."

"Okay. I'll run over to the church after I get you some breakfast." Yosef stood to go.

"Ask Vera for a pad of paper and a pen too, will you?"

"Sure, I'll be right back."

Forty-five minutes later, Brady sat up in bed, in deep thought, when Yosef returned from the church. Balls of yellow notepaper dotted the room and bed. An open Bible lay to Brady's left and his untouched breakfast to his right.

Brady looked up as Yosef entered. He shook his head. "The trash went out this morning. I'm sorry, Brady."

"Argh!" He clenched his teeth, and another ball of yellow notepaper flew past the foot of the bed.

"Just speak from your heart, Brady. Trust God to give you the words."

"Don't tell me how to do my job, Yosef."

Trust God! Why on earth would I trust God?

Yosef blinked at the angry retort. He struggled for a moment, began to speak, then averted his eyes. He placed Brady's old college Bible from the church office at the foot of the bed, gathered the uneaten breakfast and left the room.

Vera poked her head in the door as Yosef passed. "Brady, the Fire Chief and Detective Walker are here to see you."

"Sure, Vera, send them in." *Why not, I can't remember what I was going to say anyway.* Brady crumpled another wad of paper full of half-finished thoughts. He set his pad on top of the borrowed Bible and looked up to see the tall form of Detective Walker followed by the Fire Chief. The two men took in Brady's bandages and the yellow paper balls strewn about the room. For a moment, Brady thought about explaining, then decided to ignore the evidence of his frustration and focus on his guests.

"Well, Padre, we seem to be seeing quite a bit of each other lately."

"Good to see you too, Detective. How can I help you gentlemen?" Brady folded his hands in his lap and waited.

"We came to talk to you about how the fire started in your bungalow. To be blunt, Pastor, it was arson."

Chapter Twenty

Arson!

Brady's body stiffened as if it had turned to marble. Somebody had set his house on fire with him in it? Impossible.

Brady closed the Bible and set it on the table beside the bed, giving his emotions a moment to settle. He held his voice steady. "Why do you suspect arson, Chief?"

"We found traces of an accelerant in the area of the heater closet."

"You mean like gasoline?"

"Something along those lines, yes."

A.J. had his notebook open and pen ready. "Do you have any idea why someone would try to kill you, Padre?"

"Not a clue, Detective. I've only been here three months." Brady glanced at the clock and then back to the Detective. Already 2:00 p.m. He didn't have time for this.

Vera came back into the room with a lunch plate for Brady. "The Fire Chief says someone set the bungalow on fire, Vera."

She set the tray on the bed next to Brady. "Yes, the Chief told me a little bit ago. Any idea who might have done such a thing, Brady? I can't think of anyone." He could see in her eyes that this violence hurt her, too.

Vera turned to address Detective Walker. "We've both lived in Morro Bay all our lives but don't spend much time with anyone outside the church. Could it have been a prank of some kind?"

"Not likely. Seems more thought out than that."

She started picking up the yellow balls of paper that littered the floor around the bed. "Well, I will think it over and let you know if I come up with anyone."

The Fire Chief and Detective Walker questioned Brady and Vera for twenty more minutes, but nothing new came to light. Brady desperately wanted to get back to the eulogy. The clock was ticking, and he did not intend to make a fool of himself at the funeral. Finally, as the questions began to repeat, Brady brought the question-and-answer session to a halt. He pulled his Bible back onto the bed and opened it. "I'm sorry I don't have more answers for you, gentlemen. Now if you don't mind, can we finish this another time?"

"Sure, Padre, we can talk again. Ma'am," Detective Walker touched a finger to his forehead, and the two left Vera and Brady alone.

Brady reached for his sandwich, realizing that he was finally hungry.

Vera sat on the edge of the bed. "Who could have done such a thing, Brady?" Her eyes darkened with sadness and worry as she picked a piece of lint from the bedspread.

"I haven't a clue, Vera. Maybe they didn't even know I was in there."

Or maybe they did.

The morning overcast had cleared and the sun warmed him as Brady arrived at Mariners Chapel for the funeral. The full parking lot surprised him. And more cars lined the curbs up and down the street. Someone had roped off a spot next to the side door. Vera got out and moved the ropes so Yosef could pull into it. After he parked the car, Yosef got out and came around to Brady's door with the wheelchair.

Having never been wheelchair bound, Brady was gaining a new appreciation for those who were. As Yosef pushed him up the ramp that led to the church's side door, the ocean breeze penetrated his thin layer of clothing, running a chill up his back. His burned legs and lacerated shoulder could only tolerate a light t-shirt and shorts. Yosef had made a run to Mervyn's for some basics for him. The rest of what he needed would have to wait.

Inside the little church, ceiling fans silently moved the air, heavy with the fragrance of flowers. Yosef wheeled Brady over to the corner where he had a limited view of the pews filled to capacity. At the front of the church, a raised platform had been quickly constructed to accommodate Brady's wheelchair. He hadn't thought about that, but somebody obviously had.

Mrs. Post, the pianist, began to play softly. The murmurs in the room died as latecomers took their seats. Evelyn appeared at the back door and slowly followed the center aisle up to the empty front pew, where she sat alone, ramrod-straight and dry-eyed.

Mrs. Post played the introduction to "It Is Well With My Soul" while people glanced at their programs and found the page in the hymnal.

Brady sang from deep down inside, his voice cracking as the words brought fresh visions of his ruined home, his ruined life. Visions of his son, crushed and almost unrecognizable swam before him. Brady had made the identification more by his Sesame Street pajamas than his once perfectly adorable face. Karen had not been as disfigured. Her skin waxen in death, she had still been lovely but no less dead. Overcome, he no longer sang. He simply closed his eyes and listened to the words;

"Though Satan should buffet, though trials should come,
Let this blest assurance control,
That Christ has regarded my helpless estate,
And hath shed His own blood for my soul."

Brady reflected on the pain the hymn writer Horatio Spafford must have felt as he looked upon the watery grave of his daughters in the mid-Atlantic. Unlike Spafford, however, it was not well with Brady's soul. He scorned the God who would allow such pain.

Brady knew he was totally inadequate to the job before him. A simple eulogy sat on his lap, devoid of inspiration. God had not touched his heart as in times past because again, he had not asked. The words were lifeless and hollow, but he would speak them and be done. The skills of a speaker were his stock and trade. He would rely on them, because he could not rely on God.

The strains of the classic hymn faded away, replaced by sniffing and dabbing of eyes. Brady struggled for control. The painful memory of that same hymn sung two years ago in a much larger church in Wyoming tore at him, leaving him shaken and weary.

Silence permeated the white clapboard walls. Every eye seemed fixated on him. Waiting for the eulogy. Yosef came to the back of the wheelchair and rolled Brady up the ramp to face the assembled friends and acquaintances of a troubled young girl who died much too soon. He placed the notes from his lap up onto the lectern and made a show of organizing himself. He knew he needed to look up and face the grieving people and the stoic Evelyn. The truth was, he didn't want to.

Brady took a deep breath in a final effort to compose himself. He raised his head and looked out over the assembly. Few looked familiar. Here and there, members of Mariners Chapel faced him with looks of encouragement and support. Vera and Yosef had joined Evelyn. Mrs. Post sat next to Sylvia Thorndyke, and three rows back, in their usual spot, sat Charlie and his wife, Irene.

Jessica was there, too—seated all the way in the back, nearest the door—so she could bolt at any moment. At least she had come. Across the aisle from Jessica, Brady's eyes locked with Holly's. A lump rose in his throat. He wanted desperately at this moment to go to her, leave all this behind, and be alone with her to talk through what was happening in his world. He couldn't though, not right now. Her face showed her surprise at his condition. She obviously hadn't heard about the fire. He tore his attention away from Holly and back to the work at hand.

"Author David Searls once said, 'Seeing death as the end of life is like seeing the horizon as the end of the ocean.' I think Mr. Searls had a firm grasp of the transition that awaits us all. We are here today to celebrate the life of Cheri Davenport. Cheri left us this week to be present with the Lord."

Brady's eyes ran across the faces below him as he spoke. Jessica hung on each word. Her eyes were swollen and her nose red, but she listened and didn't run for the door. Holly's face was also flushed with tears, a tissue dabbing her eyes. Yosef nodded and scratched his nose a few times, but Evelyn never moved. Her eyes stayed dry and her face pale and drawn. Toward the end of Brady's eulogy, Arlen Parkfield slipped in the side door and took a seat near the back.

When Brady finished, Yosef rolled him back down the ramp to the front of the church. Several people came to shake his good left hand and thank him for his words. Holly held back until almost everyone had moved away, then came over, with eyes full of concern.

"Brady, what on earth! What happened?" She took in his wheelchair and bandages in a quick assessment.

"My house burned down last night." His words came out empty of emotion, as if it were something that happened to everybody.

"You're burned." She gently touched his shoulder. Her lovely green eyes clouded with concern.

"Not very badly, more like a bad sunburn, the doctor said. I should be up and about in a couple days. It's mostly the bottoms of my feet." He smiled up at her, drinking in her attention. "I'm glad you came, Holly."

"And who is this, Pastor Brady?" Yosef appeared behind Brady, ready to wheel him out.

"Holly Fain, this is Yosef Shankston. The kind man who has given me a place to live."

"Pleased to finally meet you, Miss Fain. My wife here tells me you have been working hard to find Brady a house."

"We have been working at it, but now it seems more important than ever."

"I could live out of a phone booth right now. I didn't even come away with my pajamas intact."

Vera patted his shoulder "Don't you worry, Pastor Brady." "We'll get you back on your feet and a roof over your head in no time. The word has already gone out."

"Do you know how it happened?"

Brady looked around and found no one within earshot. "They suspect arson."

Holly gasped, "Arson!"

"Shhh," Brady quieted her. "We would like to keep that private."

"Who on earth would do such a thing?" She looked around the now mostly-empty church, as if she half expected to see a threatening figure lurking in the shadows.

Vera slipped her hand into Yosef's. "We have no idea."

"I'm sure they will find out. Oh, Brady, I'm so sorry. To lose everything, it's just awful." She lifted her hand as if to grasp the feeling from the air and speak it.

His eyes began to burn and the muscles in his face ached as he fought the emotions. He needed to change the subject. He glanced at his watch. "I need to get over to the cemetery. Are you coming, Holly?"

She nodded.

At the Cayucos cemetery on a grassy rise, a portable awning and several chairs marked the location of the graveside service. The wind buffeted the awning and the flowers on the casket trembled, a petal or two taking flight with each new gust. Morro Rock stood sentinel down the coast to the south, its feet immersed in the frothy sea.

Brady was surprised when he arrived to find Detective Walker among the mourners. The two men exchanged glances as Yosef rolled Brady across the grass. The jostling sent jolts of pain through his legs and chest. He hadn't taken a pain pill, afraid it would slur his speech. Now he wished he had brought one. Holly joined Vera as Yosef pushed Brady's wheelchair to the front of the more intimate gathering. Evelyn sat in a metal chair at the front. Vera excused herself to join her friend.

Evelyn's eyes held the flat, hollow look of a dog left too long in the shelter. Brady tried to meet her gaze, but it remained distant and unfocused. The mischievous wind played havoc with her usual prim and proper appearance. Her hand occasionally touched her disheveled hair, but without effect.

Brady took a deep breath, swallowed, leaned over, and took a handful of dirt from the pile by the casket. "Father, we are here to commit Cheri Davenport to your most precious care. Grant her peace, Father. Grant peace to all who miss her. 'Ashes to ashes, dust to dust....'" Brady quoted the expected words as he tossed dirt upon the casket.

Then, a single tear trickled down Evelyn's pale cheek.

Chapter Twenty-One

When Brady finished speaking, Yosef went to the casket and pulled a rose from the spray that flowed over the top. He brought it over and offered it to Evelyn. She took it without meeting Yosef's eyes and laid it upon her lap. After a moment, she rose, turned her back to the casket, and moved off toward her car. Brady watched the small, slender woman wearing black make her solitary way across the grass, an impermeable figure that repelled anyone's approach.

"I'd like to speak with you for a moment, Padre."

Startled, Brady looked up to find Detective Walker standing at his shoulder. The perceived advantage irritated Brady, but there was nothing he could do about it.

"How can I help you, Detective?"

A.J. looked around and then leaned down a bit closer to Brady. "We've now determined that Cheri Davenport was murdered. Do you have any thoughts on that, Padre?"

Brady sat silent for a moment, assessing the implications. "My first one is of shock, Detective. Do you think it was someone she knew?"

"Oh, she knew who it was all right. I came to the funeral to see who would show up. Sometimes the murderer enjoys watching the funeral."

"That's sick."

"These kind of people *are* sick, Padre. You need to keep that in mind." The detective looked up again, surveying the area. "The person who torched your house didn't plan on you getting out. The window in your bedroom was screwed shut."

Another chill ran through him, but it wasn't from the wind. Somebody wanted him dead! He had rejected the thought this morning but now he couldn't ignore the bone chilling truth.

Before Brady could respond, Holly joined them, stopping so she stood facing them both.

"Hello, A.J., I see you have met my client." Her green eyes lingered on each face just a moment too long. "We are all heading back to the church for some food and conversation. Would you like to come?"

"I think I will, Holly, I think I will." A.J. turned to Brady, laying a heavy hand on his lacerated shoulder. "You have a great agent there, Padre. She sold me a house four years ago. Best investment I ever made." He winked at Holly and headed to his car.

Mariners Chapel Women's Ministry worked like a machine when it came to activities involving food. The church's community room bustled with energy and tempting aromas as food appeared and was replenished with quiet efficiency. Vera and Holly headed to the overburdened buffet table and filled plates for Brady and themselves while Brady held court of sorts. Several parishioners came over to inquire about his injuries, offer condolences, and compliment him on the memorial service. Brady took their words in stride, wishing for the comfort of the Shankston's soft bed and some solitude.

A.J. hung at the edge of the crowd, plate in hand, his eyes on those around him. Brady scanned the room occasionally as well. All he saw were well-known members of Mariners Chapel and some younger people he assumed were friends of Cheri. But his eyes always came back to rest on A.J. He couldn't keep his mind away from the relationship between A.J. and Holly. Was there one? The self-assured Detective seemed to think so but he didn't get the same impression from Holly.

A.J. finally moved back through the room to stand beside Brady.

"Pretty innocent-looking crowd, don't you think, Detective Walker?" Brady looked up at the man, hating his lower position.

"You never know, Padre." He popped a stuffed olive in his mouth. "You never know." Then he moved off again to mingle.

Holly and Vera soon arrived with their plates of food. They all gathered at an open table where Holly took a seat across from Brady.

Vera sat on Brady's right. She placed a napkin on her lap and handed a plastic fork to Yosef. "So, Holly, have you been in real estate very long? Seems I've seen your face quite a bit lately in the newspaper."

"I've had my license for five years, Vera. I'm glad you remember my ads. That means they are working." Holly smiled sweetly.

"Where do you go to church, Holly?"

"Oh, it's been quite a long time since I darkened the door of a church." She didn't look up as she assembled her turkey sandwich.

Vera buttered a roll. "Seems you broke that pattern today."

"Seems I have." Holly shot a sideways look at Brady. "You have a very gifted pastor, I think."

Brady returned her warm glance.

A.J. came up behind Holly with a refilled plate of food. "May I join you?" His hand came to rest comfortably on her shoulder.

"Of course, Detective, by all means!" Yosef motioned to a seat to his left.

A.J. seated himself across from Vera and between Yosef and Holly. Holly smiled at A.J., and he winked. She didn't move over to give A.J. more room in spite of the tight seating.

Brady's pleasure at Holly's presence at the memorial service evaporated as he watched the interplay between A.J. and Holly. Anyone who cared to look would see that the two of them were on more than a professional footing.

"So Detective, do you attend church locally?" Yosef's question drew A.J.'s attention reluctantly away from Holly.

Holly looked up at Brady. "Was that Cheri's mother in the black?"

"Yes."

"She seems so..." Holly looked past Brady and stiffened. "Why would Arlen Parkfield be here?"

Her voice dropped and Brady had to strain to hear her. "Arlen Parkfield is one of our elders, why?"

"I just settled a lawsuit that involved him."

"Really? What was it about?"

Holly looked around. Seeing A.J., Yosef, and Vera deep in conversation, she answered in a low voice. "There's not much to tell from my point of view." She moved some food around on her plate. "I sold a home about a year and a half ago. The home had a wonderful ocean view, but it had been vacant for years and a water leak had left it full of mold—what we call a scraper. The value was in the land. When we closed escrow, the new owners tore it down to build a new home. During the excavation, the contractor discovered an Indian burial ground. The construction had to stop while the various agencies investigated. Eventually, construction went forward and finished. But the owners sued me, along with Arlen. His company built the original house."

Brady set his fork down. "What could they sue you for?"

"They claimed I didn't disclose that the house was built on an Indian burial ground and sued me for damages."

"But how can you be involved if you didn't know?"

"Welcome to real estate. They say it's not a matter of if you'll get sued, but when."

"Do you think Arlen's company did anything wrong?"

"Well, he argued that the foundation footings back then did not have to be as deep as the city requires now. That's why the bones weren't discovered. But that was hard to prove." Holly cast a sideways glance at Arlen, her distaste evident.

Brady didn't have any reason not to trust Arlen. The church had found him qualified for eldership. That meant something in Brady's book. "Perhaps some of his employees did the work. Poor performance on his employees' part doesn't mean Arlen himself is a bad person."

"I suppose you could be right, but the suit cost me a fortune in attorney's fees."

"Don't you have insurance for something like this?"

"Oh sure, with a five-thousand-dollar deductible."

Brady whistled under his breath.

"Don't worry, I can manage it. I just don't like having to. Even though I didn't know anything about the burial site, I still had to defend myself. We went to mediation last week to settle everything." Holly put down her fork and leaned back against her chair.

"Holly is the best in the business," A.J. broke in. Obviously listening with half an ear to their conversation. He reached over and gave Holly's hand a squeeze. "She got caught up in the litigation net. Not unusual for California. She's had a pretty tough week all around." His hand remained on hers.

"Thanks, A.J." Their eyes held each other's briefly, before she pulled her hand away and placed it in her lap, a touch of red coloring rising in her cheeks.

Vera leaned forward and looked down the table. "Well, Pastor Brady, we're about finished here. Aren't we, Yosef?" Vera gave her husband a meaningful look. "I think it's time we got Pastor back to the house for some rest."

A.J. stood. "I'll be going myself. Nice to meet you all," He winked at Holly again and turned away into the thinning crowd.

Vera collected her sweater from the back of her chair and threw it over her shoulders. "Holly, would you like to join us?"

Brady's heart jumped. *What was Vera up to?*

Holly hesitated, looking down as she gathered her purse and stood. Then she lifted her eyes to Brady before turning to Vera. "I'd be delighted, Vera. Thank you."

Holly and Brady made themselves comfortable in the Shankston's living room. Brady had been able to hobble into the overstuffed chair that Charley had settled into earlier in the day. Holly sat on the couch next to him. Vera excused herself to the kitchen and Yosef to his chores.

"Thank you for rescuing me at the cemetery when I was talking to Detective Walker."

"A.J. can be a bit dramatic at times."

"A.J.?"

"I don't know what it stands for. Everyone just calls him A.J."

"Sounds like you took good care of him four years ago." He tried to leave room for more comment from her.

"Yes, I did." The answer hung in the air. Holly's glance flitted around the room, then down at her hands.

Stupid.

"I didn't mean to pry, Holly."

She looked back at him. "It's all right. A.J. and I became friends. He's working on my uncle's case."

"How is that coming along?"

Holly's eyes flicked toward the kitchen where Vera bustled about and then back at Brady. "Brady, I know you are busy with the work at the church, but would you perhaps have a little time to do me a favor?"

"Sure, anything. How can I help?"

"How good is your Hebrew?"

"Not too bad. Early church history is a bit of a passion, so I studied Greek and Hebrew extensively. I'm better with Hebrew, why?"

"My uncle kept a journal for as long as I can remember. Someone mailed them to me the same day he was killed. I don't think Uncle Nikko could have managed it. He couldn't get out of his wheelchair without help." She paused, checking the doorway to the kitchen again. "Nikko was a Messianic Jew. His journals were written in Hebrew. He tried to teach me some when I was young, but I am afraid it didn't stick."

"Would you like me to translate them for you?"

"If it wouldn't be too much trouble. They are the last connection I have to him. But I am particularly interested in an entry around the fourth of July, fifteen years ago."

"Why then?"

"There was a change in my uncle's relationship with a friend of his around then. I can't remember the man's name, but his face is clear in my mind. He had been a regular visitor at our home. Every Friday after work, he would sit in the kitchen with Uncle Nikko and drink a beer before heading home. The two of them would talk about work and the construction business. I remembered it was Fourth of July, because that year I helped with the fireworks display over the bay. I came home to tell Uncle Nikko, and this friend was just leaving. He brushed me aside, almost knocking me down as he came barreling out the back door. I never saw him again."

"You think that incident might have something to do with your uncle's death?"

"I don't know, but it keeps coming to mind. I haven't told A.J. about it because it may be nothing. I would just like to find out if the journal says anything about it."

"Well, I'd be happy to help in any way I can."

Brady reached over and laid his hand on hers--a simple gesture that held a world of meaning. He hoped she sensed his care. Brady started to speak and then hesitated. Her face turned toward him, the afternoon light golden on her face. She was lovely and kind. But also vulnerable. The heavy hand of loneliness dropped on his shoulder, would she ever consider giving him a chance? Maybe they could heal together.

"What, Brady?"

"Holly, would you ever consider dating a strait-laced guy like me?"

Vera appeared from the kitchen carrying a tray with a pitcher and four glasses. "Anyone for lemonade?" Her eyes fell on their clasped hands, and her old eyes glinted with mirth.

In the kitchen, the screen door slammed. Yosef hurried into the room. "Pastor Brady, look who I found!"

In his arms lay a charcoal colored mound. The mound wiggled and a pair of brown eyes found Brady. Then a stick of a tail thumped twice against Yosef's arm.

"Daisy!" Brady threw up his arms in joy and then winced as the stitches in his shoulder strained. .

Yosef placed the curled bundle in Brady's lap. Daisy's hair was charred in some places and completely gone in others. Her tail was thin and hairless and her breathing was labored. She didn't try to lift her head, but her eyes spoke volumes. She whimpered softly, her eyes locked on Brady.

"I found her under a bush by the leaky spigot. I think she settled there because of the water." Yosef tried to pet a patch of red hair left uncharred. "I heard her whimper when I went to turn on the water. I looked and there she was."

Brady caressed the little dog in his lap. His joy was unspeakable, and he ached for her condition. "We need to get her to a vet. Vera? Holly? Do you know anyone?"

Holly checked her watch. "It's after five. But there's a twenty-four hour vet in Atascadero. We could take her there."

"Yosef, help me to the car. Holly, can you drive?" Brady shuffled to his wheelchair. He was desperate to save this last small bit of his former life.

"I'll call them to let them know we're coming." Holly dug for her cell phone as she headed out the door to her car. Holly pulled her Honda down the driveway to the makeshift ramp at the back of the house. Yosef wheeled Brady and Daisy down to the waiting car.

Once the two invalids were settled in, Holly headed for Hwy 41 and Atascadero.

Brady didn't know where to touch Daisy. Every inch of her seemed damaged in one way or another. He could see her back paws were raw and swollen. A tear threatened, and he rubbed his face with one hand.

"Hang on, Daisy. We're taking you to the doctor. You'll feel better soon." Daisy's tail twitched once, then she closed her brown eyes and appeared to sleep.

"What do you think, Holly? Have you ever seen a dog in this condition?"

"Never." Holly risked a glance at the miserable little bundle. "Her hair is singed, but her skin doesn't look burned, except for her tail and paws, that is."

"She rattles when she breathes. I can feel it. I wonder if her lungs are damaged." Brady stroked the small spot on the back of her neck where some hair remained. Daisy made a small sound but otherwise didn't move.

Thirty minutes later, Holly pulled into the twenty-four hour veterinary office in Atascadero. With some effort, Holly managed to get Brady and Daisy into the wheelchair and up to the main entrance. She pulled on the door but it didn't budge so she pushed the night buzzer, and in no time a vet in a white lab coat responded.

"Oh man," the young vet exclaimed. "She looks pretty beat up. Bring her in here, and let's take a look."

Daisy refused to uncurl when Brady placed her on the stainless steel table. The vet didn't try to move her. He just gently checked her eyes and ears and listened to her heart and lungs.

He took in Brady's wheelchair and bandages. "Looks like you have both been through it."

"My house burned down Saturday night. Daisy woke me up just in time, but then she ran back toward the fire, barking furiously, as if she could drive it away. She wouldn't come when I called her." His voice broke. He paused to collect himself then continued. "I tried to go after her, but I couldn't. The fire drove me back. I'm amazed she made it out alive."

"Dachshunds can be ferocious little fighters. I think the best thing is to leave her here. We'll knock down the pain, and then I can get a better look at her."

Brady hated to leave Daisy after having her back for less than two hours. But he knew her survival depended on getting veterinary care. Holly rolled him back to the Honda, and they returned over Highway 41 to Morro Bay. The sun was beginning to set as they wound their way through the canyon. The bald head of Morro Rock was fringed by a blanket of grey. The final rays of the sun skimmed a wash of pink across the top of the foggy mist, giving the rock a rosy glow. As the sun drew below the horizon, the sky grew more riotous. Salmons and pinks mixed with turquoise. The intensity grew and spread across the sky as the minutes passed.

Holly slowed the car so they could enjoy the fading sunset. "How could someone look at that and not see the magnificence of God. We serve an awesome God, Brady. His hand is in even the smallest things. I think the fact that Daisy made it through that inferno is a miracle in itself."

"I have no doubt you're right, Holly." He reached over and squeezed her hand, his own words hollow in his ears. "What are you going to do now, Brady? Live with the Shankston's till we find you a house?"

"Probably, maybe not. I guess I don't know, really. I have deep roots in Wyoming. They are very appealing right now."

Chapter Twenty-Two

Holly had lain awake most of the night--her mind revisiting the time spent with Brady. The fellowship she experienced at the church reminded her of the happy times in the past, but it also picked at the wounds of rejection and hurt she thought were healed. Before her parents' divorce, the church had been her social world. They worshiped together, studied together, and shared the joys and sorrows of life together. She had tasted a bit of that sweetness again yesterday, but beneath it lingered bitter bile. People could be cruel in the name of righteousness.

She'd been transfixed by Brady's compassionate eulogy. He was a powerful speaker; no wonder his church in Wyoming had grown to such impressive proportions. She could still feel the touch of his hand on hers. Where had these emotions come from? She wanted no part of the church. But the church was Brady's life. In spite of that, she had allowed the day's events to move her along, the fresh wind of circumstances filling her sails. One moment she was a realtor paying respects at a co-worker's funeral. The next moment she was spending the afternoon and evening with the pastor—and liking it. He wanted to move their relationship up a notch. She spent a restless night alternately considering then rejecting the idea.

She wasn't pastor's wife material—not the sewing-circle, social type at all. She had a business to manage. And a sailboat to enjoy.

This relationship had to slow down. He wanted to date her. But Brady needed to understand that a man in his position needed –needed what? Well, not her. And she was dating A.J., sort of. A.J. was a good man too, compassionate, smart, and hard-working. He made her feel like a princess when they were together. And he wouldn't need someone to teach Bible studies and shake hands on Sundays.

Holly scrutinized her morning reflection in the bathroom mirror. Her eyes were puffy and her cheeks were red. "Ugh, what a mess!" She had promised Brady when they parted yesterday that she would come to the Shankstons this morning and bring the copies of the journals. She would have to work a bit harder with the cosmetics to repair the damage of the sleepless night.

"Father, help. What should I do? You've brought this wonderful man into my life, a man of God. But you have brought A.J. as well. Thinking about going back into the church life makes my stomach roll. Those days still hurt, Lord. I thought I'd forgiven those people years ago, but I guess I haven't. I don't see how this can work."

The smell of coffee drifted in from the kitchen just as Holly finished dressing. She poured herself a large mug, gathered her basket of study materials, and stepped onto the balcony for her morning quiet time. The moisture-heavy air collected and dripped from the edge of the patio cover onto a row of pots overflowing with impatiens, their white and pink blossoms bobbing with each heavy drop. Holly tucked a blanket around her legs, flipped on her small space heater, and shut her eyes. Her Bible lay open on her lap as she renewed her quiet conversation.

"Father, help me to go in the direction you would have me go." Immediately she felt a check in her heart. She didn't *want* to go back into the church. She knew with every ounce of her that she would never open herself up again to such hurt. The wall she had built remained intact. Her prayer lacked sincerity—and stuck in the layers of fog that hid the ocean from view.

Sunday morning at the Shankston's found Brady struggling to dress himself. He had decided that he would stay home from church today. An elder had graciously offered to speak in his place, which had come as a welcome relief for Brady. With all his study materials gone, pulling together a sermon would have been impossible. In addition, he was exhausted from working long into the night refreshing his Hebrew. He was a little rusty but had found a website on Yosef's computer with the Bible in Hebrew. He mechanically translated the words of the Torah, carefully keeping his heart protected from their power. He didn't doubt God existed. He didn't even doubt his salvation. He knew who Christ was and he understood the need for the cross as well as his need for that sacrifice. But he didn't trust God anymore. "If God is so good, why is there so much evil in the world?" He had heard the question many times and knew the answer, but that answer was for other people. How could God turn *his* ruined life into something good? The eighteen-inch journey from what he knew in his head, to accepting it in his heart, could just as well be eighteen miles. The pain and the loss were always there, just at the edge of his emotions. If he dared to touch those painful, open wounds, the tears would flow like a river. He had learned not to touch them, not to ask those hard questions of himself.

His legs burned like fire. He had suffered through a tough night until finally around two a.m. he had succumbed to the pain medication that the doctor had prescribed. He tried to pull on the long pants Yosef had bought yesterday, but it was no use. His legs couldn't stand the pressure of the pants, and his shoulder couldn't tolerate the shirt, so he donned a soft sweatshirt and shorts. His mind touched on Holly's lovely face, and a softness touched his heart. She said she would come today. No matter what, it was going to be a good day.

Brady recognized Yosef's steps coming up the hallway. When the quiet knock came, Brady answered and Yosef's head popped around the door. "Vera has breakfast on."

Brady was getting more mobile in his wheelchair, and Yosef had rearranged some furniture to give him a clear path into the kitchen. He rolled his way to the table where Vera had spread a sumptuous breakfast; biscuits, bacon, eggs, jam, and steaming coffee.

Vera placed a big cup of coffee before him. "You need all the nutrition you can get, Pastor Brady, so you can heal."

Yosef poured a cup for himself and sat down across from Brady. "How are you feeling today, Pastor?"

"If it doesn't sound like complaining, Yosef, I'm a bit worse today. Everything hurts, but I don't want to take the pain medication during the day. If I start drooling and mumbling, people will begin to wonder." In all honesty, taking his medication and sleeping for the next three days sounded much better, but helping Holly was a bright spot that got him out of bed. Her presence drove back the blackness that hovered at the edges of his life.

He realized he hadn't told Vera and Yosef she was visiting. "Holly is coming over today," he said, judging their reaction.

Vera and Yosef shared a brief look.

"That is if you don't mind of course." *Boy, this feels awkward*

"We don't mind a bit, Pastor Brady, we're delighted to have her. Will she be staying for lunch?"

"No way to know, Vera. She asked me to help her decipher some of her late uncle's journals. Apparently, they are written in Hebrew."

"That's strange. Why would he do that?"

"I don't really know. He died last Thursday. Holly told me he was murdered."

133

Yosef slowly buttered a warm biscuit, nodding his head. "I think I read about it in the paper. He was living at Hibiscus House, right?"

"That's the one. I really don't know much more."

"Paper said there was no evidence of a forced entry. Inside job apparently. Maybe he made one of the residents mad. Those old folks can trigger real easy."

Vera took Yosef's plate. "Those old folks? We're no spring chickens--and that's enough biscuits, Yosef."

Yosef's jaw dropped then snapped shut as he watched his plate disappear into the sink. He muttered something about overbearing women around his final mouthful of biscuit.

Holly pulled up to the house, turned off the car. Was it wise for her to be here? She could have hired a translation service for a small fortune and maintained her distance from Brady, but here she sat.

The fog was finally retreating, leaving everything fresh and sweet smelling. The Shankston's home had a broad front porch filled with potted geraniums, their red blossoms poking through the white pickets of the porch railing. Taking a deep breath, she got out of the car, retrieved the box of journal copies from the back seat, and followed the walk up the steps to the front door. A cool ocean breeze lifted her red hair off her shoulders. She inhaled deeply, refreshed by the tang of salt. She tossed a quick glance at a sliver of ocean between two houses across the street. Neatly framed between them a large sailboat headed north, all three of its sails hoisted and filled.

Yosef opened the door, startling her.

"Oh, hi Yosef."

Yosef looked past her. "Beautiful sight, isn't it?"

"The sailboat? Yes, lovely. I've never sailed a cutter rig."

"I understand you like sailing, Holly. You and Brady had quite an adventure, I heard."

"We made it though. Chalk up another one for experience." She lifted a hand and marked the air with one finger.

Yosef took the box from Holly and placed it on a glass table on the front porch.

"Brady thought it would be nice to sit out in the fresh air while the two of you work on your project."

"This is perfect, Yosef. Thank you."

"We'll be just inside if you two need anything." Yosef winked and stepped to the side as Brady rolled out the front door. Then the old man left the two of them on the porch.

Brady had a yellow tablet on his lap and a pencil behind his ear. "Hi there! I hope sitting out here is all right with you. The house is rather small, and this will provide us with more privacy." He eyed the box of journal copies. "I lost all of my reference books in the fire, so I will have to do this from memory. I haven't used my Hebrew in a while, but I should be able to get most of it for you. I spent some time on the Internet last night brushing up."

Holly reached into the box and picked up the top bundle. "I don't know which ones are which, but it seems he has written the dates every few pages." She pointed to an inscription at the top of one of the pages.

"Yes, that's a date. Looks like August of 1987."

"Okay, so the one I'm looking for is July of '94."

She pulled the next three bundles onto the table and Brady went through them one by one. "No, none of these."

Holly pulled out the last batch, and finally Brady found the stack they were looking for. "Okay, here is June of '94. Close enough." He turned a few more pages and began reading, occasionally making notes on the yellow pad.

They worked on through the morning. Brady translated a section and then read it to Holly. Most of it were Nikko's thoughts on a Scripture he had read that day or observations about work. Occasionally, he bragged on Holly. Brady could see that those passages were the hardest on her. Her lips would draw into a thin line and her eyes would grow moist. Then she would rally as he continued. He tried to stop a time or two but she insisted they continue as long as he was willing.

Two long hours had passed when Brady sat back and looked up at Holly. "I think I may have found what you have been looking for. Does the name Kent ring a bell?"

"Yes! Kent Haden, now I remember. He was younger than my uncle, but they had a good friendship. What does the journal say?"

"Basically, it says, 'Big fight with Kent tonight. Can't seem to get along since the last project. This thing is tormenting us both.'"

"Sounds like that's it. My uncle was definitely tormented by something. Before he died, he kept repeating that same phrase over and over. 'What the eye doesn't see, the heart won't grieve over.'" She looked at him to see if it made any sense.

Brady looked off into the distance, puzzled as well. "Let me continue reading for a bit. Maybe I can go back a few months and find something more."

Holly checked her watch. "It's almost noon and I smell lunch cooking. I think I'll go see if Vera needs any help."

Brady nodded but didn't look up, engrossed in his reading.

In the kitchen, Holly could see Vera setting glasses on the table.

"How can I help?"

"All set. Just have to wait for the chicken casserole, and we're ready. How are you two doing out there? Making progress?"

Holly didn't really want to discuss it. "The work is slow but we seem to be getting through it. That casserole smells wonderful. Reminds me of home."

Vera dried her hands on a dishtowel. "I'm glad, Holly. Where were you raised?"

"Here in Morro Bay. Never lived anywhere else except when I went to college."

"Funny how we never met. Being such a small town and all."

Holly picked up a wet plate and started drying it. Coming inside without Brady had been stupid. It gave Vera an excellent opportunity to grill her. The silence became awkward.

"I didn't mean to pry, Holly." Vera replaced the dishtowel, casting a sidewise glance.

Holly slowed her drying, then stopped. "You're not prying, Vera. I know that." She looked up. "Vera, I love the Lord with every ounce of who I am. But I can't stand His church." She put down the dishtowel and crossed her arms, her hip settling against the kitchen counter. "No, that's not accurate. I don't *trust* His church."

Holly watched and waited for Vera's response. At some deep unreasoned level, she knew that what came next would tell her a lot about what direction she would be taking with Brady.

"Meaning you don't trust me."

"Well, yes. In a sense."

"Something awful must have happened to you, child."

"Vera, I'm not a child, and yes, something awful happened. And it was good, godly church people who did it."

"And you automatically assume I am just as awful as those people?" Vera's gentle face had hardened.

"You don't know what happened."

"Oh, I can guess." Vera picked up another plate and began to dry it. "They didn't act very Christ-like. Am I right?" She didn't look up.

"No, they didn't"

"Funny that."

"What do you mean?"

"I suspect the next thing you'll tell me is that folks outside the church are nicer than those within the body." Vera stopped drying for a moment and waited for Holly's response.

"I guess I would."

"When do you clean a fish, Holly? Before it's caught or after?"

As the two women stood in silence, Brady rolled into the kitchen, inhaling audibly. "Smells great, ladies." Then he stopped, sensing the tension. "Did I interrupt something, Vera?"

"No, Brady. Holly and I were just discussing the fishing industry. Lunch is ready."

Yosef came in and washed his hands at the kitchen sink. "Smells great!"

The four sat around the simple pine table at the back of the house and reached for each other's hands.

Brady bowed his head. "Father, thank you for this beautiful day. Help me, Father to remember what I have learned so I can read these journals. Thank you for the food Vera has prepared, in your Son's name. Amen."

Yosef filled a plate with casserole and handed it over to Holly. "So tell us more about these journals you're reading, Pastor Brady. That is if you don't mind, Holly."

Yes, I mind very much. She forced back the old protective instincts and composed her face as she took the plate of food. *They're just being pleasant, making small talk.*

"Not at all, Yosef. Brady can explain them better than I can."

"Holly's uncle wrote them by hand in Hebrew, so it's slow going."

Vera brought a large pitcher of lemonade to the table. "Sounds like a big project. How's your Hebrew, Pastor Brady?"

"I'm not as rusty as I thought I would be. I'm glad I took the extra units of Hebrew in seminary. I actually enjoyed studying it, unlike some of my classmates."

"I'm sorry to hear about your uncle, Holly. When is the memorial service?"

Holly hesitated. Memorial service, who would come? "I'm still in the process of arranging the details."

Vera filled her glass with lemonade. "If we can be of any help, don't hesitate to ask."

Brady caught her eye. "You could use Mariners Chapel if you like."

Holly felt the pull of their compassion. She knew in her head that they were trying to be helpful. But her heart rebelled. Twelve years of maturity fell from her as the wounded teenager fought to the surface, wanting to strike out at their kindness, find fault in their motives, and throw it back in their faces.

She studied her lunch, knowing her eyes would betray her if she looked up. She took a deep breath. "It will probably be awhile. I have a few things to clear up first."

Vera started to speak but Yosef nudged her into silence.

When lunch was over, Brady painfully hobbled to his wheelchair and followed Holly back onto the porch.

Holly watched him struggle to get comfortable. "Can I get you anything to help?"

"The pain is worse than yesterday for some reason. I could take some of the medication the doctor gave me, but it makes me groggy. I think I'd rather hurt." His brown eyes found hers and held them. "I'm glad you stayed for lunch. Is today a busy real estate day for you?" He reached out and laid his hand over hers.

"I don't have anything pressing at the moment." She liked the feel of his hand on hers, but she also felt awkward. He definitely wanted to take their relationship to another level. "I noticed the blue tarp on the roof of the church. Is there a problem?" She slipped her hand from under his and reached down for her purse, making a show of looking for something.

"Some shingles blew off in the last storm. We have some roof work ahead of us. I was supposed to help Arlen with the job. I guess he'll have to find someone else."

"That will be expensive. Does your church have the money for roof repair?"

"Oh, you might be surprised."

She picked something up in his tone. "Surprised in what way?"

He fiddled with his pencil, then looked up. "Holly, we have a problem with the church books. I'm just not sure what to make of it. Would you be interested in a little brainstorming?"

"Of course, I'd be happy to help … if I can, I guess." The conversation had taken an awkward turn.

Brady plunged ahead, in spite of her discomfort. "It's a bit of a puzzle. Large deposits and withdrawals are going in and out of the account every week. Currently, the church has over three-hundred-thousand dollars in the account. I just don't know what to make of it. I thought perhaps you might know someone I could talk to outside of the church."

"Good grief! What does your bookkeeper have to say?" Holly sat back in amazement.

"That's the biggest problem. The bookkeeper is Evelyn, and we haven't been able to get a word out of her. I think she's been traumatized by Cheri's death."

"I heard a rumor that she was murdered."

Brady settled back in his chair with a sigh. "Yes, that's what the sheriff's department is saying.

"Brady, this is creepy. Two murders, totally unrelated, in one week?"

Brady wondered if he should tell her that his house was deliberately set on fire. "It is creepy. I don't quite know what to make of it."

Just then, Vera appeared in the doorway. "Pastor Brady, there is a young girl on the phone for you. She says it's urgent." She brought Brady his cell phone.

"Hello, this is Brady McGregor." He listened for a moment, then leaned close to Holly so she could hear.

"Jessica? What's happened?"

"I'm at the Sheriff's Department. I've been arrested. Can you come?"

Chapter Twenty -Three

Holly rolled Brady into the same vanilla room Brady had visited earlier in the week. She had been through some tough things with Jessica, but this was the first visit to the jail. They had come so far together. She should have been heartbroken. But instead she found she was angry. Jessica had been doing so well.

A.J. came through the door, looked from Brady to Holly and back again. "Well, well, well. Look at you two."

"What's that supposed to mean, A.J.?" Holly's voice held an edge.

A.J. flashed her a crooked grin and took a seat across from them. "Just doing my job, Holly. Just doing my job. I understand you two are here to see Jessica Barnes. Is that right?"

"That's correct, Detective," Brady replied. "When can we see her?"

"All in good time, Padre. Did she mention why she was here?"

"No, she just called me and asked me to come. She said she'd been arrested and that's all."

"Well, your Miss Barnes was found with Cheri Davenport's jewelry in her possession, and we'd like to know why. Perhaps you can help us get some answers."

"I'm not sure I can help, Detective. If she tells me something in confidence, it stays in confidence. You know that."

"Wouldn't you like to know how she came into possession of a dead woman's jewelry, Padre?

"I guess I'll have to ask her, Detective. Now can we see her?"

"We?" A.J. raised an eyebrow.

"Holly is with me. We're both concerned about Jessica."

"How do you know Jessica?" A.J. asked Holly.

"I was her mentor when she was finishing high school. If Jessica doesn't want to see me, then I'll wait outside." She held A.J.'s intense gaze, not allowing him to intimidate her. She had nothing to be ashamed of. She cared for Jessica and was here to help.

"Fine." He slapped his notepad on his open palm. "I'll be just down the hall if you want to talk. You know the way, Holly." He winked at her and left.

Holly let out an exasperated sigh. "Maybe I should wait in the lobby. Jessica might be uncomfortable with me here." She turned to Brady. "She did call you instead of me."

"I'd like you to stay." Brady squeezed her hand. "Let's see what happens when Jessica comes in."

"Have you ever handled something like this before?"

"Not since my days as a youth pastor. Although I have to admit that the worst offense I dealt with was the time when a couple of the boys spray-painted the pastor's prize bull."

Holly was horrified. "Did the bull die?"

"No, and the pastor taught a great lesson on respecting other people's property the next Sunday. I made the boys take notes and write a report on the sermon. Those were fun days." His eyes were far off and soft.

Holly felt herself detach a bit and observe Brady. She enjoyed his company. He was friendly, intelligent, engaging and handsome, all of which were in the plus column. The fluttery feeling in her stomach when he was near is what bothered her. No one had affected her that way in a long time. In truth, she hadn't allowed anyone close enough. *When people get too close they find ways to hurt you.*

It was a truth she'd lived by since high school. It had kept her heart safe. But Brady had somehow slipped over the walls she had erected.

Before long, the door opened and Jessica entered, dressed in an orange jumpsuit. An officer nodded to them both and closed the door.

"Thank you for coming, Pastor Brady. I didn't know who else to call." She dabbed her puffy eyes on a damp wad of tissue. Jessica cast a watery glance at Holly. "And I didn't have your number, Holly."

Holly instantly didn't believe her but she brushed the thought aside. "I'm glad you called, Jessica. You did the right thing. Why don't you sit down, and we'll talk about what happened."

"The cops came to my apartment this morning," she started as she seated herself in the metal chair, her voice trembling. "They said they found my fingerprints at Cheri's house. They had a search warrant and took all my jewelry and stuff." Her voice wound higher. "I guess Cheri's mom identified some of it as Cheri's." Huge tears tumbled to the steel table.

"How did you get the jewelry, Jessica?"

Her head snapped up. "She gave it to me, of course. How else would I get it?" Her eyes crackled with defiance. "I thought you were here to help."

"We can't help if we don't have all the facts." Brady said. He leaned back in his chair and crossed his arms, waiting.

Jesssica's defiance dropped away. She shifted beneath Brady's stern look, her eyes darting to Holly then back to Brady.

"Did you tell the officers that Cheri gave you the jewelry?" Holly asked.

"Of course, but they don't believe me. They never believe me. Cheri was my friend. We hung out and stuff. Why is it so surprising that she gave me something?"

"I thought you were just casual friends, Jessica. I didn't realize you knew her that well."

"Well I did! See, you don't believe me, either." She sat back in her chair folded her arms too, and put her chin on her chest. Her tangled hair fell over her face.

"I'm just trying to get an idea of what happened." Brady's voice was measured, steady. "I'm not accusing you of anything."

"I'm telling you what happened." She looked up, shaking her hair from her eyes, then rubbed her nose on her sleeve.

Holly leaned forward, resting her forearms on the table. "Jessica, how much jewelry did they find at your house?"

"I'm not sure. Some earrings, a ring, and a necklace, I guess."

"You don't remember what she gave you?"

"Of course I do."

"Well?"

"You guys are supposed to be here to support and help me, not give me the third degree."

Brady leaned back in his chair, palms flat on the steel table. "Helping you means being honest with you, Jessica. You need to be honest with us as well. The evidence is stacked against you right now,"

"I didn't steal anything. She gave me the jewelry." Her tone flat. She traded Brady look for look, dry-eyed and defiant.

Holly sighed, drawing Jessica's attention. "Jessica, there was a time..."

"I'm not like that anymore, Holly!" She shoved back her chair, stood and began to pace.

"Jessica," Brady said, his voice low and authoritative, "the police believe that Cheri was murdered. This is a very serious situation."

Jessica stopped pacing and turned to face Brady. "Murdered! That's crazy." She wrapped her arms around her slim waist and began to pace again. "I don't know anything about that. Who told you she was murdered?"

"Detective Walker."

"Why do they think she was murdered? The paper said suicide."

"I don't know the details, but if you are involved or know anything at all, you need to tell us the whole truth."

Jessica spun and slapped her palms down on the metal table. "I *am* telling you the truth."

Holly stood and moved around the table, stopping behind Jessica. She placed her hands on Jessica's shoulders and gently turned her so they were face to face. "Jessica, I know you've been through a lot in the past couple of years. We've walked through most of it together. You can be honest with me. You know you can trust me."

The door opened, and the guard came in. "Time's up."

"Time's up! I just got here!" Jessica protested, breaking away from Holly.

Brady rolled his wheelchair back from the table. "Jessica, it's okay. We'll come back and visit you."

She turned to Brady. "You will?"

"I promise."

Holly started the car and backed out of their parking spot as Brady fastened his seat belt. "Well, what do you think?"

"She's lying."

"How do you know?"

"Me thinks she doth protest too much." Holly wiggled her eyebrows at him.

"You think she stole the jewelry?"

"I'd bet a quarter on it."

"What a shame." Brady shook his head. "Seeing her at Cheri's funeral gave me hope."

"This may be just the thing she needs. Jessica has had a rough start. Stealing isn't the worst thing she's done in the past. But I thought she was done with that part of her life."

Helping Jessica get through high school had been rewarding for Holly, but she hadn't thought of it as ministry, really, just something she did to help a young girl get on her feet. Back then, Jessica had shown a willingness to break with her past and get her feet on a better path. She began getting her homework done and in on time. Her grades rose and finally, after a year and a half, Holly proudly watched Jessica graduate. Holly had kept their faith discussions to a minimum because of the policies of the program and Jessica's own resistance to the topic. She hoped that in time Jessica would trust her enough to take that step. Had Jessica fallen far enough to finally listen? Holly wasn't sure, but she was willing to give it a try. Jessica obviously wanted Brady to visit and perhaps Holly could come along. Maybe the time was ripe for a heart-to-heart with Jessica about Christ.

They drove in silence for a few minutes.

Brady reached out and patted her hand where it lay on the center console. The simple gesture sent a thrill up her arm. There was an assumption in the gesture that annoyed her. She pulled her hand away and placed it on the wheel as she turned a corner.

"You said you had an idea about who might help us with the bank account mystery. Who did you have in mind?" Brady asked.

"My bookkeeper, she is a wizard with accounting. I'll bet she can help you. I have to warn you though, she is a bit of a character. She is one of those people that is so intelligent they are a bit eccentric. Do you want me to call her?"

"It's worth a try."

Holly got her on the phone and was pleased that her friend was available this afternoon. Holly told her they would be right over. She smiled to herself. This would be an interesting meeting.

Chapter Twenty-Four

Glynnis Hoving lived in San Luis Obispo, about twelve minutes south down Hwy 1. Holly always enjoyed the ride through the residential area on the north end of town. A tunnel of ancient trees shaded the early fifties homes, their huge branches joining hands across the street. Holly pulled onto the cracked concrete driveway of a small, light turquoise house. The meticulously groomed landscaping bordered a molded concrete retaining wall and a cobbled pathway. The flowerbeds were a tumble of colors and texture. Ornate metal sculptures peeked from the foliage and hung jewelry-like from the house.

She pulled into the driveway and parked. "Uh, oh."

"Uh, oh what?"

"How am I going to get you into the house?"

Brady scanned the front yard. The front approach to the house was definitely not wheelchair accessible. He was able to walk, but it was extremely painful to go so far, and stairs were out of the question.

Holly turned off the car. "Maybe we should do this another day."

"No, I need to get to the bottom of this money mystery."

Just then, a figure in flowing robes came onto the front stoop. She was tall and majestic. Her long, thick black hair held at the nape of her neck with a silver clasp. When she saw Holly, she smiled and waved them in.

"Come in, Holly, come in. Bring your friend."

Holly rolled down her window. "Glynnis, we have a problem."

Glynnis came over to the car and stooped down to look in the window.

"And what is our problem?" The scent of gardenias drifted in.

"Glynnis, this is Brady McGregor. He's in a wheelchair right now because his feet and legs are burned. How can we get him into the house?"

"Come to the back." She motioned them to follow her down the driveway to the garage, her long black ponytail swaying in rhythm with each step. She disappeared into the garage for a few moments and then re-emerged with an aluminum ramp that fit in special brackets at the back steps. "Ta da!" She threw her hands into the air.

Holly helped Brady out of the car, and before long they were up the ramp and in the house.

Glynnis' home was sunny and warm. Nothing had been updated since the home was built, but everything was in immaculate condition. Built-in linen drawers lined the hallway to the living room where an explosion of color filled every space. Great bunches of fresh flowers graced a large fireplace mantle to the left. Under the front window, a bright couch and two chairs were stacked with pillows, and vibrant throws tumbled across them. Wood-framed windows with deep, thick sills were capped with a lemon yellow valence. Everywhere were paintings, all full of color and totally modern. Brilliant swooshes of red were mingled with magenta and green in one. In another, yellow was the dominant color with bits of antique jewelry providing accents.

Glynnis watched Brady's reaction to her work. "I see my art has attracted your attention." Glynnis smiled and nodded. "I find it catches the eye of those who appreciate inspired work."

Brady paused and looked up at the one with the embedded jewelry. "It is definitely inspired."

"The Holy Spirit guides my hand to portray God's beauty. This one, for example, conveys the jewels in the crowns of the saints. You know that the saints will have crowns, don't you?"

"Brady is the pastor of Mariners Chapel in Morro Bay, Glynnis."

"Oh, well then, I am sure you sense the Spirit moving in my work."

"Absolutely." Brady looked about the room at the other works of art as Holly wheeled him to an overstuffed chair by the fireplace. After positioning the wheelchair as close as possible, Brady hobbled two steps to the chair and settled in.

"So, how can I help you two today, hmmm?" Glynnis took a seat across from Brady and Holly.

"Well, Glynnis, Brady has discovered some irregularities in the church bookkeeping. I suggested we come visit you. Maybe you can figure out what is happening."

Glynnis looked over at Brady. "So what seems to be the problem?"

"In a nutshell, large amounts of money are moving in and out of the account every Thursday. Not money from the church but from some other source."

"How much money?"

"Last I looked, we had over three-hundred-thousand dollars in the account. Sums of around one-hundred-and-fifty thousand move in and out regularly. I picked up the last six months' bank statements, and that seems to be the pattern."

Glynnis settled back into the couch and arranged her robes, considering. "What does your bookkeeper say?" She played with the heavy beads about her neck.

Holly and Brady exchanged glances. "The bookkeeper lost her daughter recently. She's been rather hard to approach since." Brady said.

"She obviously knows something about the transactions. She's been balancing the books every month."

"I can't imagine she has anything to do with the money. She's a simple widow who has been doing the books for years."

"She may not have anything more to do with it than to cover it up. Don't you think she suspected something when the first transaction hit? Have her monthly financial statements reflected the true picture of the account?"

"No, the last statement we received showed we had about ten-thousand dollars, not the three-hundred-and-some thousand."

"My guess is that there is some sort of money laundering going on with your account and your bookkeeper is involved."

"That's a lot of money." Glynnis glanced at Brady's bandages. "Perhaps somebody would be willing to kill to protect it."

"We're talking about members of our church, elders who have served for years if not decades," Brady protested.

"The deposits don't have to be made by someone who signs on the account, Brady. If the bookkeeper is involved, she could maneuver the money herself." Glynnis' bright blue eyes looked steadily at Brady.

"If you saw Evelyn's lifestyle, you wouldn't include her. She lives very carefully. She's a widow on a tight budget."

"I wouldn't rule her out so quickly. We've all heard plenty of stories about little old ladies who were worth millions when they died, and no one ever knew." Glynnis sat forward and addressed Brady. "You may have stumbled onto a very dangerous situation, young man. If I were you, I would watch my back."

Brady became very quiet, eyes locked on a spot just past Glynnis' head. One finger tapped his leg.

The clock on the mantle ticked away the moments as Holly watched the various emotions play across Brady's face, the struggle behind his eyes evident for all to see. She exchanged glances with Glynnis, who also acknowledged his struggle.

"What worries you, Brady? Are you afraid to die?"

He shifted his gaze back to Glynnis. "No, I'm not afraid to die."

"Then what is your struggle?" The words were gentle.

The silence grew between them as Brady fought for control, Glynnis' gentle hazel eyes willing him to speak.

"Brady, we serve a very big God, you and I. Your struggles are known to Him, you know that."

"Brady, what's troubling you?" Holly leaned forward, resting her hand on his arm.

Brady looked around the room, his eyes stopping on the front door. He looked like a rabbit trapped in a snare.

Beads of sweat appeared on his forehead and upper lip and his breathing became labored. Alarmed, Holly stood up and went to him. She placed a hand on his shoulder.

"Brady?" She knelt next to the chair where she could look up into his eyes, but they were far away and unfocused.

Glynnis came over and placed one hand on Brady's shoulder, raising the other into the air. "Abba God, Ruach HaKodesh, touch this man. Comfort him and heal him. You see what no one sees. You see into our hearts. Abba, comfort him with the comfort only you can provide."

Brady closed his eyes and Holly placed her hand over his where it rested on the arm of the chair. His skin was cool and slick with perspiration.

"Abba, Brady carries anger in his heart. You know about it, Abba, and it grieves you."

Glynnis moved to stand in front of Brady. "The Lord has a word for you. 'I will never leave you or forsake you.' He wants you to remember that." She reached out and laid both hands on his head and prayed quietly. The clock on the mantle ticked off the seconds as Brady sat in the chair. Glynnis' prayers continued quietly, interspersed with long periods of silence. She occasionally mumbled words Holly couldn't quite catch.

Holly's lips, however, were silent. The prayers for Brady wouldn't come. She felt his pulse racing beneath her hand. She knew he was caught in an emotional war zone, the battle raging between opposing forces. His rapid heart rate a witness to the intensity of the struggle. She should pray. Intervene on his behalf. But she remained mute.

Finally Brady's breathing became steady, his pulse slowed, and he opened his eyes. Glynnis looked down on him. "God answers when we ask, Brady. If you do not have answers, it is because you do not ask."

Brady nodded and wiped his face. "Thanks, Glynnis. I get a little overwhelmed sometimes. Could I have a glass of water?"

Glynnis went to the kitchen leaving Holly and Brady alone for a moment. "Are you alright now, Brady?" Her green eyes showing worry.

He smiled down at her and patted her hand. "I'm glad I met you. Have I mentioned that?" He brushed a lock of hair back from her forehead.

She didn't return his smile. Glynnis returned with a pitcher and three glasses.

Once back in the car and headed home, Brady turned to look at Holly. "I know it's early, but would you like some dinner? I've never been to San Luis Obispo. I hear they have some great restaurants. What do you say?"

"Thanks, Brady, but I need to get home. I've been away from work for a couple of days now, and I really should check in with my other customers." She hoped he would easily relent. She wanted to take him back to the Shankston's, drop him off, and tell him they should not date anymore. If it meant losing a customer and an escrow, so be it. His touch, their close proximity all day, had sent her emotions on a crazy ride. He was pulling her back into her former life, a life she had turned her back on years ago. The prayer, the ministry, the whole church package was not part of who she was anymore. If Brady had been a nice Christian man other than a pastor, perhaps she could have made a life with him. But he *was* a pastor. The church *was* his life. She didn't want it to be part of hers.

All afternoon, painful memories had flitted through her mind. She could still remember the smell of the youth pastor's cologne as he sat with two other kids in his office. She recalled the conversation, reliving the pain and rejection . . .

"Holly, I know you have worked hard in the leadership of the youth group for two years and we really appreciate all you have done."

Her breath came heavily as she fought tears. The two girls that sat with him wouldn't meet her eyes. One of them had a father that had left church leadership because adultery was ruining his life and marriage. It had been a humiliating blow for the petite blond, a young girl accustomed to popularity, and her family's central role in the church.

"I know it may be hard for you to understand. However, I think it's best for you to step down from your youth ministry responsibilities."

She slapped her leg in frustration. "But why?"

"Please, Holly." He lifted his hand to calm her. "I know you have been through a lot over the past few weeks."

"Yes, I have. But haven't I done my job? I've been on time and I'm always prepared for the studies. Has someone complained?"

The young pastor's eyes darted to the two girls in the room. It was a telling lapse.

Holly turned to the petite blond in rage. "I am not responsible for my father's behavior and my parents problems have nothing to do with my ability to minister."

"No, Holly, you are not responsible for your parents' behavior. Unfortunately, their behavior does affect you in more ways than you may be aware. For the time being, Maggie will be taking over your junior high girls."

The brunette sitting next to the petite blond examined her nails, refusing to meet Holly's outraged stare.

"I can't believe I'm getting fired from youth group because my father is a jerk!" Holly screamed, then ran from the room and slammed the door behind her.

The memory misted her eyes, the pain alive again in her heart.

"I promise I won't keep you late tonight. You could be home by seven at the latest." Brady wasn't giving up.

She forced her face to soften before turning toward him. "No, Brady, really, I have a business to run. Thanks anyway."

Once they arrived at the Shankston home, Holly helped Brady back to his wheelchair and then stepped around to face him. Sitting on the cement step leading up to the back door, Holly met his eyes. "Brady, there's something I have to tell you." She felt her throat begin to tighten and took a long breath to fight it off. "I have been doing quite a bit of thinking these past few days. You are a gifted teacher, and you love the Lord as much as I do, but you need someone who can help you in your ministry. I'm not that person, Brady." She choked back tears. They glistened on her eyelashes, and she blinked them away. "I have never dated a man like you. You're kind and smart and have a great gift. I would stand in the way of all that. Do you know what I'm saying?"

Brady sat in silence, his eyes registering pain and disbelief.

"God will guide you, Brady."

He threw his head back, staring at the cloudless sky, chuckled weirdly, and looked back at Holly. "God doesn't seem to have done a very good job so far." His eyes flashed anger, and then it was gone. "Thanks for introducing me to Glynnis. She was a great help in clarifying the money mystery. Tell her thanks when you see her next." Their eyes locked for a painful moment. Then he winked at her and rolled himself slowly up the ramp and into the house.

Chapter Twenty-Five

It's better this way. The thought battered her as she drove home. Her mind again ran the scene when she told her mother and uncle that she had been removed from youth ministry ...

"Well, sweetie, I can't say I'm surprised." Her mother had whispered in her hair as Holly sobbed on her shoulder.

"Nothing in the church surprises me anymore."

The slamming of the back screen door pulled them apart as Uncle Nikko arrived home. He hugged her then held her by the shoulders. "What's this? Why the tears Hollyhock?"

"I was removed from the youth ministry team today."

Uncle Nikko nodded and smiled, as if it was all perfectly understandable. He seated himself at the kitchen table of their small home and opened his evening beer.

Holly sat at the table across from him. "You don't seem to be upset, Uncle Nikko. How could they do this to me?" Her ready tears infuriated her.

"So you think it was them. Them who, Hollyhock?"

"That she-witch Maggie and her blonde sidekick Christa, of course."

"Hmmm, maybe not. Who else could it be?"

"Uncle Nikko, honestly I hate it when you only ask questions. Just tell me who you think it was."

"Who is ultimately in control of your life? Who allows all things to work together for His good purpose?"

"You think God allowed this? That's craziness. Why would God want me out of ministry for something I had nothing to do with?" She looked to Mom for support.

She was wrapped in a heavy sweater and sipped a cup of tea. Her once dark red locks now showed streaks of silver. Lately she was always cold.

"Momma, you're not saying anything?"

"You're Uncle Nicholias is on this kick about God being in charge of all the bad that happens."

"No, Elizabeth, that's not what I've been saying. What has happened to Holly is a perfect example."

"How so?"

He turned back to Holly. "When Christ went to the cross, who sent him there?"

"Judas."

"Try again."

"Uncle Nikko, I know the story, everybody does. Judas betrayed Christ."

"If Judas hadn't been available, do you think Christ would have been crucified?"

"Of course, it had to happen to bring salvation."

"So?"

"It was God who ultimately caused it to happen, Holly. Your uncle and I have been down this road many times since we moved in with him."

"So you're saying it was God who caused—'"

"Allowed," Uncle Nikko interrupted.

"Allowed me to be removed from ministry. That's crazy." Holly dismissed the thought with a wave of her hand.

"There you have the core of our ongoing discussion," Mom said over the rim of her teacup.

"Holly, I suggest you open your heart to God and ask him to show you why this has happened. The Lord is watching how you react to this, trust me." Nikko waved a thick, calloused finger in her direction.

"So you're saying that this has nothing to do with Mom, and Dad, and all of that."

"Exactly."

"Impossible, Uncle Nikko, why would God do such a thing?"

"That is what He wants you to discover, Hollyhock. Your growth as a Christian rests upon it."

That had been over twelve years ago, but it felt like yesterday. Her uncle had urged her to return to church, but the anger and hurt ran too deep. She never went back. The thing that had hurt the most was that no one from the church ever called. No one seemed to care that she had disappeared.

Did she want to return to the source of such hurt? Brady was a wonderful, brilliant man, but he came with baggage. That baggage was the church.

The click of her house key in the lock had a hollow, lonely sound. Holly didn't flip on the light, allowing the sunset coming through the French doors to drench the living room in salmon and gold. She crossed the room and stood gazing down past Morro Rock to the fire-touched sea, undulating and peaceful. The evening fog bank hung like an immense somber curtain off the coast, waiting for the cooling of the land and the calming of the winds before it crept on shore.

Holly chided herself for her abruptness with Brady, She had hurt him, and he didn't deserve that. But he would survive and so would she. She never did master being gentle with such things, like taking off a band-aid. Better fast than slow.

A blinking red light on the kitchen phone told her she had a message. She went over and hit the button.

"Holly, this is A.J. Give me a call."

Funny that he hadn't called her cell phone. She took it out of her purse and realized she had turned it off. Three beeps told her she had messages when she turned it back on. All of them were from A.J.

She dialed his cell phone from memory. He picked up on the first ring.

"Hey, Holly, glad you called. Did you hear my messages?"

"No, I just got home."

"Well, I'm in the mood to celebrate. I just solved a drug case and wondered if you were up for dinner. My treat."

She glanced at the clock, five forty-five.

"Holly, are you there? I made reservations at Windows on the Water for six-thirty. You game?"

"Sure, A.J." She looked around her darkened condo. Dinner with A.J. was better than a lonely night at home.

"Great! I'll pick you up in forty minutes."

The word no formed on her lips, but he had already hung up. She would have preferred meeting him there, avoiding the inevitable and awkward good night on her doorstep. A.J. never pushed her hard, but he always pushed. Tonight she felt vulnerable.

Thirty-five minutes later Holly had changed into a simple black dress. Her mother's pearls draped her neck, and a creamy silk shawl protected her shoulders from the night chill. A quick spritz of cologne and she was ready.

A.J. was on time and whistled appreciatively when she opened the door.

"I'm the luckiest man in town tonight." He twirled her around and offered his arm with a grin.

Holly couldn't suppress her pleasure as he escorted her down to his car. She was crazy to be going and glad she was. The clear, crisp evening lifted her spirits. She inhaled deeply of the thick ocean fragrance filled with kelp, salt, and that something that she called the breath of the ocean.

They arrived five minutes early, so Holly and A.J. enjoyed a glass of wine overlooking the bay. Pinpoints of light danced on the water around two of the moored boats, indicating someone was aboard for the night. Holly loved sleeping on the water—for her the most relaxing experience on earth.

A.J. slipped an arm around her waist and pulled her next to him. They watched a seal break the surface and survey its surroundings before re-submerging without a ripple. "How long did it take you to solve your case, A.J.?"

"I have been working on it for almost a year. Can't tell you the details, of course, but it was a tough one. You'll probably read about it in a few days."

"I'm happy for you. I know how hard you work. Did you stay out of trouble this time?"

His boyish grin gave him away. Sometimes he looked like a mischievous teenager. "Oh, Holly, you know me too well. Let's just say I got the job done. The boss got a little tense with me but I still have my job."

She looked up at A.J. The full moon highlighted his face, accentuating his lean, handsome features. He bent down and kissed her.

His voice was husky against her neck. "You are very beautiful tonight."

"Thank you." Her body, flushed by the contact, brought heat to her face.

Drawing back, he fingered her pearls. "These are lovely."

"They were my mother's."

"Your uncle's sister?"

"Yes." A little sadness crept into her voice.

"I'm sorry. I didn't mean to ruin the moment."

"That's all right. Let's go inside, I'm getting chilled."

The hostess escorted them to a table overlooking the water. A woman at the next table nodded and waved as they passed by. Holly searched her memory for who the woman might be and then realized she was the piano player from Mariners Chapel.

As the waitress left with their order, A.J. leaned forward. "Tell me more about your uncle, Holly. Why were those journals written in Hebrew?"

She buttered a wedge of fresh bread slowly, then answered. "My uncle was a Messianic Jew."

"What's that?"

"He was raised Jewish which included learning Hebrew. As a young man he came to understand that Christ was the Messiah."

"Wow, I bet that doesn't happen often."

"There are several Messianic Jews in our area. I have probably met most of them. The contractor he worked for when he was young was a strong Christian and held Bible studies during lunch. Over time, my uncle accepted Christ but never let go of his Jewish roots."

She took a sip of her wine. "How about you, A.J.? Where do you stand?"

"I don't know, Holly. That's pretty personal stuff." He sat back and looked out the window, obviously uncomfortable with the topic.

"Nope. You're not going to get off the hook that easily. This is an important issue to me."

"And it's a very private issue for me. Can't you respect that and let it go?"

"I respect that it is a very private issue. But it's also an important issue. I think it's fair to say that we enjoy each other's company, A.J. Our relationship has gone beyond business, and for me, it's important to know that we both share the same basic view of the way the world works. Does that make sense?"

"What makes sense is that you've been hanging around with that padre too much. I'm not going to let you get away without a fight, Holly."

Without a fight? She bristled. She wasn't a prize to be won. "He's just a customer, A.J. Nothing more."

"You never came over to my apartment when we were house hunting together."

Holly hesitated.

"Bingo."

The rest of the day and into the night, Brady found that the pain medication helped more than just the pain in his legs and shoulder. Yosef had invited Brady out to the kitchen for dinner, but Brady preferred the darkness and the drugs. Sleep was his only friend. When he was awake, the pain in his heart drowned out the physical discomforts. So many losses, so much betrayal by a God he had once trusted with his life. The pain turned to anger over the course of the evening, burning within him until he thought it would consume him. When Yosef brought him dinner on a tray, Brady kept silent, not wanting to lash out at the one kindness he saw in an otherwise dark and disappointing world.

At the end of two long days in self-imposed isolation, Brady received a message delivered on his lunch tray by Yosef. The vet wanted to talk to him about Daisy.

Daisy. She was worth getting up for. Deciding to forgo any more pain medication, it took Brady almost an hour to shower, shave, and make himself somewhat presentable. The blisters on his feet and legs were healing to the point where he could stand comfortably, although shoes were still out of the question, Yosef had found him a pair of sandals that did the trick.

When he came out of his bedroom and into the living room, the sun made him squint. The fragrance of lemon oil filled the house.

"Pastor Brady! What a delight to see you up and about." Vera gushed with joy as she set down the furniture polish and went to greet him. The enthusiasm annoyed him, but the mask he had learned to wear dropped into place with practiced ease.

"Thanks, Vera, I guess I went into hibernation for a bit, but it seems to have done the trick." He looked down at his legs and feet. The skin was peeling but the open sores had a fresh covering of pink tissue. "They itch though," he bent down and rubbed his hands up and down his legs. Flakes of skin fell like snow around his feet. "Oops, sorry, Vera." He smiled sheepishly. "I understand the vet called?"

"Yes, as a matter of fact, he did. He wants to give you an update on Daisy." She brought him a phone.

Brady settled himself in the overstuffed chair in the corner, the one he had sat in when he had touched Holly's hand. He winced at the thought and punched in the numbers.

"Mr. McGregor?" the vet's voice came on after a short wait. "I want to give you an update on Daisy. Your little girl has a strong and determined spirit. Her skin is healing up pretty well, and the hair is coming back. The sores on her pads will take more attention, but I think they will eventually heal if we can avoid infection. As far as her lungs go, that news isn't as good. I'm afraid there was quite a bit of damage. She will survive, but she will always be short of breath. She may even wheeze if she overexerts herself."

"When can I bring her home, Doctor?"

"Well, she can go home today if you want. She just needs rest and care from this point forward."

"I'll be over this afternoon. Thank you, Doctor. I appreciate all the work you've done." Brady hung up the phone. At least Daisy had survived. It wasn't much but it was something.

Vera stood in the doorway wiping her hands and waiting for the news.

"Is it all right with you, Vera, if I keep Daisy here till I figure out what to do?"

"Of course, Brady." She waved away his concern. "Daisy is a delight and a very well-mannered little girl. I'll go get the dog bed and water bowl out of the basement."

"Then I think I'll go over now and pick her up." He rose.

"Do you think you can drive all right?"

"I'll be fine, Vera. Your good food has done the trick. When I get back, I'll start work on Sunday's sermon." He winked at her and headed for his car.

Chapter Twenty-Six

Holly threw herself into work, trying to make something happen in the tepid real estate market. One or two new homes came on the multiple listings daily in Morro Bay, and as many as ten or twelve more up the coast in Cayucos, Cambria and over in Los Osos. Most were short sales, and the banks weren't cooperating. The challenge of it all kept her focused on work and off of Brady.

Holly did most of her work in Morro Bay, but it didn't hurt to be on top of the other coastal communities. She spent several hours Wednesday morning driving around previewing the new listings that had come on the market. She had found over the years that buyers expected her to have seen every listing. She also found this knowledge helpful when she counseled her sellers on their market position. Going from house to house was exhausting and time consuming but had paid off many times over in completed sales.

By early afternoon, she was satisfied that she was caught up. Back at the office, she pulled a name and address from her purse and typed it into the MapQuest program on her computer. A little red dot indicated the residence of Kent Haden, her uncle's friend from years ago. She grabbed her purse and headed back out the door. Ten minutes later, she arrived at a tidy little two-story home on the north end of town—a charming place with a white picket fence and children's toys on the lawn. But something wasn't right with that picture. Kent Haden would be in his mid-forties. Had he perhaps started a family? Holly knocked on the front door. A young woman with an infant on her hip answered.

"Hello, I'm looking for Kent Haden. My name is Holly Fain." She handed the woman her business card.

She glanced at it without interest. "He lived here before we did. But we've been here about three years now. I heard he is living on a boat in the bay."

"Do you know which one?"

"Haven't a clue." Something crashed inside the house and a child let out a wail. "Sorry, gotta go." She closed the door, leaving Holly pondering her next move.

Holly went back to her car and sat in the sun, considering her next move. She hadn't really thought about why she wanted to find Kent, except that he was a connection to her uncle and perhaps had an idea about what had been troubling Uncle Nikko in the end. Tracking him to this point had been a simple matter of a few phone calls to friends at city hall. Finding out which boat he lived on and getting to it could prove a bit harder.

She drove to the launch ramp parking lot at the south end of the Embarcadero. Down at the dock, Holly approached a large man in a faded green jacket who sat in a dinghy working on the motor. "Excuse me."

"Huh?" The big man looked up, his bearded face browned by years in the sun. "Hi, can I help you, ma'am?"

"I'm trying to find Kent Haden. I understand he lives on one of the boats in the harbor. Would you happen to know which one?"

"I do, as a matter of fact. Do you wanna talk to him?"

"I'd like to talk to him if I could. Can you take me to his boat?" The man eyed her, taking in her tall heels and tailored suit. "I'll pay you for your time."

He waved the offer away. "It's not that, ma'am. It's just that Kent is a bit ornery. Not somebody you talk to, exactly."

"I'd like to try. It's important." She pulled a twenty from her purse and offered it to him.

"You can keep your money. I'll take you out there, but I'm not let'n you get on his boat."

"That's fine." Holly peered over the edge of the dock and examined the bobbing dinghy.

"I'm Hank," he said. He wiped his hand on a dirty rag and reached up to help her down to a seat in the bow. Holly's nose told her he was a hard-working man with an aversion to soap and water.

Once Hank started the outboard and pushed away from the dock, Holly risked a breath. In a moment, they were motoring across the bay, the wind filling her lungs and nose with clean salt air. Hank headed south around the old fuel dock toward a field of moored boats off of Bayshore Bluffs. A white sailboat with a peeling red stripe had clothing draped over the lifelines. A rusting barbeque hung from the stern. The presence of an aluminum dinghy pulling at its tether, indicated Kent was home.

"Hey, Kent, you up?" Hank called as he shifted the motor into neutral and drifted over to the tethered dingy.

A shaggy head popped up from inside the boat. "Who wants to know?"

"It's me, Hank. You got a visitor."

Kent came up on deck dressed in a stained tee-shirt and shorts. A thick beard made it difficult for Holly to be sure he was the same person who had shared an after-work beer with Uncle Nikko so many years ago. He seemed thinner now, and darker, too.

Hank shut off the motor and grabbed onto Kent's dinghy to hold their position against the tide. Holly kept looking at the man for something familiar.

"What do you want?" he glowered.

"Kent, its Holly Fain. Do you remember me?"

The man's posture stiffened. "Don't know anybody named Holly. Go away." He waved them off and began to go back below.

"Wait, Kent. You were friends with my Uncle Nicholias. Don't you remember him?"

Kent paused and turned.

"You worked together. Do you remember now?"

Kent reached down into the cabin and brought up a bottle of liquor. He took a swig and wiped his mouth on his arm. Then he straightened and glared at her. "Nick, the tractor guy?

Holly nodded. "Yes. Nick, the tractor guy. I'm his niece."

"Then you need to get outta here." He made a menacing gesture, scowling. "I don't want to talk to you. That all happened a long time ago."

Hank leaned forward and whispered. "I think we should go, miss."

"Kent, please, just a quick question or two. My uncle died last week and he left me with some unanswered questions. I just want to clear a few things up."

"No questions! I don't want to talk to you! Now leave me alone!" He thrust his head forward, his face a threatening snarl.

Hank started the outboard and let go of the dinghy. Holly saw her opportunity drifting away. She had to try again.

"Kent, do you remember a phrase 'What the eye doesn't see, the heart won't grieve over?'"

Kent shook his fist and ducked below. Hank hit the gas and sped toward the marina. Holly looked over her shoulder to see Kent emerge with a shotgun. "He's got a gun!" she yelled over the roar of the outboard.

"I know. That's why we're outta here." Hank ducked his head and accelerated. The motor roared as they made toward shore.

Back at the dock, Hank helped Holly out of the boat. Her hands were shaking and she wasn't sure her legs would hold her. "How long has Kent been on that boat?"

"I've been here five years, and he lived there when I arrived. He's drunk most of the time. Comes ashore once a week and never talks to nobody. Not real social, as you can see."

Back in her car, Holly felt a growing frustration as she returned to the office. When Brady was translating the journals on Tuesday, Jessica's call had interrupted him. Holly left the journals with Brady, planning to continue the translation work later in the day. But by breaking off the relationship with him, she had tossed away that key to knowing what the journals said. A.J. hadn't given her any answers at dinner, either. His team was still working on their translation, and he had assured her he would call when he had any news. After the visit to Kent's boat, Holly feared she was in the middle of something much bigger. But more than that, she still wanted to know her uncle's thoughts over the last few months of his life. He had been her rock of faith. But in the end, he seemed to waver and doubt his salvation. She had to know he had remained strong to the end.

Arriving at her office, she found the message light blinking on her phone. She punched the button and listened as she sat, dropping her car keys in her open purse. "Hi, Holly, this is Margaret Brown. The listing you have a backup on just fell out of escrow. Is your buyer still interested? Give me a call as soon as possible. I'd like to get this house right back into escrow. Thanks."

Holly hung up and stared into space. This development meant a call to Brady. Maybe she could give the escrow to another one of the agents in the office and take the referral. She would lose seventy-five percent of her commission from the sale, but it would avoid a painful few weeks of having to work closely with Brady. On the other hand, the full commission would help her recover from the expenses of the lawsuit. She looked at the phone. *Lord, what should I do? I don't want to just chase money, Father. If I am supposed to pass this off to another agent, please make it clear.*

"Holly, line two," the receptionist called across the office.

She picked up the phone. "Holly, this is Vera Shankston. I hope I am not being too forward, but I want to invite you to our women's Bible study on Monday evenings. I know you haven't come to Mariners Chapel but that one time for the funeral. But inviting you has been on my mind all afternoon, and I don't like to ignore those … well, proddings. Do you think you might like to come?"

"Business is keeping me pretty busy right now, Vera."

"We meet at seven o'clock in the evening. We are just starting a new Beth Moore series, so you would be coming in right at the beginning," she persisted.

Holly knew that Vera was just being kind but she had no intention of joining the study. She searched for an out. "I'll give it some thought. Can I call you in a day or so?"

"Of course."

"By the way, Vera, is Brady around?" Her heart twisted as she asked the question, not sure which answer she hoped for.

"No, he went to Atascadero to pick up Daisy. He should be on his way back by now. Would you like his cell phone number? Yosef picked him up a new phone yesterday."

"Thanks Vera, I have it.

Hanging up the phone, Holly thought it over for a moment and then dialed.

Brady waited in one of the examining rooms while the vet fetched Daisy. After what seemed like an eternity, the vet arrived with Daisy nestled in his arms, her paws still bandaged and her tail resembling a hairless stick. Nevertheless, it wagged furiously when she saw Brady.

"Wow, little missy!" The vet juggled her in his arms as she squirmed to get to Brady.

Brady went to the other side of the table and received her enthusiastic wiggling, careful not to disturb the burn sites. She leaned up against his body as he bent down to give her a hug, dutifully cleaning his chin with her quick pink tongue. The dog couldn't maintain traction on the slick stainless surface of the examining table, so she soon settled down and curled up next to Brady's stomach.

The vet slid a finger down her head where the hair remained glossy and red. "Overall, she's doing remarkably well. Her bandages can come off in a week." He went through the various medications and instructions and saw them out the door. Brady paid the small fortune in fees without a second thought. Minutes later, Daisy was happily nestled in Brady's lap as he headed west back to Morro Bay.

The sun lingered just above the horizon as he crested the coastal hills separating Atascadero from Morro Bay. Daisy slept on his lap. Her presence brought him a joy he hadn't experienced in ages. It would be just the two of them now. Holly would have made three, but that plan had fallen through. A dog made a good companion, but he wanted more-- a life partner. And if Holly had rejected the man he pretended to be, she most certainly would reject the man he truly was.

Life had become a painful sham. His lofty goals of bringing God's word to a hungry congregation had crumbled. Deep inside, Brady longed for the relationship he once had with God, but his calloused mind and wounded heart rejected the notion. Even though he had dedicated his life to God's work, God had chosen to rip his heart out in one fiery moment. None of the placating words that all pastors say had helped him. He had to admit, at least to himself, that Holly had done the right thing. He was a wreck of a man, not life-partner material.

HONK! HONK!

The car behind him blared its horn. He glanced at his rear view mirror, but couldn't see much of anything behind him. The setting sun's glare bounced off the car's windshield. Even his own forward vision was limited in the brightness.

HONK!

Whoever it was wanted him to move closer to the edge of the road to make passing easier. The car swerved toward the center of the road and then back again in a dangerous dance, to check oncoming traffic. *Crazy nut. This section is dangerous enough without trying to pass.* Brady pulled as far to the right as he thought safe. His tires bumped over loose, fallen rocks as he hugged the hillside.

The car pulled up next to Brady, intent on passing. Then the driver inched closer and closer. Brady honked and looked at the other driver, but the windows were darkened. Daisy stirred at the noise and the jerking vehicle. Brady's right tire hit a large boulder, and the rocky cut in the hillside loomed close on his right. He glanced again at the other car as it nudged Brady to the edge of the road. Having passed the section of mountain, a drop off was coming up on the right. The big car lunged forward, clipping Brady's front bumper with its back right corner as it slipped into the lane ahead. Brady's car spun from the impact and broke through the guardrail to his right. Brady gripped the steering wheel, as Daisy yelped and scrambled to the floor. As the tires left the pavement, the engine revved a roar, and then Brady's Lexus soared through the air, hit the sloping ground hard and careened toward the bottom of the ravine.

So this is how it ends. The realization that he was about to die was but a brief flash, then nothing.

Chapter Twenty-Seven

Beep...beep...beep. The steady sound coming from the IVAC reassured Holly that Brady was still with them.

"Brady?"

His eyes fluttered.

Her warm hand took his cool one. "Brady?"

She squeezed, and he squeezed back.

"Brady, its Holly. You were in an accident. But the doctor says you're going to be all right."

Brady opened his eyes and then shut them tight again.

"You have a concussion but nothing is broken."

He squeezed her hand again.

Holly thanked God one more time that Vera had called her. She hadn't thought twice about coming. It looked to be a long night ahead, so Vera and Yosef had gone to the cafeteria for coffee, just moments before Brady started to stir. A large bandage covered his forehead and both eyes were black. Because of a large gash in his scalp, all his hair had been shaved off, and another bandage curved across the top of his head. She knew that it would be important for him to know what had happened, and that he would be all right.

But Daisy wouldn't be. She had been thrown out of the car and died on impact with the ground. How would she ever tell him? They had found her broken little body not far from Brady.

Holly had never known anyone who had lost so much. She knew it happened to other people, but not to anyone this close. "God, I offer up Brady to you," she whispered. "He has been through so much. I ask for your tender mercies to comfort him. I don't know how to help him, Lord. Thank you that he's not badly hurt. Grant him a swift recovery, Abba. In your Son's most precious name. Amen."

Amens came from behind her. She looked around to see Vera and Yosef in the doorway. Vera handed her a cup of coffee.

"Thanks. He woke up for a moment and squeezed my hand." She inhaled the fragrance from the hot black liquid before taking a sip.

The clock above Brady's bed read ten. Holly felt the urge to pray again. She moved to the foot of Brady's bed and bowed her head, placing a hand on his foot. Yosef and Vera also moved to the bed and laid hands on Brady's still body.

Holly saw a tear trickle down Brady's cheek. Her heart ached. "Father, I know you have great plans for Brady, plans to prosper him and make him whole. You have gifted him with the ability to reach people with your word. Father, touch him now. Comfort him. Draw him to you, Lord, and make him whole."

"Lord God," Vera continued, "Let Pastor Brady know how much we love him. He is your servant, Lord. Hold him close and keep him safe."

In the depths of Brady's mind, he stood in an open field. The cool wind brushed his skin and danced across the grass, bending it into changing patterns as it raced toward the horizon. He realized someone stood next to him. He looked and saw himself.

"What are you looking for?" the other Brady asked.

"I'm not sure." He looked again at the horizon. The grass in front of him parted, and a low wall began to rise from the ground. The wall stretched as it rose, into the distance in both directions. Brady looked past the wall and saw a man dressed in white robes moving toward him across the field. Soon Brady was craning his neck and standing on his toes to catch a glimpse of his face before the rising wall blocked his view. Brady stepped up to the wall and ran his fingers across its dark, rough surface. The wall continued to rise until it blocked the sun. The shadow it cast, cold and dark.

"You built the wall, you know," the other Brady said.

Brady looked up, trying to see the top. "I know," he admitted.

The knowledge pierced him. He placed both hands on the wall's bitterly cold surface. The cold spread into his hands and began to move down his arms. The chill beneath him began to creep into his feet and up his legs. He couldn't move. He didn't want to move.

He dropped to the ground, his hands clutching the grass. Sobs wracked his body as the cold moved closer to his heart.

"You do not have because you do not ask."

"I asked and asked!" Brady screamed into the ground.

"You asked for what you wanted, not what God wanted."

"I wanted the church to grow. I wanted people to know God."

"No, you wanted the church to grow because you wanted people to know *you*."

"That's not true! It was always for Him."

"Really?"

"Yes! People were coming to Christ. The sheep were being fed. We were doing great things."

"We? You and who else?"

The words landed like mortal blows, driving him onto the grass. Brady's mind raced through the strategy sessions and press conferences, prayer meetings and public events. He could see the power of the Holy Spirit growing dimmer and dimmer over the years. "This isn't about God anymore, Brady. It's all about you." Karen's words pierced him. She held their precious son in her arms. "I'm going for a drive." Then she was gone.

"I'm sorry, I'm so sorry. Karen, I'm sorry," he pleaded, but no one answered.

"Behold I stand at the door and knock."

The words gripped him with fear. He didn't dare look up. He felt vulnerable-- stripped naked before the Lord. The mask ripped off, his deepest thoughts laid bare.

"Behold, the eye of the Lord is on those who fear Him."

"Oh, God!" He tore at the grass, writhing in the pain of his exposure. "I've let you down. I've relied on my own flesh. You gave me everything and I squandered it. I'm not worthy of your gifts. Lord, I need your healing. I rebuilt the wall between us that you tore down at the cross. I got what I deserved, Lord—separation from you."

The numbing cold had reached his heart. Brady knew he had lost the only thing that ultimately mattered. He had built the wall, brick by brick. Each time he moved in the flesh, each time he gloried in the headlines, another brick was laid. He was alone and without love. The emptiness engulfed him. So this was eternal separation from the Lord. It was unbearable and forever.

Chapter Twenty-Eight

Brady opened his eyes just as the sun peaked above the mountains to the east, trailing its warm light across his bandaged face. Holly's head rested on the foot of the bed. Yosef snored in a chair by the window. He turned to his left to see Vera stretched out on the bed in the adjoining space. Brady's heart swelled.

"Thank you, Father," Brady whispered, "for this glorious day. Thank you for these friends with me, and thank you for Holly. Thank you for breaking down the wall and allowing the light to stream back into my life."

He reached over and caressed Holly's tumbled red locks. She murmured in her sleep and then her eyes flew open. "Brady!"

Vera and Yosef jerked upright and rubbed their eyes.

"Pastor Brady!"

Brady grinned, amused at their surprise. "I guess I took another long nap."

Holly squeezed his hand and he squeezed back.

"What happened? I don't remember a thing once I left the vet's office."

"Your car went off the road. The police said it was nothing short of a miracle you weren't killed. The car flew through the top of a large oak tree, which broke the fall and flipped the car over so it landed on the tires instead of upside down. You have a concussion, but other than that you're fine."

"I don't feel fine. I feel like I've been pulled through a knothole. Everything hurts." He paused and looked at Holly. "How is Daisy?"

Tears welled up and glistened in Holly's beautiful eyes. She shook her head.

Brady turned his head away and closed his eyes. *Okay, Father. You have my full attention now.*

Holly rested her hand on his arm. "I'm so sorry, Brady."

"Me, too." He squeezed his eyes shut. *She was just a little dog, Father, but she was all that was left.*

A nurse came into the room. "Excuse me, folks I'll need you all to step into the hallway. It's time to check on Mr...um...." She looked at the chart. "...Mr. McGregor's bandages." It shouldn't take long. Then you're welcome to come back and keep him company."

When the door closed behind them, Vera stretched her arms and yawned. "I'm heading for another cup of coffee, anybody want anything?"

Holly and Yosef shook their heads.

"Be right back then." Vera headed down the antiseptic corridor, dodging carts and nurses on their rounds.

Holly and Yosef leaned back against the pale green wall, letting the morning bustle pass. "What day is it?" Holly asked, rubbing her face.

"Thursday, all day." Yosef's eyes twinkled at his attempt at humor.

She crossed her arms and exhaled. I wish we could do something to help Brady. He's under so much pressure."

"I've been thinking on that. On top of everything else, we have a little money issue at the church."

"You mean the deposits and withdrawals?"

Yosef turned his head, the surprise evident on his face.

"Brady told me about it." She was embarrassed to be party to such personal church information. "We have spent quite a bit of time together lately, looking at real estate, of course."

"Obviously." Yosef's steady look unnerved her.

This is awkward.

"How much has Pastor Brady shared?"

"I have a very good accountant. We went over to see her and get some ideas about what might be happening."

"Did she come up with any thoughts?"

Holly didn't answer. She wanted a moment to read the old man's eyes. "Not much, really, except that it might be dangerous for Brady to pursue because of so much money being involved."

"Do you think the car accident had anything to do with the money situation?"

"Who knows, maybe?" She pushed away from the wall and turned to face Yosef. "Look, Yosef. Brady confided in me. I didn't pry the information out of him."

"I'm still surprised that he shared so much about church business with—"

"With his realtor? So was I, frankly. But now that I do know, I'd like to help. I've never seen someone lose so much in such a short time." Holly glanced toward the closed door. "He's a good man, Yosef."

Yosef rubbed the side of his nose with one finger, glanced down the corridor for Vera, then leaned forward, closer to Holly's ear. "Those deposits and withdrawals always happened on Thursday. I wonder if I could recognize someone going in and out of the bank. We could do a stake-out, like Mike Hammer." He wiggled his eyebrows, his eyes dancing.

"Not by yourself, you don't. I'll go with you. That way we can spell each other for food and other necessities."

"If you really want to help, Holly, I'd be glad to have you. Just a warning though, it will probably be pretty boring, but I don't think it will be dangerous."

"I might as well. The only good client I have right now is in that hospital bed." She looked at her watch. "It's eight-thirty. The bank won't be open till ten. How about we meet in front of the bank at nine forty-five? I'll pack a cooler."

Vera appeared at the end of the hallway with her coffee. Yosef waved to her, then turned to Holly. "Don't tell Vera what we are planning. She is such a Nervous Nelly. She would never agree."

"All right, I'll meet you at the bank." Holly winked at him just as Vera returned. After everyone said their good-byes to Brady they headed for home.

Once back at her condo, Holly took a long, luxurious shower and ate a big bowl of oatmeal. Her eyes were dry and sore from too much caffeine and too little sleep, but the idea of catching the mysterious money man was worth staying up for.

She dressed in jeans and pulled an old sweatshirt over a tee shirt. Comfort, not fashion was the idea. She dumped the ice from the icemaker into the bottom of her cooler. Hard-boiled eggs, chips, apples, and four sodas filled up the rest of the space. She filled a grocery bag with paper towels, wipes, and a few paper plates.

Glancing at the clock, she spent the remaining half hour checking the Internet for e-mails from customers, hoping no one wanted to see property today. Experience told her most buyers wouldn't wait for her. They would simply call another agent, and she would lose the deal.

One e-mail caught her eye. The house Brady had the back-up offer on. Rats! She'd forgotten to talk to Brady about it. Maybe if Brady could get this house, he would reconsider returning to Wyoming. Is that what she wanted? She fingered her cell phone case, her thumb hesitating over the dialing pad.

Then, making a decision she punched in the number and was frustrated when she got voice mail. "Hi, Sharon, this is Holly Fain. I got your message about the house I have a backup offer on. I can pick up a check for you today, and we can have it back in escrow by this afternoon." A click on the line told Holly that Sharon had picked up. "That sounds fine, Holly. When I didn't hear from you yesterday, I had to put it back into the MLS. I'll pull it off as soon as you fax over a copy of the check."

"I'll call you when I fax it so you know I have it. Thanks, Sharon." She had been hoping that Sharon would pull the listing back off so they wouldn't lose it, but Sharon had done the right thing. Money greased the wheels of real estate. She knew that and so did Sharon. Holly debated running back to the hospital to get the check, but she would be late for her meeting with Yosef. Besides, Brady was in no condition to rethink such an important decision. "Father, please just keep that house out of escrow today. Give me a chance to get that check from Brady," she prayed as she gathered her things.

Holly lived three blocks from the bank. She could have easily walked except for the cooler. She placed it in the back seat of her car and headed over to the bank. Arriving four minutes late, she found Yosef waiting in his pickup truck right across the street from the bank, just as they had agreed. Holly pulled up behind Yosef's truck, got out and went up to his window.

"I have snacks, Yosef. Do you want to sit in my car? We have a good view from there, too."

Yosef reached across the passenger seat and opened the truck door. Holly recoiled at the sight of the passenger seat. The stuffing spilled out of the cracked vinyl like dirty shaving cream. On the floor lay a tangle of fishing gear, buckets, cables and several unrecognizable treasures. The smell of dead fish and diesel oil combined for an odd paring that stung her eyes and made her nose run.

Yosef watched her face as she scanned his truck's interior. "What?"

"My car, Yosef. Definitely my car."

His bushy brows came together. "I don't see why. I can clean you out a spot. We have a nice high view from my truck, better than your itty bitty car."

"Yosef, I'm not sitting in here." Holly met him scowl for scowl. The seconds ticked by.

"Oh, all right! I don't understand you women. Vera won't ride with me either."

"Small wonder," Holly muttered.

Yosef climbed into Holly's passenger seat a few minutes later. The scent of fish and diesel lingered but wasn't overwhelming.

"Well, here we are. How long do you think we have to wait?"

"No way of knowing. The deposits didn't have a time on them. I suppose there's a record somewhere. I didn't think of that." Yosef frowned.

"That's okay. I don't have anything else to do today, and I have my trusty cell phone." She patted the phone next to her. "If anything comes up at the office, I'll get a call." She adjusted her seat for a more comfortable position and closed her eyes. No! Not a good idea. Sleep would rapidly overtake her. She moved her seat back upright and took a drink from her water bottle.

Yosef yawned. "Sleepy? I know I am."

"Well, I assume this won't take that long." Holly sounded more hopeful than she felt.

"No way to know."

Holly sipped a soda and watched the clock on her dash mark the passing time. Yosef had recommended they take turns napping in half hour shifts. By two-thirty, they had gone through most of her snacks and were reasonably rested. When Yosef returned from the gas station restroom up the street, Holly decided to get a conversation going. FORD; family, occupation, recreation, dreams. She used the skill again.

She kept her eyes on the front door of the bank. "So, Yosef, tell me how you and Vera met."

He chuckled. "That's quite a story. First time I saw her, she was in her pajamas. I was at a camp out with the Boy Scouts. Vera's older brother Martin was in my troop. We were in Yosemite, and Vera's folks decided to come camping, too. They were a couple of campsites away. Vera's folks didn't do such a good job of putting their food up, and a black bear made a midnight visit." He chuckled again at the memory.

"I never heard so much screaming and yelling in my whole life. We all piled out of our tents and ran to help. I went running up, and there stood

Vera, hollering up a storm. The bear burst out of the tent, followed by her mom swinging a broom and using language that wasn't proper back in those days."

Holly chuckled at the visual Yosef painted for her.

"They were yellow."

"What were yellow?"

"Her pajamas. And I was smitten." His eyes twinkled and Holly saw a glimpse of the younger Yosef.

"How about you, Holly, have you ever been married?"

She took a long breath. She hadn't intended for the conversation to swing back to her. "No, never married."

"Well, I don't mean to pry, but you and Pastor Brady seem to be sparking a bit."

"Brady is a remarkably gifted man, Yosef. You're right, we do 'spark' a bit as you say." This was the last thing she wanted to talk about. She shouldn't have gone to the hospital yesterday. She had sent an unintended message to Brady, Vera and Yosef. But when she received word of the accident, she hadn't thought about anything but getting to the hospital and seeing Brady.

Their brief interaction in the hospital now took on a deeper significance. The squeeze of his hand, the new light in his eyes, told her he had misread her intentions in being at his bedside. Her mind switched to her date with A.J. She couldn't help but compare the two men. When rested and shaved, A.J. was handsome in a craggy, high Sierras kind of way. He'd made her feel like a queen on their last date. Even buying her roses from a young lady who had passed through the dining room of the restaurant.

Then their conversation about faith had ended in embarrassment, especially when Brady and the journals had come up. Asking for Brady's help had seemed natural at the time. Could A.J. be jealous of Brady? That seemed so high school.

Praying at Brady's bedside with Yosef and Vera had strengthened the bond they all felt as fellow Christians. That sweet bond seemed to be the only thing lacking in her relationship with A.J. And sharing the vigil at Brady's bedside with Yosef and Vera had reconnected her with a time in her past where deep understanding and mutual unspoken support were part of the natural rhythm of who she was. Yes, she missed those days. Admitting that surprised her. Her close bond with Uncle Nikko had filled some of that void over the years, but that chapter had closed.

Holly rubbed her eyes. *God, why did you bring Brady into my life? I'm not a suitable wife for him, I think I fit more with A.J. But ...*

Yosef broke into her thoughts. "Pastor Brady could use a woman who loves the Lord by his side." He glanced around him, trying to seem casual about his comment.

"True. And Brady also needs a wife who can be a helper to him, someone who is as devoted to the church family as he is. He doesn't need a woman who works long, crazy hours and stays out way past dinnertime. How would it work, Yosef? I can see it now. I'm heading off to the Monday night Bible study, bundt cake in hand, and the phone rings." She turned in her seat to face him. "What do I do? If I don't meet with my customers, they will just call someone else to write the offer, no matter how long I have been working with them."

"I imagine the women would have to go without their bundt cake." A simplistic answer to a much more complex issue.

"I've been in the church, Yosef. We both know the answer. The pastor's wife is in the spotlight every waking moment. I remember when women came over to our house after church. They spent twenty minutes discussing the outfit the pastor's wife had worn that day. I'm not interested in subjecting myself to that."

"So it's not the job you're worried about, it's the gossip."

Ouch. In real estate, she stood on her performance. They didn't give you awards for your perfectly-appointed wardrobe. She received recognition for her business sense, which translated into dollars. She couldn't care less what others thought about her. Her numbers told the story. Uncle Nikko often cautioned her about her drive for success. She could still hear his voice: "You can't serve both money and God you know, Hollyhock." She felt she had been successful in both, though. She supported an orphanage in India, and felt she had a good relationship with the Lord.

Could God be calling her back into the church? She rejected the thought. This past week, old wounds had reopened. Anger lingered closer to the surface, making her vulnerable.

"I've been supporting myself for a long time, Yosef. I've built a successful business, and I don't see myself leaving it anytime soon. I like real estate. And, I'm good at it."

"I don't see your career getting in the way of being a loving wife to Pastor Brady."

"A pastor's wife has duties. I don't see how someone like me could fill those shoes *and* run a business."

"I think that would be between you and Pastor Brady. Don't you?"

"Yosef look, I ...well ...let's just say that I have some history with going to church, and it wasn't all positive."

"The church is made up of people, Holly, just folks the same as you."

Holly shifted in her seat, looking away from Yosef and back toward the bank again. This conversation needed to be redirected, fast.

"This is a pointless discussion, Yosef. I ...look!" Holly pointed to the sidewalk in front of the bank.

Arlen Parkfield was entering the front door of the bank. He pushed his dark glasses up onto this head as the door closed behind him. Holly looked at Yosef in surprise. "Yosef, you don't think it's Arlen, do you?"

Yosef sighed and shook his head. "His daddy was as honest as the day is long, but Arlen has always skirted the edge a bit."

"Isn't he an elder at the church?"

"Yes, and he's also one of the biggest supporters of the church."

They sat in silence, watching the bank for several minutes. Holly remembered Arlen from the mediation meeting. Could he really be laundering money through the church account?

Holly jumped when the back door of the car opened and Arlen slipped in. "Looking for me?"

Yosef looked over at Holly for help. "Arlen, we ah, we were..."

Arlen pulled a gun from under his jacket. "Let's go for a little drive."

Chapter Twenty-Nine

Holly sucked in her breath. The gun was huge. Its black eye pointed at her face. Arlen held it below window level so they could both see it, then pulled his jacket over his hand, leaving just the end of the barrel showing.

"Drive, Miss Fain." He ground out the words.

"Drive where?" Holly couldn't move, her eyes locked on the gun.

Arlen's attention shifted to Yosef. The old man's hand moved to the door handle.

"Don't even think about it, Yosef." The muzzle of the gun followed Arlen's focus of attention.

"Hello, yoo hoo," a singsong voice called from the sidewalk next to the car. Mrs. Thorndyke waved at them as she passed by on the street.

Yosef nodded and smiled, acknowledging her. Holly's mind raced. How could she get Mrs. Thorndyke's attention? She opened her mouth to call out.

"No!" Arlen hissed from the back seat.

Holly's mouth snapped shut.

"Head out of town, we're going for a ride."

Holly started the car as Arlen glanced over her shoulder at the dashboard. "Good, a full tank. That should get us there."

What should she do? What could she do? Holly glanced around for something to ram with the car. She didn't want to hurt anyone. The fire hydrant wouldn't stop the car. She looked farther up the road. She had a clear shot at the pharmacy wall. She glanced over at Yosef, but he stared straight ahead, beads of perspiration forming on his temples.

Holly felt pressure through the back of her seat. "If you try anything funny, I can shoot right through the seat. You'll die and then Yosef. Want to be responsible for that?"

"Where are we going?"

"For a little ride to the mountains."

Brady pushed what was left of his last hospital lunch away from the bed. In an hour or so, he would be heading back to Vera and Yosef's. Every muscle screamed when he moved, but the ache in his heart was gone. God had exposed the lie he had been living for so many years. He was humiliated and exhilarated at the same time. Since he had awakened from the accident, he had mentally traveled back over his time spent in Wyoming. Brady revisited the success of his church and how that success had subtly pulled him further and further from the source of that success. The slide downhill had been gradual. At first, he remembered no warning signs, no red flags. However, as he became more honest with himself and earnest in his prayer, he realized that the signs had been everywhere.

His prayer life had slowly become mechanical, an expected thing with no real substance. He began to rely on his instincts rather than promptings from the Holy Spirit. The shift had been subtle and spiritually deadly. Long hours away from home had also taken their toll on his marriage with disastrous results. Some of his closest advisors had tried to warn him, but he found ways to justify or ignore their heartfelt advice. Those trusted friends had slowly been marginalized and they finally moved on, leaving him with 'yes men' instead of men of wisdom, and courage of conviction.

In the beginning, as the Wyoming church had grown, Brady had walked with the Lord on a moment-by-moment basis. No decision had been too small to prayerfully consider. Back then, he had diligently protected himself from those very things that had ultimately destroyed him, pride and arrogance. Then as the radio interviews had become expected, the speaking engagements second nature, he began to think of the church's success in terms of his own leadership abilities.

The return of prayer to his life was the sweetest gift of all. The connection with the Lord that he had clogged with his own pride was finally reopened. For several hours this morning, he prayerfully examined his downward slide, purging the pain and guilt. Earlier in the day, the nurse had found him on his knees. "Oh, Mr. McGregor. Did you fall? You shouldn't be out of bed." She reached for his arm. "Let me help you back into your bed."

Brady chuckled in spite of the pain as he allowed her to help him stand. "I guess you haven't seen many folks on their knees in prayer."

Holly eased the pressure on the accelerator and dropped the notion of running into the pharmacy. The pressure on her lower back focused her on how close she was to death. She had no doubt that Arlen would use the gun. A dog had bitten her as a child. That dog had the same look in its eyes. Focused, desperate, dangerous.

"What is this all about, Arlen?" Yosef tried to turn in his seat.

"Eyes front!"

Yosef snapped back around. "For heaven's sake, Arlen."

"Pretty stupid of you two, sitting in front of the bank like that. Didn't you know I'd see you?" The words were biting, mocking. "A little bird told me the pressure was on. You shouldn't have frozen the account, Yosef. That was very naughty. I need that money." He snapped his fingers. "That's it! You can go in and get the money. They will give it to you. Turn around, Holly, and head back to the bank."

"I don't know anything about freezing the account, Arlen. But if it is frozen, not even I can get any money out."

"Ahrgh!" Arlen reared back and kicked the back of Yosef's seat, knocking him forward. His face slammed against the dashboard.

"Yosef!" Holly reached over to him.

"Drive!" Arlen commanded.

Holly's eyes snapped back to the road. She continued to the highway, casting nervous glances at Yosef. Drops of blood seeped from his nose. Holly drove with one hand and fished out a wad of tissue from next to her seat. She looked into the rear view mirror and caught Arlen's eyes.

"I think his nose is broken."

"That's what he gets for sticking it in other people's business. Take forty-one over to Atascadero, and then head north to Paso and over to Kettlemen."

"Where are we going, Arlen? Why on earth do you want us?"

"You two are my little insurance policy until I get my money. Now drive." He shoved the back of her seat for emphasis.

Back at the Shankstons, Brady made notes for his sermon for Sunday in spite of his throbbing head. The aroma of dinner on the stove caught his attention and drew his mind from his work. Several tightly-written pages sat neatly to his right. The Holy Spirit had blessed him richly this afternoon, and time had simply vanished.

Vera appeared at the door. "Dinner is almost ready, Pastor Brady, but there is no sign of Yosef. I'm not sure what to do."

"Did you call around?"

"Everywhere I could think of. He might be down at the boat."

"I could use a break, Vera. I'll run down to the boat and check. He probably just lost track of time."

"Do you think you should drive?"

"The doctor gave me a clean bill of health. Just a few bumps and bruises. Nothing a little aspirin won't fix. I'll be fine." He waved away her concern as she handed him her keys.

Down at the dock, Brady couldn't see any sign of Yosef. His sailboat bobbed gently in its slip. Yosef's truck wasn't there. Puzzled, Brady approached a man who lived on a nearby boat.

"Good evening, have you seen Yosef today?"

"Not hide nor hair."

Strange, Brady thought. He drove by the church to see if Yosef might be working on something, but the parking lot was empty. He had been gone for forty-five minutes by this time, so he headed back to the house, hoping to see Yosef's ratty truck in the driveway.

By the time they had driven an hour and a half, Holly needed to go to the bathroom. They were passing through Kettleman City. She looked in the rear view mirror and caught Arlen's attention.

"I have to go to the bathroom."

"Tough."

"So do I." Yosef's words were thick. His nose had stopped bleeding. Dark circles were beginning to form under both of his eyes. He squinted from the pain.

"Keep driving, we'll stop outside town."

Several minutes later, Arlen leaned forward and motioned toward a farm road that stretched out into the distance to the south. "Pull over here."

"Here?" Holly was incredulous.

"You wanna pee, we stop here."

Holly turned and drove down the farm road until she came to a wide spot. She pulled over and Arlen stepped out of the car. He positioned himself where he could see both Holly and Yosef. Holding his gun steady, he motioned them out. The cars on the highway half a mile away hummed by, unaware of their plight. "Well, go ahead." He waved them toward an irrigation ditch next to the car.

Holly measured the distance from where she stood to a field of tall grape vines. She glanced at Arlen and back to the vines.

"I can read you like a book, girl. Go ahead and run. Let's see how steady my hand is." He fired off three shots in quick succession. A tin can at the bottom of the ditch jumped three times.

Holly swallowed.

"I'm waiting, go ahead. I won't watch."

His smile gave Holly the creeps.

"This is sick, Arlen." Yosef sounded like he had a bad cold.

"Dis is sthic," Arlen mimicked him. "Tough. You wanna go? You go here."

Holly resigned herself to the embarrassment. She turned her back on the men and took care of business. In spite of the awkwardness, relieving her bladder felt good. Yosef did the same, and soon they were back in the car, heading east on Highway 41.

Holly remembered reading one of those e-mails that everyone sends around about carjacking. She was supposed to throw the keys and run. That advice would do her no good now. Her stomach growled.

"Hungry, girl?" Arlen asked. "No point in wasting food on you. You may not be around long enough to digest it."

Vera was starting to panic. "I've put a call in to the prayer chain. Some of the ladies are on their way over." She put Brady's dinner on the table. "This just isn't like Yosef. His stomach has an alarm clock. He never misses a meal." She twisted the towel in her hands.

Brady reached out and took her hand. "Lord God, we offer up Yosef to you tonight. Lord, wherever he is I pray your shield of protection around him. Send your mighty angels to guard and protect him. Amen."

"Thank you, Pastor Brady." She whispered before turning back to the kitchen sink.

Brady swallowed his last bite of beef stew when the first of the ladies arrived. Charlie's wife, Irene was joined by the church pianist, Mrs. Post. Vera busied herself with making tea and setting out plates of cookies. Sylvia Thorndyke bustled in a few minutes later, and they all joined Vera and Brady around the kitchen table. Brady allowed them some brief questions about his own health before turning the discussion to Yosef.

"Any idea where Yosef might be, Pastor Brady? Did he go sailing today?" Irene's face showed her deep concern.

"I checked down at his boat, Irene, he's not there."

Mrs. Thorndyke accepted a cup of coffee from Vera. "Well, I saw him around after lunch down the street from the pharmacy. He was in a car with Holly."

Brady's breath caught for a moment and dread clutched his heart. Holly had been with Yosef, and Yosef was missing.

Brady pulled his cell phone from his hip pocket and dialed. He let the phone ring until her voice mail came on. "Holly isn't answering her phone. Looks like it's time to pray." He reached out to the ladies on either side. Again, the sweet connection between him and the Lord filled him with awe and joy.

"Father, we come before you on behalf of Yosef and Holly. You know where they are and what they are doing. Prompt them to contact us, I pray that a simple oversight has occurred and they are safe in your will ..."

And so the evening wore on. The diligent group prayed and petitioned God for Holly and Yosef's safe return. About eight-thirty there was a knock on the door. Vera rose to answer it and Evelyn stepped in.

Her face was pale as wax, a strand of gray hair hung over one eye. Noticing the others, she hesitated, tucked the strand behind her ear and dabbed her nose with a tissue. Sniffing once, she stepped across the room and knelt beside Brady's chair.

She looked up into his eyes and took his hands in hers. "Pastor Brady, I've come to ask your forgiveness . . . and the forgiveness of Vera and ... Yosef." She looked over at Vera then back up at Brady. "I know who set the fire."

Chapter Thirty

Evelyn wept and clutched Brady's hands. "Lord, forgive me, I was so frightened."

"Frightened of what, Evelyn?" Brady tried to keep his voice calm and gentle, but inside his heart pumped with conflicting emotions, realizing Evelyn could have been involved in the destruction of everything he had brought with him to California, and even his own life.

Love the sinner, hate the sin.

He thought about a lifetime of photographs. A legacy from his father, gone.

Seventy times seven, forgive them.

Karen and Jeremy.

Love your neighbor as yourself.

"You were pushing me for the books. I knew you had discovered what was happening, but he told me that I would go to prison if anyone found out. I didn't know what to do. When the bungalow burned down, I knew it was him."

"Him?" He was lost for a moment. "Who, Evelyn?

"Arlen! He's dangerous, Pastor Brady. His father sent him away to get help for him, but it didn't work. Holly's Uncle Nikko knew the truth, and it got him killed!" She pulled her hands away and wiped her eyes. "I hoped and prayed someone would read his journals in time. Nikko wrote it all down. He had me mail them to Holly. But ..."

Across the room Sylvia Thorndyke gasped, her hand went to her throat. "When I saw Yosef and Holly this afternoon, I also saw Arlen. He was in the back seat of the car, and . . . ."

"Arlen--at the bank?" Evelyn's head snapped around and she stood to face Sylvia.

"Yes, well, outside the bank, anyway. That's where I saw them together, in Holly's car."

"Oh, dear Lord." Evelyn grabbed Brady's sleeve, terror in her eyes. "I froze the bank account yesterday. I knew it all had to stop. I just hadn't worked up the courage to confess until now. If he can't get to his money, he'll be furious. You don't know him the way I do. He's been passing money through the church account for over a year now. He hides it from the IRS somehow that way. And that's why he killed my Cheri!"

Arlen killed Cheri? This was all coming too fast.

Evelyn sniffed and looked around the table at the other women. "When she came home, our relationship was going better than ever. We were having fun. I had my daughter back. One night, Cheri came over and found me crying. She badgered me until I told her why—about the church bank account. Well, she had been dating Arlen. He was probably the father of her child. My ... only grandchild." Her voice quivered. She took a moment to gather herself then continued. "I think she tried to blackmail him and he . . . he ..." Evelyn buried her face in her hands and sobbed.

"Vera, would you please call Detective Walker." Brady kept his voice steady, but inside his guts twisted and pulled. His head pounded as his blood pressure rose. "I'll try Holly's cell phone again."

He said as walked out onto the front porch and dialed.

Holly's phone rang again. She reached for it.

"I don't think that would be a healthy decision, Holly." Arlen told her from the back seat." Give me that phone. It may come in handy."

She held it for a moment, not wanting to give it up.

Arlen reached up and grabbed a handful of her hair, jerking her head back. The car swerved into the next lane, narrowly missing a semi. "Watch the road, girl, and gimmie that phone."

She handed it over her shoulder.

Arlen looked at the illuminated display." Well, waddya know, Pastor Preachy Britches." He answered the phone and pressed the speaker key.

"Holly?"

"Well, hello, Pastor. Holly is busy right now. You'll have to settle for me."

"Arlen?"

"The one and only."

"Where is Holly?"

"She's with me, and for the moment, she's fine. You can keep her that way if you want to."

"What do you want?"

"Three-hundred-and-sixty-five thousand dollars. Cash."

"And if I can get it, then what?"

"Then Yosef and Holly return to Morro Bay, and I get on with my life. Simple."

"Where do you expect me to get that kind of money?"

"The money is in the church account. You know that by now. It's mine. I want it back."

"How do you want me to get it to you?"

"I'll give you directions. If you tell anybody, all bets are off. I can disappear into the woods, and you'll never find me. But you will find Holly and Yosef. Dead."

Twenty minutes later, Detective Walker arrived at the Shankston's followed by two officers. Brady and Vera rose to meet them in the living room. Detective Walker eyed the women gathered around the kitchen table. They sat with their heads down and eyes closed. Some moved their lips, and others were still. A.J. raised an eyebrow in Brady's direction.

"Prayer group. We called them when we realized something was wrong,"

"Whatever works for you." The detective flipped open his notebook and looked expectantly from Brady to Vera.

Vera dabbed her nose and looked to Brady. "You start."

Brady filled in the detective as quickly and concisely as he could. As he talked, part of his mind wrestled with the desire to reveal his phone conversation with Arlen. No, the risk was too great. He would get the funds himself.

A. J.'s face hardened at the news of Holly's involvement. When Brady finished, the two men stood silent for a moment, sizing each other up. "Why do I feel you're holding something back, Padre?"

"I can't help you with that, Detective." Brady met the lanky detective stare for stare. Like two alpha dogs, ruffs up, legs stiff. Brady was acutely aware that to a great degree, he was responsible for Holly and Yosef's danger. Arlen's call had given him a chance to redeem himself.

A.J. backed off and turned his attention to Vera, who slowly told him all she knew. It was a long process. She cried, steadied herself, started to talk, and then cried again.

Brady motioned to Evelyn, who had joined the prayer group, and by this time had composed herself. Her spine ramrod straight, she confessed everything, including Arlen's suspected part in Cheri's death.

"Well, this fits into what we are piecing together from another murder."

"Do you mean Holly's uncle?" Brady interjected.

"So you know about that?"

"Holly asked me to help her translate her uncle's journals. I didn't get very far, but she did recognize a name, Kent."

"Kent Haden. We picked that up as well. He's a retired city inspector. We have already had a chat with him. Arlen Parkfield is hip deep in this thing. I'm not surprised he was planning to run. I'll have the phone company start a search for Holly's cell phone. With the new technology today, we can locate her phone within fifty meters provided she is in an area that has coverage."

Evelyn spoke up. "Do you suppose Arlen might have taken them to his cabin?"

A.J. turned at the question. "His cabin?" His voice crisp with tension.

"Up in the Sierras, on the way to Yosemite, the cabin has been in his family for years."

"Lousy cell phone reception up there, do you have an idea about where this cabin is exactly?"

"Yes, my husband and I used to go up there with Arlen's family before Cheri was born. It's up in the mountains above Hunters Lake. We never used street names when we went there, just landmarks. I remember we would turn right at the red mailbox and go so many miles, then a left at the big pine tree stump. I couldn't tell you *how* to get there, but I might be able to show you. Back then, it was just a maze of dirt roads. It might be different now."

Brady turned his back on the conversation. He flicked the living room curtains aside and stared out at the moonless night. Time was passing and Arlen was getting farther away. *Lord, hold Holly and Yosef in your hands. Bring angels to guard them.*

A.J. made a phone call, and then rejoined the group. "The phone company has started their search. I have everything I need for now. As soon as we get a fix on the cell phone, I'll contact you. Mrs. Davenport, you need to come along with me." He shook hands with Vera and Brady and escorted Evelyn out the door.

Holly's eyes burned, and her neck felt stiff and achy as she drove along the south shore of Hunters Lake in the Sierras. She'd never been here before and wished it were under happier circumstances. The lights from homes across the lake danced like fireflies on its mirrored surface as they wound along the water's edge. On Arlen's command, she made a right, heading away from the lake. Arlen peered into the darkness. "Slow down, make a right here," he motioned to a dirt road that wound up through the trees.

Holly slowly made the turn, her front bumper scraping the ground as she maneuvered through a drainage ditch and up the other side. The road was more of a path, rutted and potholed. An owl flitted through her headlights, startling her.

Arlen peered over her shoulder again, his head bobbing from side to side as they lumbered uphill through the darkness. The path became more and more like a trail the longer they drove. Holly's headlights fell upon a huge tree stump.

"Turn left," Arlen barked.

She could just make out two narrow strips of clear dirt she assumed was the way through the towering pines. Her headlights jumped around in a crazy dance as she negotiated up the long track. She finally came into a clearing, and her headlights caught a glint of light on the windows of a rustic cabin. To her left, the mountain dropped off from the edge of the meadow, leaving a narrow shelf where the cabin sat. The track led in a circle up to the front of the cabin. She glanced over at Yosef. The old man stared straight ahead, his face was unreadable, hidden in the shadows.

"Stop here," Arlen commanded.

The silence inside the car was profound. Only the occasional click of the engine cooling down disturbed the pristine silence of the place. Arlen got out of the car and moved around to the front of the cabin. He climbed the steps, a brilliant dome of starlight providing sufficient illumination. Once Holly's eyes adjusted to the night, she could see Arlen clearly at the top of the steps. He motioned toward the cabin with his revolver. "Okay, climb out and keep your hands where I can see them."

Yosef climbed stiffly from the car. Holly stood on the other side of the car watching Arlen from across the roof. The keys were still in the ignition. Could she jump back in, start the car, and get away? She watched Yosef move slowly over to the foot of the stairs and glance at her.

Arlen turned the gun to the old man's head and looked at Holly. His eyes as hard as concrete. "Go ahead ... run."

Brady stood alone in his darkened bedroom, the conversation with Arlen sending his mind racing, creating and rejecting one plan after another. He couldn't get the money from the church account because he would have to have someone co-sign with him to unfreeze the account. He would have to use his own funds. Striding across the room, he started to open the bedroom door then stopped, turned back to the bed and sat. There was nothing he could do tonight. He looked at the journals in their box by his bed. He had let Holly down by not discovering Arlen's involvement earlier. In a way, he blamed himself for the kidnapping. Brady pulled back the curtains of the front window. A passing car's headlights filtered through the evening fog.

About an hour later, Brady's cell phone beeped. He opened it to find a text message giving him directions to the cabin with the final words. *"Come alone!"*

Holly winced as Arlen gave a final tug on the ropes that held her arms to a wooden straight-backed chair. Yosef sat near her, also tied. She worried about him. He hadn't said a word in hours. His swollen nose took a definite jog to the left. The sight of it made her stomach lurch.

The cabin was rustic but well-maintained in spite of its shabby exterior. Inside it was clean, dry, and well-stocked. It was a man's environment to be sure, but a woman had once tried to soften its rough-hewn character. Faded curtains hung at the windows, and wildlife pictures dotted the walls. Cordwood was stored by the fireplace, and the last visitor had laid the makings for the next fire in the hearth, ready for a match. Arlen went to the simple kitchen and pulled a bottle and a glass from a cupboard. He returned and dropped into a leather armchair across from Holly and Yosef. He placed the bottle of Jack Daniels next to him on a side table and lifted a half-full tumbler to his lips, studying them across the rim.

"Now, what am I going to do with you two? This would have been real simple if that old busybody Thorndyke hadn't wandered by. She sure complicated things."

"You could let us go," Holly answered.

"Not likely, sweet thing. You two are the only bargaining chips I have. Evelyn told me Brady was starting to press. I was nearly ready to go, too." He took another pull on his Jack Daniels. "Things never would have turned out this way if those folks you sold the house to hadn't decided to tear it down. I warned you to settle at mediation. Don't you read your mail? Nobody would have known. Cost me a fortune to make that go away."

"*You* wrote the letter! Known what, about the bones?" Her eyes widening as she realized what Arlen was telling her.

"To the bones," he saluted with his shot glass. "They were tucked away nice and pretty. Nobody would have known."

"So you built that house. You knew about the bones and covered them up."

"What the eye doesn't see, the heart won't grieve over, sweet thing."

Holly's mouth dropped. "And you killed my Uncle Nikko!"

Arlen put his tumbler down. "Well, sorry 'bout that. He might have talked. He would have died soon anyway."

"Argh!" Holly clenched her teeth and took a stab at Arlen's shin with her foot.

"Easy there, tiger. I said I was sorry." He smirked and reached for his glass. Then he downed another shot.

"I have plenty stashed now to go anywhere I want, but I'd like to get that last bit out of the bank. Kind of a hard decision. Life would be a bit sweeter with an extra three hundred thousand in my jeans."

The evening wore on as Holly and Yosef watched Arlen get drunk. His words started slurring and he sunk deeper into the chair. "You think you're better than I am, always looking down on me cause I'm not a goodie two-shoes like the rest of you. Only reason I get any respect is because I shovel money into that piece-of-junk church." He waved his glass, sloshing a bit of the amber liquid onto his pants. He stood and wobbled over to Yosef, his liquor-laden breath washing over them both in a noxious wave. "You know what makes me better? Money. Money makes me equal to anybody." He waved the glass again and took another gulp.

Yosef remained silent, his face taut. Holly could see the older man's leg muscles tighten. Did he plan to kick Arlen?

"You act awfully brave when we're tied up." She wanted the attention away from Yosef.

"Oh, ho! So you want to take me on, do you, sweet thing?" He stumbled over to stand in front of her. His eyes were bloodshot and unfocused. His breath reeked.

Holly fought down the bile that rose in her throat.

Arlen leaned down and put his face inches from Holly's head. "Play nice and I might let you go." He leaned over farther and tried to kiss her.

Do it! Now!

She took his drooling lower lip between her teeth and bit down. Hard!

Arlen yelped and drew back. A drop of blood appeared. He wiped his hand across his mouth, examining the blood on his palm. "You little ..."

Crack! His hand connected with her face. Stars erupted in her head as she felt herself falling backward. A picture above her came down on her shoulder, then smashed to the floor. Her chair wobbled on one leg before falling sideways, crushing Holly's right side. A sickening crunch and pain shot up her arm.

She lay still, dazed by the impact. Arlen settled himself back in his chair and studied them both as he finished off the bottle. The throbbing in Holly's arm was almost unbearable. She suspected that she had broken her wrist, but she also felt a loosening of the chair back. Feigning unconsciousness, she watched Arlen through slits. He was slowly succumbing to the effects of the alcohol. Finally, his eyes closed, and his breathing became deep and rhythmic. Soon he was snoring loudly. She waited a few minutes longer and then tried to move. The pain caused her to gasp.

Yosef looked down. "Are you okay, Holly?" he whispered.

She nodded and tried again. Moving different muscles and avoiding pressure on her wrists, she was able to sit up with the back of the chair still held by her bound arms. Carefully, she stood, leaning against the wall for support. She watched Arlen for any sign of movement, but he was out cold--his head tilted at a crazy angle, drool pooling on the arm of the chair.

Holly tiptoed over to Yosef, her eyes trying to convey her intentions. She turned around and placed her tied hands in front of his mouth. He got the message and began pulling at the knot with his teeth. All the time, Holly kept close watch on their slumbering captor. With each tug, Holly had to bite her lip to keep from making a sound. The pain in her wrist made her knees weak. Spots began to appear before her eyes, and the room started to spin. She dropped to one knee, trying to stay conscious. Nausea threatened to overwhelm her.

Lord, help us please! We have to get out of here. Keep Arlen asleep and give me the strength to overcome the pain. Taking deep breaths, Holly made it to her feet again as the spinning subsided. She repositioned herself before Yosef, and in a couple more excruciating minutes, the ropes dropped from her wrists. Holly caught the back of the chair with her good hand before it hit the floor. She examined her right wrist. The swelling in the joint, and dark bruising spreading under the skin, grim testament to the damage. She couldn't move it without searing pain. Yosef waited and watched. How could she untie Yosef with just one good hand?

She knelt behind him and examined the knot. Once she developed a strategy, she set to work with her teeth and her uninjured hand. Arlen's steady snoring marked the passing minutes until she worked the knots loose. Finally, Yosef stood beside her, rubbing his bruised wrists. He nodded toward the door, and the two of them silently crept across the wood floor.

Holly's cell phone sat on the arm of a couch by the front door. Her hand closed around it as ...

Squeak!

A board protested beneath Yosef's foot. They both glanced at Arlen and watched as he stirred. His eyes opened, and he surveyed the room dumbly. Standing, he lurched toward the empty chairs and lifted the ropes that had once held his captives. "Argh!" he threw them at the wall and turned.

Holly and Yosef stood rooted to the floor next to the front door. The light from the kitchen did not reach them. As Arlen surveyed the small cabin, his eyes missed them in the shadows on the first pass. He turned his back, and Yosef took the opportunity to reach for the door handle and turn it.

The sound brought Arlen around in a crouch, the abrupt motion causing him to lose his unsteady balance and fall to one knee. Taking this small chance, Yosef and Holly bolted through the front door, down the steps, and into the blackness of the night.

Chapter Thirty-One

Holly gasped for breath as she stumbled after Yosef, the altitude robbing her lungs. She stopped briefly, listening, breathing hard. She heard the distinct sound of Arlen swearing and the rustling of the trees and brush behind them. Fear pushed her forward, just barely keeping Yosef in view. His stamina amazed her as he made steady progress ever higher into the woods, pine needles muffling their footsteps. Holly peered into the darkness for any sign of danger. Her imagination played tricks on her; the deep murk of the forest danced before her eyes, taking on dim shapes, then dissolving into nothing.

Holly's nose ran from the cold. She rubbed it with her sleeve, releasing all sense of propriety for the sake of survival. Her heart thundered in her chest as she followed Yosef's dim outline in front of her. She pressed on, making her way around boulders and over fallen trees. Her hands were numb with the cold. Perspiration made her thin cotton shirt clammy beneath her sweatshirt, increasing the discomfort. She cradled her injured wrist, wincing when she stumbled. If she held it still, she could tolerate the pain, but any sudden twist or jar made her grit her teeth. She wondered if Yosef could sense her struggle.

The sliver of moon blinked out as heavy clouds rolled across the night sky. A brisk wind moaned in the treetops and sent shivers down her spine. Without the moon's thin light, the forest became almost impassable. She could just make out Yosef's white sweatshirt, a blob of pale movement ahead of her, as she struggled over yet another fallen pine.

The transformation didn't happen all at once, but over several minutes the forest changed. She caught up to Yosef and they stopped to catch another much-needed breath. A hush settled around them. The wind died down, and she found herself listening and waiting. She felt a cold touch on her cheek and then her hand. She looked down as white flakes melted on her jeans.

"We're in trouble," Yosef whispered, looking around. "We have to find shelter and fast. No way of knowing if this snow will last." He studied the earth where the large pine rested on the ground. Crouching, he ran his hand along its side. Crab-walking a few feet, he followed the fallen mammoth through the woods, checking every so often at its base. Holly followed him, not wanting to be separated. Finally, he found what he was searching for and motioned Holly over. He pulled pine needles and brush away, exposing a depression beneath the tree and motioning Holly down into the small space. She lay on her belly and slipped down into the dry shelter. A thick mat of pine needles kept her off the cold, damp earth.

She heard Yosef clamber over the top of the big tree. Twigs and dirt cascaded into the depression as Yosef piled brush up against the other side of the fallen pine, blocking out the wind. Then he climbed back over the log and pushed great handfuls of pine needles into the depression.

"Pile this over the top of you, Holly. The needles will help keep us warm."

When their little cave was completely full of pine needles, Yosef slipped down next to her, pulling two large pine boughs into the opening, effectively sealing the entrance. Then he burrowed beneath a thick layer of pine needles and lay still.

She couldn't say she felt warm, but she certainly wasn't as cold as she had been a few minutes ago. Their combined body heat filled the little space quickly, making her marginally comfortable. Outside, the wind had picked up again, occasionally finding its way into their little nest with bitter puffs. Holly shivered where she half lay, half sat next to Yosef.

"If you'll excuse me, Holly," Yosef spoke through the darkness." I don't want you to take offense, but for the sake of survival we should huddle up."

She could hear the embarrassment in his voice but understood the wisdom behind his words. "I'm not offended, Yosef. It's scriptural. 'If two lie down together they keep warm.' I think it's in Ecclesiastes. God wrote that just for us tonight." She smiled at him in the darkness and then moved over, pressing her back against his chest. He wrapped his arm around her waist, and they settled in to wait out the storm.

Holly listened intently for any sound of Arlen's pursuit. In their haste to seek shelter from the snow, Holly hadn't considered what small, skittering creatures they might have disturbed beneath this tree. Although she had no knowledge of the insects that inhabited the forest, she assumed that spiders would most likely be found, possibly in abundance.

As if on cue, something crawled across her stomach. She started to investigate, but her wrist screamed in protest. She swung her elbow down and across her stomach, hoping to squish the intruder. A tickle on her neck alerted her to another invader. Suppressing a squeal of panic, she worked her left hand free from under her head and investigated her neck.

Nothing.

In her mind's eye, she visualized an army of spiders descending on her little nest of warmth and protection.

Her ankle.

She rubbed furiously with her foot.

"Holly, are you all right?"

"Spiders, Yosef. There are spiders in here."

"The weather's too cold for spiders, Holly. They're hibernating."

"Really?"

"Yes, really. They won't be out "til the snow is gone. Another month at least. You're just feeling the pine needle pricks."

"Oh."

"Try to rest."

"Okay. Thanks, Yosef."

Hours later, Holly opened her eyes to complete darkness. Her hips ached, and her left shoulder and arm were numb. She started to move, but pain shot through her right arm. She had forgotten about her wrist. Yosef's heavy breathing ruffled her hair and warmed her neck, their shared warmth holding off the cold. Listening, she realized that the wind had stopped. Darkness and silence. Not even a glimmer of light penetrated their haven. Yosef's arm rested heavy and limp on her waist. She could feel cold patches where the protective pine needle layer was thin, but she didn't want to move and break the warm barrier that had built up around them.

She knew she had slept because she had dreamt of strolling along the beach with a man. They held hands, the sun warm on her back. Up ahead in the distance, two small children built a sand castle, their hair deep red like hers. She closed her eyes and tried to drift back to that moment, to feel the warmth of his hand in hers. She could just catch wisps of the dream. Whose hand was she holding? Whose heart had captured hers?

Then the cold intruded and the dream fled. Was she going to die? Was this how her life would end? She drove the thought away. What had Uncle Nikko always said? God had bigger plans for her, plans to prosper her. She held onto that promise with fierce intensity. She was too smart to die this way. They would find a way out if they stuck together. Yosef was old, and injured too, but they couldn't be that far from civilization. When morning came, they would travel down the mountain. Surely they would come to the lake, and the lake meant people. They would be rescued.

Arlen's eyes swam before her in the darkness. Where was he now? She remembered him stumbling and swearing behind them as they scrambled up into the forest and away from the cabin. The chase had gone on for what seemed like forever. Had he returned to the cabin, or was he caught out in the snowstorm as well? She hoped he lay frozen and dead. The thought alarmed her, but with Arlen out of the picture, they would have a better chance to get to safety.

Her thoughts turned to food and water. She had heard that it wasn't a good idea to eat snow, but she didn't know why. If it came down to it, water would probably not be a problem. Food though, that was a different matter. What if they were trapped up here for days? Jesus lived in the wilderness for forty days while he fasted. She knew that with available water they could last quite a while if they minimized their activity.

When she was a child, her best friend had been a Girl Scout, but Holly had never taken a liking to the group. Now she wished she had spent more times in the out-of-doors. How could she ever have known that some day she would be trapped on the side of a mountain in a snowstorm? The Lord knew, and that comforted her. He knew where she was. He would either lead her out or lead her home. Someone at church used to say that all the time.

Yosef stirred next to her. She could tell by his breathing that he was awake.

"You slept." She said

"I guess I did."

"What time do you think it is?"

"I could look."

"Don't, it will let in the cold. It doesn't matter that much anyway."

Yosef listened for a moment. "I don't hear any birds. Probably still nighttime."

"The wind stopped. Do you think it's still snowing?"

"No way to know. I bet we're warmer because the snow has filled the gaps, keeping the warmth in. Snow is mostly air you know, great insulator."

"What do you think we should do, Yosef?"

"Wait here till morning. Then we'll know which way's east and head for the lake."

"I thought that, too. Do you think anyone is looking for us?"

"I know Vera will be worried. Sylvia Thorndyke saw us together. Maybe they will put two and two together. They'll never figure we're up here in the mountains though. I think for now we're on our own."

The thought strengthened Holly's resolve. She was not going to give in to this situation. She was smart and healthy. If they were careful and planned their moves, they would get out as long as Arlen didn't show up. But before all that, she wanted to pray.

"Father, you know where we are and the trouble we are in. You know we need help. I've never been in a situation like this before. Please grant us courage and wisdom, Lord."

Yosef continued. "Keep Vera calm, Lord. Keep her safe 'til I get back. She worries so, Lord, and that's not good for her heart. Show us how to get out of this pickle. I don't know how to pray about Arlen. I trusted him, and he betrayed us. I now know what you must have felt like with Judas way back then. I don't want him to die, but please make him miserable in his sin. Amen."

"Amen to that." Holly gave Yosef's hand a squeeze and closed her eyes.

Snuff, snuff snuff.

The sound woke Holly, and she instantly froze then wiggled her shoulder to alert Yosef.

Wuffle, wuffle, grunt.

Something large was nosing into their hiding place. The moments ticked by as the large creature probed and pawed at the branches. Next, it went over the top of the fallen tree and investigated the other side of the small depression.

A bear. Holly knew it in her bones. It was spring and a bear would be hungry, but didn't they eat berries and rodents? She had heard of bear attacks but never had heard that anyone had been eaten. She hoped she remembered right.

Yosef pulled her closer. She could feel his heart beating hard against her back. She tried to keep her breathing slow and steady as the big animal probed their hiding place. She heard the brush crackle at her feet. Her eyes were drawn to the light that filtered past the large black nose pushing its way through the brush.

"No! Get out!" Holly kicked at the black bulb invading their den.

195

The bear yelped and pulled back, leaving a hole to the outside world. Holly heard it trotting away into the trees. Cold air puffed in on Holly's feet from the breech in their insulation. Yosef moved his foot and pushed pine needles up into the gap, sealing off the hole. They now had further information about the outside world. The stars were out, and a layer of snow covered them, so the storm had passed.

"Good job, Holly."

"You think it will be back?" Her heart racing from the encounter.

"No. I don't know much about bears, but I think you thoroughly scared that one off."

"Yosef, I know we're going to get out of this."

"Yes, we are. We're not far from help. I'm sure of that. When the sun comes up, we'll poke our heads out and see where we are, then we'll start down the mountain."

Holly closed her eyes again and steeled herself for the journey ahead.

Brady woke to a slate gray morning and packed what few clothes he had in a grocery sack. He grabbed one of Yosef's warm jackets from the hall closet and stashed everything in the trunk of Vera's car.

When Vera came into the kitchen at eight-thirty, Brady had coffee going and eggs and toast on the table. "Thank you, Pastor Brady. I overslept." She accepted a mug of coffee and sat down at the table.

"Vera, I have to borrow your car this morning. Is that all right? I may be gone for awhile."

"Of course, Pastor. Help yourself. I won't be going anywhere until I hear from that detective." She sipped her coffee and stared at the chair where Yosef should be sitting.

Brady finished his breakfast and spent the next forty-five minutes in prayer before heading to the bank. Asking for over three-hundred-thousand dollars in cash was unusual, but he didn't anticipate it would be a problem. The money was in his account, and he should be able to get it out. However, three hours later he emerged empty handed. He had been as persistent as legally possible, but in the end the bank had won—citing their printed regulations about pre-notification to withdraw large sums.

Standing in the parking lot, Brady went over his options. The story of the nation of Israel stepping out in faith to cross the Red Sea came to mind. He searched around inside Vera's car and found a map of California. Determining his route, he headed for Hunters Lake.

Chapter Thirty-Two

The beauty that surrounded them would have been breathtaking if the air hadn't been so cold. For a moment, Holly doubted their ability to survive as she grabbed the cuff of her sweatshirt with her teeth and pulled it down over her hand. Then she gingerly covered the other hand, wincing at the pain, and cradled her broken wrist across her chest.

Snow spread a pristine blanket across the landscape. Now that the sun was up, they could see that they had taken refuge at the edge of a small meadow. The tracks from the bear that had visited them in the night cut across the meadow and into the woods on the other side. The sun peeked over the top of the mountains and glistened on the snow. Here and there, steaming patches of soil emerged as the morning sun crept over them. Holly moved out into the sunlight and turned her back to its warmth. She watched as Yosef went into the middle of the small meadow, pulled up the sleeve of his sweatshirt, and took off his watch. Holly came over to see what he was doing.

Yosef faced the sun and turned the watch so that the hour hand pointed at it. Then he looked off across the mountain, pointing. "That way is east. That should take us to the lake."

"That's amazing! How did you figure that out?"

"I picked up a few tricks over the years. You should know this one, Holly, it's a good sailor trick." He winked at her. "Shall we?"

Holly looked around and then back down at the hollow under the log where they had spent the night. She wasn't sure about leaving its safety, but they had to do something. She looked back at Yosef. She had been so steady in the face of danger in her boat last week. Where was her courage now?

"I know, Holly, but we can't stay here and starve. If nobody knows where we are, then we are on our own."

She pulled her cell phone from her back pocket and activated it. No bars—no signal. She removed the battery put it in her pocket. She hoped they could get service down lower on the mountain, and she wanted to have enough battery power to call out.

They moved off in the direction Yosef indicated. The pine needles under the snow were slick, so she took care where she stepped. Nevertheless, her feet, wet and numb, caused her to stumble often. She tried to catch herself with her one good arm but wrenched her broken wrist in the process. At such a slow rate of progress, Holly began to doubt they would reach help in time.

At the Shankston's, Detective Walker was filling Vera in on the progress of the case when Evelyn arrived with Mrs. Thorndyke who, along with her husband, had paid Evelyn's bail that morning. The rest of the prayer group soon followed.

"We got a fix on her cell phone north of Fresno. The signal was weak but enough to find them. Looks like they *are* heading to that cabin." He turned to Evelyn. "Get your coat; we're going for a ride."

"I'm coming too, and we need to let Pastor Brady know," Vera said over her shoulder as she headed for the coat closet.

"Suit yourself, ma'am. Where is the Padre?"

"He had to borrow my car this morning. He said he would be gone a while."

"Did he say where he was going?" A.J. paused and turned to look at Vera.

"No. He has a cell phone. We could call him and let him know where we're going."

Mrs. Thorndyke fussed with starting a fresh pot of coffee in the kitchen. "We'll call him, Vera, and then stay here and pray. Call us when you hear anything."

A.J. turned for the door with Evelyn. Vera close on his heels.

Brady chafed in frustration as he followed a slow truck up the winding road into the mountains. Trying to hold Holly loosely and turning her over to God was at the edge of impossible. He had turned a corner in his relationship with the Lord, but trust was a brittle thing. Everything he had clutched to his heart had turned to wisps and memories.

Please, Lord, don't take Holly. If it is your will then let it be so, but please, if there is any chance, please preserve her.

Brady remembered the look of determination on Holly's face as she had worked to reattach to jib on the sailboat, saving them from crashing on the rocks. He prayed that the same determination would see her through this as well.

His phone beeped once. He checked it and saw that he had missed a call from the Shankstons. Then the service dropped, and he turned the phone off.

Holly and Yosef had been trudging downhill for several hours; the going was slow through areas of thick brush, outcroppings of rock, and dense forest. A swift-flowing stream provided a refreshing, but chilly drink. They lingered on a slab of sun-bathed granite, drinking their fill since there was no way to carry the water with them.

Yosef sat in the sun examining a crumbling piece of stone, his face lined with worry.

"We'll get out of this, Yosef." Holly spoke in hushed tones. She hadn't heard anything that would indicate Arlen was near, but she was nervous.

Yosef let the small stone dribble from his fingers down the rock face and into the stream. Then he looked over at Holly and sighed. "I've known Arlen since he was a boy, and I believe his faith is real. I just can't seem to get a hold of what happened to him."

The deep heat of anger tightened Holly's chest. She knew all too well the betrayal that Yosef felt. . A sharp response rose in her throat, but she clamped her teeth against saying it. Instead, she looked out across the tops of the pine trees. A breeze tugged at their tips and a large hawk balanced on the updraft.

"When he went away to college, he was involved in Campus Crusade for Christ. I even sponsored him on a mission trip to Mexico. Then his dad fell ill, and Arlen had to give up college to run the construction firm. His disappointment showed for everyone to see. Over time, I assumed he had adjusted. I guess you never know what might make a man crack. You can read about plenty of God-fearing folks in the Bible who did bad things. Look at King David. He murdered a man and took his wife. Yet no one doubts David's devotion to God."

Holly tossed a rock into the snow at their feet. The vision of Uncle Nicholas' frail body made her eyes sting. He didn't have a chance when Arlen came for him.

"I think he had had enough of the construction business and was ready to get on with his life. He just didn't think it through all the way."

"When the bones were discovered, and he was hit with a lawsuit, I think that probably accelerated his plan. But why Cheri? How does she play into all this?"

"We may never know."

Crack. It was a subtle sound, but Holly heard it. Someone or something had moved in the forest above them. Holly caught Yosef's eye. He had heard it as well. Then their eyes followed the footprints they had left back through the thin crust of snow into the trees. The white blanket surrounding them would betray their every move.

Brady followed Arlen's directions up into the mountains and emerging in the meadow where the cabin sat in afternoon shadow. He climbed out of the car and called out for Arlen.

No answer.

He peered inside Holly's Honda. The sight of bloody tissues made his jaw tighten. In spite of his sore feet, he took the steps leading to the cabin porch two at a time and shoved open the door.

The broken chair, lengths of rope, and the empty Jack Daniels bottle were silent witnesses to what Holly and Yosef must have faced. Since Holly's car was still at the cabin, Brady made a quick inspection of the small dwelling and concluded that the three of them must be in the surrounding mountains. He bent down and picked up the rope where it lay next to the broken chair. Then he saw the Jack Daniels bottle again and squeezed his eyes shut, trying to block the bone-chilling images his mind conjured up. He slung the rope across the room and kicked at the broken chair. The pain didn't matter.

Back on the porch, he surveyed the meadow. Patches of snow clung stubbornly to the shadows, pristine and untouched. He thought about trying to find evidence of a trail but let the idea go. If he did find where they had entered the forest, he would only get himself lost.

"Lord, I'm not sure what to do here. Should I call A.J. and let him know that I found the car? Maybe Yosef and Holly will make it back here on their own. But what if Arlen returns and I've called the police?" He spoke out into the cooling afternoon air.

Twenty minutes later, Brady rose from his knees and went back inside the cabin. No clear word of direction had come to him. He didn't know what to do, so he chose to do nothing but wait. He sat on a couch under one of the front windows with his feet up. Reclining slightly, he had a clear view of the cars and the meadow beyond. The long afternoon shadows muted the colors and darkness crept into the cabin as Brady waited and then slept.

Yosef held still, his granite grey eyes surveying their surroundings. Down the mountain to the right, the trees opened up and the ground was clear of snow. He put his finger to his lips and motioned Holly to follow him. He led her to the clear patch of ground and, when he stood directly in the middle of the clear ground, made a hard right and went back up the hill to a large granite outcropping. The boulders poked up through the thin skin of earth, their surface crumbly to the touch. The ground around them was dotted with protected snow patches, which Yosef skirted.

As they climbed out onto the exposed granite, Holly fought to keep her footing on the crumbly surface, slipping once and leaving a white mark on the pepper speckled rock. Her brow furrowed in an apology to Yosef who shrugged it off and helped her up onto the top of the outcropping.

Motion up the meadow in the trees alerted them to Arlen's location. He came out into the clearing below, having followed their tracks to the unyielding granite. Squatting down, he appeared to study the surface and then surveyed the area.

Holly and Yosef ducked down just as he lifted his eyes to the surrounding boulders.

A.J. waited outside the ladies room at a gas station in Fresno for Evelyn. He was just finishing up a phone call when she came out. "I'm in contact with the local sheriff. Two units will be waiting for us at the turnoff for Hunters Lake. I sure hope you can remember how to get to the cabin."

"If things haven't changed too much over the years, I should be able to find it."

Vera soon came out of the bathroom and made her way across the parking lot to join them. She dabbed her nose and then tucked away her tissue and got back into the car without a glance or a word. Her features were becoming more haggard by the hour. Evelyn and the detective exchanged glances and then resumed their journey up into the hills.

An hour later, they were at the intersection. Two squad cars sat in the shadows, only their grills facing the passing cars. A.J.'s Lincoln nosed into the turnout. Everyone but Vera got out. They were met halfway by two armed officers dressed in camouflage fatigues.

After the necessary introductions, A.J. introduced Evelyn as their guide. She tried to explain the landmarks she would be looking for. As she went further and further into her description, flickers of doubt touched the faces of the local officers.

"Ma'am, how long has it been since you were up here?"

"Probably twenty years, why."

The tall blond officer's face hardened. "Ma'am, things have grown quite a bit since you've been here."

"Well, that's the best I have. If the good Lord wants us to find them then we'll find them. We're wasting time here." Evelyn turned back to the white Lincoln.

The officers exchanged glances. A.J. spoke into the silence. "This guy may have already killed one woman and an old man on the coast, and he has a bundle of cash he would like to get his hands on. I think we may have a hostage situation. He is probably going to use the old man and the girl as bargaining chips. According to my sources, he's a skilled hunter and tracker. He hunts deer in these mountains and knows them well. If we can catch him in the cabin and keep him contained, we may have a chance. If he gets into the hills, we'll lose him."

The hair on Brady's arms stood up, alerting him that he wasn't alone anymore.

"I know you're awake, Brady." Arlen's voice came from above him.

Brady opened his eyes and could make out Arlen looming over him in the darkness, the muzzle of a revolver inches from his nose.

"Did you bring my money?"

Brady's body flushed with heat. He swallowed down the rising fear and cleared his throat. "That depends. Where are Holly and Yosef?"

"Haven't a clue, but that doesn't matter, does it. Your car is out front. I assume the money is in it." Arlen lifted one dark eyebrow. A grin teased the corner of his mouth as he took a step back and allowed Brady to sit up.

Arlen lowered himself into the chair where the empty Jack Daniels bottle lay and lit an oil lamp on the side table. The golden glow revealed Arlen's mud-encrusted pants and torn jacket. His hand quivered as he blew out the match, but his gun hand held steady, the barrel pointed at Brady's chest.

"You're a hard man to kill, Brady. I would have sworn that tumble off the road would have done the job."

"So that was you."

"Yep."

"What happened, Arlen? How did all this start?" If he was going to die, he at least wanted to know the reason.

Arlen lifted the Jack Daniels bottle and examined it, sniffing the opening and checking the bottom for any remaining liquor. "What's it to you, Mr. Preacher? Doesn't much matter now anyway." He set down the empty bottle and turned his attention to the darkness beyond the window above Brady's head.

"Was Cheri carrying your baby, Arlen?"

A flicker of something in his eyes, then it was gone. "Yes."

"Is that why you killed her?"

"No!" He bit off the word. "She tried to blackmail me." He thrust himself out of the chair and turned away, then whirled around, the gun snapping back to target Brady's top shirt button. "Guess she figured she'd be safe because she carried my kid and all. But kids aren't in my plan."

"You've been planning this escape for awhile then."

"Ever since my old man died and I got stuck with the company. Every day was another step backward, away from where *I* wanted to go."

"And where was that?"

"Anyplace *but* Morro Bay. I was made for greater things."

Brady clasped his hands in his lap to stop them from shaking. "On that we agree."

"You see! You know what it's like to move in the power circles. I knew you would understand when I saw that interview you did on television. You've rubbed shoulders with those people." The muzzle of the gun dropped an inch. "I couldn't get my old man to see the big picture. He was small town all the way."

"But I *left* all that and came to Morro Bay." Brady knew the direction of the conversation could get him killed.

"Yah, that didn't make sense to me. Why you came, I mean. I figured a guy like you would have a good reason. That I could learn something from you, Brady." Arlen dropped his head back and looked up at the ceiling. The gun settling in his lap. Then his head came up and his eyes locked again with Brady's, the gun following his gaze.

"Why did you have to get nosey? I was almost there."

"How many people would have died, Arlen?"

"Nobody else. I just wanted to get my money and go."

Brady's heart thudded in his chest. "You're lying."

The whole room stilled. Like the moment the birds stop their singing just before lightening strikes.

Chapter Thirty-Three

Holly was reluctant to leave the shelter of the boulders, but night was rapidly closing in on them and dark clouds once again threatened snow. The sun-warmed granite had lost its warmth, leaving her chilled. They hadn't heard a sound for over an hour, so Yosef risked a quick look.

"Looks like the coast is clear. We better get moving," he said and started down out of the rocks.

With shelter their top priority now that Arlen seemed to have left, Holly popped the battery back into her cell phone and checked the signal. One bar blinked briefly and was gone. She lifted the phone into the air and moved it around, trying to find the signal again. Nothing. She shoved it back into her pocket and followed Yosef down into the jumble of boulders.

Yosef scanned along the edge of the rock strewn surface. "I'd like to find a cave or overhang of some sort. You go a bit over that way. See what you can find."

As they spread out looking for cover, Holly kept Yosef in sight. Finally, Holly spied a place where two boulders rested against each other, leaving a shallow overhang about four feet high and six feet wide. She waved him over.

"Yosef, would this work? Can we use some branches and block the opening?"

He came to the spot and peered inside. "This will have to do. We're running out of light."

Yosef worked quickly for half an hour. Holly, hampered by her broken wrist, struggled to help. Yosef broke off branches and Holly dragged them over to their shelter where she leaned them against the opening. When they were finished, their little cave had an interwoven windbreak about four feet thick, with an opening at one end to allow them to crawl in. Holly set aside a bough to pull in behind them to seal the hole.

Yosef crawled in first and lay with his back against the hard stone of the small cave. Holly followed, slipping in and pulling the bough in behind her to block the opening. They had just enough room for the two of them to lie next to each other. Holly rested her head on her good arm and gingerly positioned her throbbing wrist.

Yosef dropped an arm across Holly's waist as he had the night before. Their shared warmth helped some, but her hands and feet burned with the bitter cold. She wiggled her toes to keep the circulation going.

"How far do you think we have to go before we reach the lake, Yosef?"

"No way to know. I am figuring that if we continue east, we will hit a road or something."

"How do you know that east is the right direction?"

"Old habit from my fishing days. I always watch the sun and keep my bearings. When we drove up here, the road that ran toward the lake ran mostly north and south. I just kept track of where the sun was as we drove. Gosh, I'm sorry I got you into this, Holly."

"We did this together, Yosef."

"I could have gone in the bank and reopened the account. We didn't have to go with Arlen. It's my fault we are in this fix."

"You didn't know what Arlen would do." When he didn't reply, Holly kept silent for a while. Then, "Do you think we'll make it, Yosef?"

"If the good Lord is willing and we keep our wits about us. We're finding water around, in the snow if nothing else. Food is a problem, but with enough water I think we'll make it if we take it easy."

Holly's thought about A.J. Did he know she was missing? Would he come looking for her? His strong, handsome face drifted through her mind's eye and was then replaced by Brady's. She warmed as she thought of him. He stirred emotions in her that A.J. didn't touch. When with A.J., her emotions were steady, and she was in control; with Brady, her heart leapt. Was that love? Her common sense told her to run from a relationship with a pastor and everything that kind of life entailed. Then her heart joined in the discussion, and common sense fled.

The little search party traveled for almost twenty minutes along the length of the south shore with no sign of the red mailbox. A.J. pulled his Lincoln onto the shoulder of the road and waited for the other cars to park. They all got out and gathered in a tight huddle. Evelyn rubbed her arms briskly.

"That mailbox could be on any one of those dirt roads we passed. Any ideas?"

A dark haired officer pulled out a notebook. "I know a guy who works at a title company in Wishon who owes me a favor. He could do a property search. What's the guy's name?"

A.J. gave him the info. "Make the call."

Vera and Evelyn stood to one side in uneasy silence. Vera's eyes darted from face to face, her shoulders hunched against the cold, her frame rigid with anxiety. The lake shimmered in the distance, and the air smelled of snow. She glanced at the heavy clouds building on the horizon, slowly encroaching on the brilliant night sky. She glanced at her watch and then moved over to the officers, interrupting them. "We have three cars, all together. I think we should split up and each take one road. Follow it for five minutes and then regroup and compare notes."

She was met with stony silence. It was the first time she had spoken in hours.

Three of the officers nodded, liking the idea. Vera felt A.J.'s eyes on her for a moment then he pushed away from where he was resting against the fender of his car. "Worth a shot."

A.J. decided that Vera would ride in the car that Officer Barnes drove and Evelyn would stay with A.J. Half an hour later, Vera and Barnes were back at the rendezvous point. The others were already out of their cars and standing in a huddle around a map spread out on the hood of A.J.'s car. Evelyn was talking in animated tones as they arrived.

"I'm sure now. We have to make a right and go a ways up Sand Valley Road." She looked up as Vera approached.

"I haven't been up here in years, it took me awhile to remember, but I'm sure now." Her eyes pleaded for Vera to believe her.

Vera ignored her. "We didn't see anything on the road we took."

A.J. shrugged, folded the map with quick, taught motions, and slapped it on the roof of his car. "Seems we have no other options. Might as well get this wild goose chase rolling."

Evelyn hugged herself against the cold. "I'm right, you'll see."

In just a few minutes, they turned onto Sand Valley Road and resumed the search for the red mailbox. Officer Barnes with Vera and Officer Williams followed at the end of the caravan, all hoping against hope that they were finally on the right track.

"They've been gone for over twenty-four hours now, Officer Barnes. They could be anywhere. What if we *are* on a wild goose chase? Maybe they never did come up here," Vera finally voiced the concern she suspected they all had.

Barnes spoke up. "I still think it's the best shot we have, ma'am. We know they came up this way. We haven't had a fix on the cell phone for quite a while. Service is spotty at best up here, so we have to just keep hunting for—"

"Stop the car!" Vera grabbed his arm as she peered into the darkness.

Barnes braked and pulled to the side of the road. Vera got out and hurried past the headlights and across the narrow road. She bent over and peered into the bushes, then reached down and lifted a battered red mailbox.

Barnes blinked his headlights rapidly, the agreed signal. Up ahead, taillights blinked as the other cars stopped and turned. In a moment, all three cars had gathered and Vera proudly displayed the much-sought-after mailbox.

"That's it! Vera, you found it." Evelyn threw her arms around her friend.

The two women stood in a fierce embrace for a moment before A.J., glancing around in embarrassment, cleared his throat. "Ladies, we're short on time here. Evelyn, where do we go now?"

"We go up this road to the stump of a big pine tree. You take a left there and the cabin is just up the road in a clearing."

One of the officers examined the surrounding area with his flashlight. "A car went up this road recently. No doubt about it."

A.J. motioned the other officers away, out of earshot of the women. Vera and Evelyn exchanged looks. Vera didn't like being outside of the planning. She knew the officers had experience in such things, but she had a serious interest in their plans. The bitter cold drove Evelyn into A.J.'s car, so Vera wandered over to listen in on the planning session.

A.J. turned as Vera approached. "We're going to go up and find the pine stump. Then Barnes and Williams here will go in on foot to get the lay of the land. We don't want to put your folks in danger by making our presence known."

"This is taking a lot of time, Detective."

"Listen, Ma'am, I'm just as concerned about Holly and your husband as you are." His eyes were hidden in dark shadows, but the intensity of his statement left no doubt in Vera's mind that Holly and Yosef's rescue was in good hands.

The little caravan set off up the rutted track and into the darkness. Their world narrowed to the illuminated strip of road just before them and the bobbing taillights ahead. Vera watched as the car twisted and turned up into the forest and seemed to be climbing to the very top of the mountain.

Forty minutes had passed since Barnes and Williams had disappeared down the dark track toward the cabin. Evelyn came over to join Vera in Barn's car. Snow was dusting the windshield twenty minutes later when Vera saw the interior light go on in the car up ahead. Maybe they were back.

The snow was quickly getting thicker, and Vera began to get worried about their ability to get out if they needed to. Through the snow, a dark figure came down the line of cars. The interior light made her blink as A.J. climbed into the front passenger seat and brushed the snow from his coat. "The cabin is just up the road across a meadow. Holly's car is parked in front and so is yours, Vera, so we seem to have found them all. The boys got a look inside. Arlen is there with the Padre, but they didn't see Holly or your husband, Ma'am. They may be in another part of the house."

Vera clutched his jacket sleeve. "What are you going to do?"

"Now that we've identified their location, we can call for help and start again in the morning. The storm should be over by then according to Barnes."

"That may be too late! They may leave. Can't you and your officers go get them?"

"That wouldn't be wise. We need backup and sunlight."

Vera started to protest but bit her lip. Her big eyes filled with tears.

Evelyn patted her shoulder. "Vera, these men have been through things like this before. They know what the best thing to do is. We need to trust them."

Vera shoved Evelyn's hand away. "If it weren't for you, my husband wouldn't be in this mess!" The two women glared at each other, like two mad cats in a corner.

Barnes slipped into the driver's seat. "We need to get out of here. I'll start backing slowly down the road," A.J. nodded, climbed out, and returned to his car.

Evelyn stayed in Barnes's car with Vera. He turned and looked behind him. She could see that his view was filled with thickly falling snow. "This is impossible," he muttered. "What a mess."

Chapter Thirty-Four

A.J. eased his car backward, straining to see through the gloom. The view out the back window of the two thin tracks behind him would soon be obscured by snow. At the moment, the large, wet flakes melted when they hit the ground. Soon the temperature would drop and the snow would accumulate. He began to perspire. A cramp started in his shoulder and crept up his neck, forcing him to stop and look forward for a moment. The car in front of him, also backing down the slick hill, was barely visible through the whiteness.

He looked back again, undoing his safety belt in order to turn more fully around. The track swung sharply to the right and dropped down. A.J. eased his car onto the drop off, guessing where he was going for the moment because he couldn't see. The car began to slide to the right. A.J. hit the brakes but the car continued to slip down the little hill, careened sideways across the road, and ended up against a tree.

"Argh!" He slammed his hand against the steering wheel. He knew the next car would reach the drop off soon so he jumped out of his car and hurried up the rise, slipping back one step for every two he took. He made it to the top and jogged up the track waving his arms to catch the attention of Officer Barnes. The car's bumper edged within a few feet of A.J. when the brake lights came on and the car stopped. A.J. went around and Barnes rolled down the window.

"I slipped off the side of the embankment. My car is up against a tree and the road is blocked." The statement was simple and clear. A.J. had messed up and put them all in danger.

Barnes got out of the car and strode up the road to stop the other car before the situation got any worse.

A.J. stood at the top of the rise where Barnes joined him. "Can we move it?"

"I don't see how. Its back tires are off the road and deep in the mud."

A.J. stood in the snow stomping and beating his arms across his chest to keep warm. Soon the bundled form of Williams emerged from the snowy gloom.

"I understand we have a problem."

A.J. explained, exasperated at his bad luck.

Williams went over to the edge of the hill and studied A.J.'s car. He spat into the snow and returned. "Well, we're stuck here. We can't stay out in the snow all night. We're in a dead spot so our radios don't work. I say we go to the cabin. We'll get close and then we," indicating himself and Barnes, "will do another quick recon on the structure. See what's going on and if there are weapons. I suspect he's armed."

A.J. nodded. It was the only plan that made sense under the circumstances.

Everyone managed to fit into the remaining two cars that headed farther up the track toward the cabin. When they were just around the corner from the opening to the meadow, A.J. signaled the cars to a stop. The snow had subsided, and the new moon was playing peek-a-boo with the clouds as Williams and Barnes headed toward the cabin.

Arlen kept an eye on Brady while he rummaged in the kitchen for something to eat, his pistol at the ready on the counter.

"You had a great business, Arlen. Why did you feel that was a step back?"

"I had big plans. I was studying international business. I was going to see the world and make money doing it. Spending the rest of my life in a dinky California tourist trap didn't fit in with those plans."

"And getting Cheri pregnant didn't fit either, I gather."

"Cheri was a parasite. She had always been a parasite, ever since grade school. She was always figuring the angle. Blackmailing me was her last big mistake. She threatened to tell you about my plans if I didn't pay up."

"So you killed her."

"Yah, I killed her. One quick shove and she was over the cliff. And I was done."

"No regrets, no remorse?"

"Don't play the pastor game with me. I know where I stand."

"Where you stand with God?"

Arlen paused from his snack of sardines, his eyes hard and flat. "Yah, where I stand with God. I paid my dues to the church, did all the right things."

"And that's enough?"

"Yah, that's enough." He pushed a sardine into his mouth and chewed slowly.

Brady let the comment hang in the air for a heartbeat. "What about Jesus?"

"I was baptized. Went to youth group. I'm saved."

"Ever heard of the unforgivable sin, Arlen?"

"Yah." He thought for a moment, chewing. "Never really knew what it was though."

"Some people think it's any sin that is unrepented."

"So you want to know if I'm sorry about Cheri and the old guy."

"What old guy?"

"Holly's uncle."

Brady stilled inside. He would never have pegged Arlen—the elder—as a cold-blooded killer. "You killed him, too?" Brady couldn't mask his shock. "Arlen, aren't you at all sorry?"

"I wish I hadn't had to do it, but they were in the way. I wasn't going to let anybody or anything else get in my way." He returned to his chair, his legs splayed and the handgun resting casually in his lap.

"So now you're on the run. Do you really think you'll get out of the country, Arlen? I'd say your dream is over. You killed it yourself."

"I have my money and I have your car. Seems I hold all the cards."

"Then you're right. You won. Only problem is, this isn't a game."

Arlen's eyes were hooded in the shadows, the flicker from the lamp giving them a yellow tint. "That's where you're wrong Pastor Preachy Britches. This is the biggest game there is. Winner takes all."

"No, the real game was over before you were even born."

"Don't try your religious crap on me." Arlen glanced once more out the window. "I think it's time to go." He rose and leveled the gun at Brady's heart. "I'll take that money now."

Time compressed down to a single crystal clear moment for Brady. He knew it was okay for it all to be over. Standing, he met Arlen's gaze.

"There is no money."

Arlen blinked. Then blinked again. Brady felt the muscles tighten in his belly, bracing for the bullet that waited a foot away in the chamber of Arlen's gun.

"Then I guess we both lose."

A creek on the front porch drew Arlen's attention. He moved to the side of the front door, back against the wall, gun raised and ready. The moments ticked by and then -

BANG!

The back door flew open, and Williams burst into the room, hitting the floor and coming up with his gun ready. Everything seemed to happen in slow motion. "Freeze!" Williams demanded.

Arlen's gun was moving as Williams fired three times.

The front door crashed open, and Barnes rolled into the room and came up with his gun trained on Arlen who was now sinking slowly to the floor.

Blue gun smoke drifted across the ceiling as Brady rushed to Arlen's side.

"Stay back!" Williams demanded.

"I'm a pastor!" He said it as if it explained everything. Brady knelt down.

Arlen's breath came in weak gasps. Blood-specked foam trickled from his nose and mouth. His eyes traveled the room then locked on Brady. They widened with terror. His hand lifted an inch from his lap and Brady slipped his fingers into Arlen's palm.

"Pastor Brady. I ..." He blinked, confused.

His hand trembled in Brady's.

He gasped and tried to speak but nothing came out.

Brady squeezed his hand and felt a flicker of response from Arlen.

Brady closed his eyes. "Father, I offer up Arlen to you. Only you know the heart of a man. Only you know the heart of this man. We see the sin, but you see what the eye doesn't see. The person you see is the person your son died for. Help us all to see the person beneath the sin. Help me to love this man the way you loved him at the cross. From the heart."

Brady opened his eyes and looked into Arlen's.

"I ...am ...so sorry," he whispered. Then his chin dropped to his chest and he was gone.

Morning at the cabin dawned bright and clear. Blue jays skimmed across the meadow in search of breakfast. A steady drip drip developed on the east side of the cabin as the thin layer of snow on the roof lost its battle with the sun. Inside the evidence of Arlen's bloody end had been partitioned off by a sheet hanging from the low ceiling. As Evelyn and Vera had known him since childhood, the officers had spared them the sight of his gruesome final moments.

Vera was stumped when it came to fixing breakfast. She finally settled on two cans of Spam fried up in an old iron skillet. It wasn't much, but it would have to do. At least there was plenty of coffee.

A.J. traced a slow zigzag path across the meadow squinting at his cell phone display. Then, he stopped and abruptly dialed. Vera's heart leapt as she watched him from the window.

"Looks like he found cell service," she announced to everyone as they sat around the room. She sipped her coffee and waited. Eventually, A.J. made his way back across the meadow and up into the cabin.

"Well, I got through. We'll have a tow truck up to move my car in about an hour, and they got a fix on Holly's phone. They are sending in a search team. If Holly and Yosef sit still, I think we'll find them.

Holly struggled out from the shelter into the morning light. Her broken wrist was swollen and ugly, and she shook from hunger and pain. Yosef had two black eyes along with his crooked nose. He took her by her good arm, and the two of them started down the mountain again. After a minute or two, her cell phone beeped.

Fear punched her, then guilt. "I can't believe I forgot to take out the battery! Oh, Yosef. I'm so sorry."

Yosef helped her fish it out of her back pocket and take out the battery. Holly hoped there it had enough life left in it to make one phone call.

The morning sun had warmed the evening's snowfall, leaving a pool of water in a depression in one of the boulders. Holly and Yosef took turns drinking it down to the dregs and then sat again in the sunshine.

Holly couldn't stop shivering. Her strength was about gone and that scared her. She considered telling Yosef to go on without her. She could wait in the protected shelter until he brought help. She looked out across the meadow to her right. Was this where she was going to end? Cold, hungry and exhausted? Yosef had so much more stamina. She was only holding him back.

Lord, she prayed silently, *I don't want to die on this mountain. I am not ready to finish my time here.*

"Ready to go again, Holly?"

"What if you went on ahead, Yosef. I can go back to our shelter and wait for you. You can move faster without me."

"Nonsense." He came over and sat next to her. "I'm sure we don't have far to go, just down through those trees, I promise."

"You can't promise that."

"You callin' me a liar, young woman!" He puffed out his chest, hands on hips. His crooked nose and blackened eyes making the mock anger all the more comical. If he only knew how awful he looked.

Holly giggled.

He nodded and winked at her, offering his arm.

Brady sat at a linoleum-covered table inside the forestry station. They had been there for almost two hours now. The ancient stone fireplace that roared to his left, and a large wall-to-wall pine bookcase filled with used paperbacks to his right added a homey touch to an otherwise utilitarian building. Behind him in what passed for a kitchen, Vera poured two cups of coffee and joined him at the table.

"Well, Pastor Brady, this whole thing with Evelyn has been quite the revelation, hasn't it? Just when you think you know someone ..." She looked back toward the small kitchen where Evelyn was wiping down the counters and making more coffee. Vera's face pinched in anger. She shook her shoulders and turned her gaze back to Brady.

"Do you think Evelyn is all that different from the person you've known all your life?" Brady said, setting his cup on the table and meeting her eyes.

"But the horrible things she's done. I've never known someone of such a stripe. She should be locked up for life, if you ask me."

"You're pretty angry at her." Brady held her eyes until Vera looked away.

She took a sip then set her cup down. "Aren't you?"

"Do you think you could kill someone, Vera?"

Vera threw her shoulders back, leaning away from Brady. "What! Never."

"Which is easier to do, Vera? Commit murder or forgive someone?"

"Well ...I suppose ...well, Pastor." She narrowed her eyes, leaning in. "What are you driving at?"

"In the Sermon on the Mount, Christ taught that anger was a heavier sin than murder. So in God's economy, who is the greater sinner, you or Evelyn?"

"You're putting me on a par with that woman?" She pointed into the kitchen.

"We're called to a higher standard than the world, Vera. A higher standard than the Pharisees and the teachers of the Law. The world sees our actions, but what the world doesn't see is the condition of our heart. That's what He looks at, and that's what grieves Him."

Vera settled back into her chair. "We trusted Evelyn with the church finances, and she let us down." She drew little patterns on the table with the moisture left from the coffee cup. "You were nearly killed, twice, and now Yosef and Holly are missing."

"Vera, we let Christ down every day, and he doesn't abandon us. I think Evelyn needs us now more than ever. What do you think?"

"You sound like you forgive Evelyn. f she had come forward sooner, Arlen would have been stopped. You lost everything in that fire. How can you forgive her?"

"Forgiveness has two parts to it, Vera. Acknowledging that it's God's job to punish and making a conscious and continual decision to forgive."

"But what she did was wrong! She hurt people. Cheri might be alive today if she had told someone."

"Don't you think she lives with that reality every moment of every day? Evelyn asked me for forgiveness, and I forgave her. Every time I get angry, I forgive her again. And I'll keep on as often as Satan brings it to my attention." He watched the struggle play across her face. A struggle he fully understood. Did his forgiveness extend to the drunk driver who killed Karen? Did he forgive God?

"But..." Vera's anger and frustration contorted her features. She clunked her mug on the table, sloshing coffee on its gold-speckled surface. "This is just not right."

"No, it's not right. Nothing will ever be right on this earth outside of God's intervention. We live in Satan's domain."

"*My* husband was kidnapped by that monster, *my* property that was burned down."

Brady weighed her words. She was correct, of course. None of this was fair. Fairness left this world when Adam and Eve fell. But ultimate justice still prevailed. "I nearly lost my life in that fire. Every earthly thing I owned down to my pajamas was in that bungalow. God has stripped me of everything that's ever been important to me." He sighed and sat back in his chair. "Trust me, I understand your anger. I am just now beginning to understand how hard it is to forgive. I can't tell you how many times I've preached on the subject, but I never knew what I was talking about till

217

now. What I do know is that the bitterness that springs from unforgivness does more damage to *me* than anyone else. Living in bitterness is a waking nightmare that colors . . . everything." The last words came out a bit husky. He took a sip of coffee and glanced into the kitchen. Evelyn continued cleaning. He watched her as she slowly knelt down and started wiping the floor with a towel.

The hint of emotion in Brady's voice brought Vera's eyes up to meet his. She squirmed under the pressure of his gaze, then she seemed to deflate. A tear rolled down her rosy cheek. "If I forgive her, then it makes what she did okay."

"Her sin was already forgiven at the cross, Vera. Forgiveness is for our benefit, not Evelyn's.

Vera nodded and slowly stood. Turning to the bookcase behind her, she selected something at random and went to the other end of the room, settling onto a tattered couch.

Fear crept into Brady's thoughts. What he had told Vera wasn't entirely true. He hadn't lost everything, yet. Would Holly be taken from him too? Could he forgive God yet again?

To whom much is given, much is required.

The words swirled in his thoughts. At one point in his life, he had been given much, and he had squandered it. In his memory, Holly's green eyes sparkled and her red hair danced in the wind. If the Lord decided to take her, she was the Lord's to take. That was a truth that remained, whether he liked it, acknowledged it, or accepted it. It was simply true. What he did with that truth was what ultimately mattered.

Chapter Thirty-Five

A sound came from Holly's right; it wasn't an animal sound. She knew it was a human sound. Arlen had found them again. Holly panicked, stumbled, and dropped to one knee. Yosef reached down and lifted her to her feet, keeping a finger to his lips. His eyes searched their surroundings until he found what he was looking for. He led Holly to the base of another granite outcropping and began to climb the face. Holly stood at the bottom and watched. He motioned her to start up. She pointed to her arm and shook her head. She couldn't climb up the crumbly boulders. Frustrated and flushed, Yosef scrambled back down the boulder. Landing next to Holly, he looked around, and then followed the outcropping to where it joined the mountain. In a few moments, he found an opening between the rocks hardly wide enough for Holly to fit into.

Yosef leaned close to her ear. "You slip in here and hide. I'll go up on top and push rocks down on him if he finds you." He pointed at the cold, dark small cave.

Lacking a better idea, Holly slipped into the darkness. When the sides of the opening narrowed, she dropped down to her knees and worked her way back further. She could see out but it would be hard for anyone to see her, wedged as she was back in the space.

The sound of Yosef's footsteps faded, and then she was alone.

The moments dragged by as she waited. Her mind began to wander, tormenting her with the horrifying possibilities of their situation. What if Arlen found Yosef and killed him? Would Arlen come looking for her? If she ended up alone, could she make it out? *Shut up!* Panic wasn't helpful, and those were panic thoughts. She focused on what she would do if she were found. A rock lay just a few inches from her good hand. She shifted her weight, wincing at the sound she made, and pulled the rock to her. At least she had done something.

Her right leg began to cramp, starting slowly in her toes and working its way up into her calf. She wiggled her toes but they locked, increasing the cramp. She had to move but dared not. She steadied herself with her good arm and stretched her leg back, wiggling her toes again in an effort to relieve the pain.

Something moved behind her.

The sound started slowly, a clack clack, chatter chatter, buzz.

Rattlesnake!

Holly pulled her leg back underneath her, taking care to move with caution, and then ever so slowly started to crawl out of her hiding place. As she reached the opening, she heard footsteps coming up alongside the rocks. The buzzing behind her remained steady. She pulled her legs beneath her, as far away from the sound of the snake as she could get and still be somewhat hidden within the small cave.

A pair of heavy, black boots stopped at the cave entrance. His feet pivoted once and then moved on. Holly waited. The boots were back, moving more slowly. Holly's heart thundered and her body flushed with fear.

Growl.

Her stomach betrayed her and the boots turned toward the entrance of the cave.

Growl.

Holly's stomach spoke again, and the boots stopped just steps from where she was hiding. Her hand closed around the rock.

She tensed her legs, preparing to spring and run. Then came a noise she didn't recognize, and the boots fell over sideways. A groan and a scuffle followed.

"Holly! Are you in there? Come out quick, I've done something terrible." Yosef's voice was a welcome relief, but alarming as well.

Holly scrambled from her hiding place, emerging to find Yosef bending over a large man in camouflage gear and a ball cap that identified him as a County Sheriff.

"Oh, Yosef, what happened?" She rushed to his side and patted the unconscious deputy on the shoulder, not sure what to do.

"Oh! I thought it was Arlen. I was up above you, watching to be sure you were all right. I saw this fella get too close to your cave, so I dropped that rock on him." Yosef nodded to a chunk of granite the size of a football.

"Yosef! You could have killed him." Holly turned her attention to the prostrate rescuer.

"But I thought it was Arlen! My old eyes aren't as good as they used to be, I guess." He patted the man's arm and looked around helplessly.

"He must have someone with him. Why don't you go and look." Holly glanced back the way their rescuer had come, then at the opening to the cave. No sign of the snake.

When Yosef had gone, Holly turned her attention to the man who lay before her. Her rudimentary first aid skills told her not to move him. She examined him slowly, starting with his head. When she got to his belt, she saw what she thought was a radio wedged beneath him. She tugged at it, but he was a big man, and she couldn't pull it out of his belt. Her mind worked on the problem. She found a short branch and began digging beneath the radio. In a few moments, she had it in her hand.

Finding the knob that turned on the power, she pushed the transmit button.

"Hello? Can anybody hear me?"

The radio squawked, and Holly jumped. "Caller, identify yourself please."

"This is Holly Fain. I'm lost up in the mountains."

"Is there an officer with you?"

"He's unconscious." She eyed the deputy. "It was kind of an accident,"

"Do you know your position?"

"I have no idea."

The deputy stirred and rubbed his face with his hand. "Wait, he's waking up!"

"Hello? Are you all right?" She patted his shoulder. The muscle beneath her hand was like patting a rock.

He started to sit up. "Maybe you should lie down for awhile."

He rose to a sitting position and shook his head. When he removed his cap, Holly could see a large bump beginning to form on the side of his head.

"Oh, ouch."

"Yah, ouch." He touched the damage gently. "Are you Holly Fain?" He replaced his cap.

"Yes, and I'm so sorry you got hurt. Yosef thought you were Arlen, and he dropped a rock, and I'm so sorry." She absently patted his knee.

"I'm all right, Miss Fain. Just a bump on the head."

"Are you still there?" The radio next to Holly squawked.

Holly jumped in surprise and handed the radio back to the deputy with a sheepish shrug.

A.J. came into the break room where Brady and Evelyn waited. "We just had contact with Holly. Somehow she got hold of a radio and called in." He crooked a finger in their direction and returned to the communications room.

Brady, Vera and Evelyn joined the rest of the crew around a radio. Evelyn and Vera exchanged quick glances and took up positions on opposite sides of the room. Brady jumped as the radio crackled to life. His ears straining for word of Holly.

"This is Parker." The voice on the radio said. "Officer West has been injured but is ambulatory. We have found the subjects and will proceed north to South Shore Road. We will need medical attention upon arrival. Estimated arrival to road at eleven thirty hours."

Vera put her hand on the young ranger's shoulder. "Who's hurt?"

"I don't know, Ma'am"

"Well, ask!"

Yosef and Holly were positioned between Officers Parker and West as they made their way down the mountain toward civilization. West led the way after taking a reading on his GPS. Holly's arm was splinted and resting in a sling, courtesy of Parker. West had a bandage over the lump on his head, and Yosef's nose was taped.

Yosef apologized several times for his poor eyesight and lack of judgment. West graciously accepted each time until Yosef lapsed into silence.

Moving helped warm Holly as she skirted stubborn patches of snow that hid from the sun. She had an emergency blanket wrapped around her, but her shoes were wet and her toes ached in the cold. She had gratefully accepted a protein bar and water, which had revived her spirits a little. Having the deputies with them gave Holly renewed energy to make the final push down the mountain. The officers had offered to send for help to carry her out, but Holly felt she could make it.

In their brief radio exchange, she had learned of everyone who had been involved in the search for them. Her heart leapt into her throat when she heard that both Brady and A.J. were in the group. Their presence gave some urgency to the painful reality of her impossible situation. Soon she would see them both and what they each represented to her. Did she dare take a chance with Brady? The pain of her memories hung heavy in the crisp morning air. Then her mind jumped to A.J. He loved her, she had no doubt of that. He was honorable and steady. She could have a good life with A.J., but it was Brady who made her heart rejoice.

Father, what am I to do? Why would you bring this wonderful man into my life and then make it impossible for us to ever have a chance at a lasting relationship? I know you want me to trust, and I do. Well, to be honest, maybe I don't. I want to be in your will. Is it your will that I return to the church? I can't imagine doing that. Those people drove us away when we needed them the most. I'm not sure I can trust the church again.

The trip off the mountain took another forty minutes. Glimpses of the lake helped gauge their progress. At last, Holly heard the whirr of tires as they stepped out onto the road. The lake was directly across from them, its broad shoreline basking in the sun.

The group made their way over to the shore and found a sunny place to sit while Parker called in their position. Yosef came over and sat near Holly.

Looking at him brought a tired chuckle. "You look awful, Yosef."

"You should see the other guy." He winked and winced.

"I'm glad to be off that mountain." She looked up the way they had come. "Last night, I wasn't sure I was going to make it."

"Well, the good Lord has a way of seeing his sheep through. He sent us a couple of great helpers." He nodded at West and Parker.

She tucked an errant red strand of hair behind her ear. "Where do you think Arlen is?" Even in the secure company of Parker and West, the thought of Arlen still out there and able to get to them haunted her.

"I have no idea. I figure he went back to the cabin when he didn't find us. I know it's not very charitable of me, but I would rather that he froze to death actually."

"Me, too. He's an animal." She shuddered and pulled the solar blanket closer around her shoulders.

Tires crunched on the gravel at the side of the road. Holly and Yosef looked up to see three patrol cars, and an ambulance pull up. They had barely stopped when the doors popped open. Vera jumped out and hurried over to throw her arms around Yosef. Brady approached as well, but slowly. A.J. held back.

Yosef gently drew Vera into himself. Tears of relief welled up as she sobbed on his shoulder. He patted her and spoke softly into her ear.

Brady paused and smiled at Holly, unsure of his next move.

Holly looked past him to where A.J. stood by his car. Brady turned to see where she was looking. A.J., taking Holly's look as an invitation, came forward. Just brushing Brady's shoulder as he passed, he pulled Holly into his arms.

Holly yelped.

"What!" A.J. drew back with concern.

Holly opened the solar blanket, exposing her injured arm. "I think I broke it."

"Oh, I didn't know."

"Excuse me, sir, we'd like to get these folks to the hospital." The ambulance attendant moved in between them.

A.J. stepped back and found himself next to Brady. The two men's eyes locked, and Brady turned to face A.J. They were of equal height, with A.J. heavier in the chest and shoulders. A moment, then two, passed before Brady broke away from A.J.'s glare and returned to his car.

At the edge of the scene next to AJ's car stood Evelyn, her arms wrapped around her slender frame in a fierce hug. Her face was set and unreadable as she watched. Then without anyone noticing, she returned to one of the cruisers and sat in the shadow, invisible, unnoticed, and forgotten.

Chapter Thirty-Six

Holly pushed the side table away with her good hand, amazed at how great hospital food tasted if you hadn't eaten in two days. A cast now encased her arm, and a nurse with a large, toothy grin had helped her take a long, hot bath an hour ago. She pulled a pillow up behind her head and reached for the remote.

"Interested in visitors?" Yosef's head popped around the corner and the rest of him followed. He wore a hospital gown, his white, bowed legs poking from beneath giving Holly a chuckle. His nose had been set and was held firmly in place with tape. Vera followed Yosef into the room. "I hope you don't mind a visit, Holly. Yosef and I thought we'd come over and have a chat."

"You two are always welcome in my room." Holly set the remote aside. "Your husband saved my life, Vera. I can never repay him."

"We worked as a team, Holly. We did it together."

"Say what you like, Yosef. I would never have made it out without you."

Vera took a seat on the edge of Holly's bed. "Holly, I know you are exhausted, but something is on our minds. I don't like things to sit when I get a prompting."

Holly's guard came up. "What is it you want to talk about Vera?" She looked from Yosef to Vera and back to Yosef again.

"Now don't get your back up, Holly. We've been through a lot, you and I. We only have your happiness in mind."

"Okay, but what is it?"

"Well, it's delicate."

"What concerns us, Holly, is your well being. You are terribly important to Vera and me. We truly have your best interests in mind."

This tiptoeing around the issue was getting on her nerves. Again, Vera was treating her like a child. "What is it?" she demanded. "Just tell me."

Vera took a deep breath and dove in. "Well, Yosef and I have been talking, and we were wondering about your relationship with Detective Walker." Her old hands twisted in her lap.

"We both know that it is none of our business, Holly, it's just that we know Pastor Brady has ...well, he—" Yosef started to rub his nose then winced.

"He loves you, Holly," Vera continued. He won't ever tell you, but I will. I don't know Detective Walker all that well. But I can tell you that Pastor Brady is the finest man I know, and before you get carried off by some tall, handsome detective, please give Pastor Brady a chance."

Holly started to speak, but Yosef stopped her. "I know the whole pastor's wife thing scares you to death, but he's a man who loves God with all his heart. You're not going to find that just anywhere."

"Find *what* just anywhere?" A.J. stood in the doorway with an armful of red roses.

"Uh...hello, Detective Walker." Yosef stood and greeted A.J, offering a hand.

A.J. stepped into the room and grinned at Holly. "I see you already have company. I thought these might brighten up this boring room," he indicated the velvet, red roses in his arms.

Yosef and Vera exchanged glances.

"They are lovely, A.J., thank you."

Vera stood and reached for the flowers. "I'll go see if the nurses can help me with a vase."

A.J. hesitated.

"Thank you, Vera. They will stay much fresher in water."

After Vera left the room, Yosef turned to A.J. "I'm glad you are here, Detective, I was wondering if you could fill us in on a few things. Vera told us about the search and Arlen and all, but I want to ask about how Arlen killed Holly's uncle and why?"

A.J. settled himself into a chair next to Holly's bed, with his hand coming to rest on Holly's lower arm. He winked at her and turned to answer Yosef's question.

"Since they are both dead, there's no reason not to tell you. Between the journals and our conversation with Kent Haden in Morro Bay, we concluded that Holly's uncle unearthed a Chumash archeological site back when they were building the original house. Arlen was foreman on the job and ordered the bones reburied. Apparently, he paid off Haden as well as Holly's uncle." He paused at this point, eyes on Holly for her reaction.

"I can't believe that, A.J. You never met a more honest man in your life than my Uncle Nikko."

"One thing you learn in my business, Holly, is that everybody has a price."

226

"I don't believe it," she whispered, tears flooding her cheeks.

"He was tormented at the end, Holly. You told me that yourself, and the journals confirm it."

"He had dementia," her words barely audible.

"'What the eye doesn't see, the heart won't grieve over,' was repeated often in the journals after your uncle moved to Arizona."

Yosef sat forward. "That's the phrase Arlen used."

"My uncle repeated it over and over at the end."

A.J. nodded and continued. "He found the bones, and Arlen paid him to cover them back up. The whole project would have been scrapped if the authorities found out, and Arlen's father's company would have taken a huge financial hit if that had happened. Arlen found it economically expedient to pay off your uncle and Haden rather than lose the whole project."

"Poor Uncle Nikko! He was so miserable at the end. He kept talking about being unclean. I couldn't understand it. His faith in Christ was as strong as any man I ever knew."

"We all slip up sometimes, even your Uncle Nikko." Yosef brought her a box of tissues. "That doesn't make him any less the man you loved."

Holly nodded and blew loudly into a tissue.

"What I can't get past is how Arlen had us fooled all these years." Yosef started to rub the side of his nose again, winced and stopped. "I thought he went away to college."

"Boy's school, actually. He didn't last long." A.J. leaned back in his chair and crossed his legs.

A nurse appeared in the doorway. "There you are, Mr. Shankston. The doctor has released you. And you as well, Miss Fain. So, if you all will excuse us, I'll help Miss Fain get dressed and ready to go."

A.J. squeezed Holly's arm. "We'll talk later. I'll wait for you downstairs." He bent down and kissed the top of her head.

Vera came back in with the roses in a vase of water. "We'll see you downstairs, Holly," she patted Holly's arm and in a conspiratorial whisper said. "Maybe we can talk again later."

Holly was the last one to arrive in the lobby, A.J.'s bouquet in her lap.

A.J. moved over to where she sat in her wheelchair. "We've been discussing the ride sharing arrangements, Holly. We have two cars, and six people. I suggested you and I take your car, and Brady here can drive Vera, Yosef, and Evelyn."

"Holly, if it's all right with you, I'd like to ride in your car," Evelyn jumped in, giving a meaningful look at Vera. The tension between the two women as thick as Vera's country gravy.

"That's fine, Evelyn. We have plenty of room."

A.J. started to protest, anger flashing briefly in his eyes.

Brady, a few steps away, caught Holly's eye and nodded. Her heart gave a little flutter, and her mouth twitched into a shy smile. He hadn't visited her in the hospital. She realized that she was disappointed. But, perhaps it was just as well.

The drive home gave Brady time to think and pray. Yosef and Vera sat in the back seat holding hands and talking quietly. They had been inseparable since Yosef came out of the woods. He envied their relationship. Seeing Holly in the lobby of the hospital had been difficult. He had gone to her room once and heard A.J.'s voice from the hallway. In a painful flash, he realized she had made her decision, and A.J. had wasted no time solidifying his victory over her heart.

At least she's alive, Lord. Thank you for that. Grant her a happy life, she is a special lady.

Over the past twenty-four hours, the Lord had worked on Brady's heart. Once Holly and Yosef were safely in the hospital, he had rented a hotel room, pulled the Gideon Bible from the bedside table, and settled in to wait for sleep. That night the Scriptures had come alive in his hands in a way that had thrilled him to the core. Not in many years had he simply sat and read God's Word purely for the joy of it. Reconnecting that way with his Lord and God had been worth all the pain of separation.

He would see Karen and Jeremy again; he knew that and took consolation in the fact. When Holly's face had come to mind, he had thanked the Lord for having met her, and released her back to Him. If the Lord led her to A.J., then it was best for them both. His heart ached with the loss of the relationship, but he sought and found comfort in the Scriptures.

Now, driving down the road, Brady could see her in the car ahead. He knew he loved her. When she had met his eyes over the bouquet of roses in the hospital lobby, everyone else in the room had faded away. Then A.J. had pushed her wheelchair to the car, and she was gone.

"I wasn't sure I would see this house again." Yosef looked around his living room with new appreciation.

Vera cleared some cups from the kitchen table into the sink and returned to the living room with a tray full of cheese, crackers, and three glasses of iced tea. "Looks like we missed church. First time we've missed in years, Yosef."

Brady settled into the overstuffed chair in the corner. "I called Sylvia Thorndyke when we knew Holly and Yosef were safe. She said the elder board had things under control. I'll pick up next Sunday."

Vera and Yosef exchanged glances. Vera nodded at her husband.

"What?" They exchanged a look that only years of marriage could interpret. "Oh, all right, woman!" Yosef turned to Brady, opened his mouth, and closed it again. Looked over at Vera and then back to Brady.

"What, Yosef? What are you two cooking up?" Brady sipped a glass of tea and waited.

"Aren't you going to fight for her, Brady?"

Brady looked from Vera to Yosef and back again, then he, took a sip of his tea. They were being good friends. Dear friends. Still, he was a bit annoyed. He pushed the emotion away before responding. "No, Yosef. She's made her choice."

Vera rose and came to sit by him on the sofa. "I wouldn't be so sure, Pastor Brady. Being a woman, I have a different perspective than you men do. I don't think she's made her mind up at all."

After dropping Evelyn at her home, A.J. drove Holly to her condo. Her sense of relief at returning home safely was sweet. She moved from room to room turning on lights and relishing being alive. She had never come close to death before. The whole experience had given her a new appreciation for life. Eventually, she settled in her favorite chair looking out over the ocean, her broken arm propped on a pillow. A.J. stood in the center of the room watching her.

"It's good to be home, A.J. Thanks for everything."

"Good doesn't begin to describe how I feel, Holly." He came over and dropped to one knee in front of her. Taking her hand, he looked into her eyes. "Holly, I don't want to take the chance of losing you again. I wanted to ask you this morning at the hospital, but you had company."

"Ask me what, A.J.?"

A.J. took her other hand and looked intently up into her face. "Holly, I want you to be my wife."

Holly's hand came to her lips as their eyes locked. "This is so sudden, A.J. I don't know what to say."

"Say yes." He drew a ring box from his pocket and slowly opened it to reveal a stunning diamond engagement ring. The large central stone catching the light and sending a rainbow of color against the far wall. Smaller diamonds collared the larger stone in an elegant platinum setting. A.J. took the ring from its tiny box and slipped it onto her finger.

"A.J., it's ... lovely," she whispered as he stood and drew her up into his arms.

"Not as lovely as you are." His voice husky as he gently kissed her, holding her close and warm.

When he finally released her, they settled onto the couch, A.J. holding her hand.

She admired the ring on her finger, watching how the fading afternoon light danced in its depths. Was she really engaged?

She looked up from her hand. "I guess I have some planning to do."

"No rush. I figured we would sell both our places and buy something with a little land, maybe up Santa Rita Creek Road. I know of a nice little operation up there that's been for sale for a while. Maybe we can go see it next weekend when you've had some time to rest up." He rose from the couch.

"I meant the wedding."

He held up a hand. "Let's not rush things, Holly. We'll get our households settled, then we can talk about all that." He bent down to kiss her. "I have to go back to the Department and file a load of paperwork. I'll see you tomorrow."

"But A.J. I ..."

A.J. touched a finger to her lips "Shh. We'll talk tomorrow. You rest." He winked at her and was out the door before she could protest.

Chapter Thirty-Seven

Twenty minutes later, Holly opened Glynnis' back door. Her friend looked up from a steaming pot of soup.

"Holly! I was worried sick. Your name was all over the newspaper this morning, talking about your being lost in the mountains and all. Let me have a look at you!" She held Holly at arm's length and examined her closely. "Well, except for the broken arm, you don't seem too much worse for wear." She pulled Holly into a soft, warm hug.

"I hope you don't mind my dropping in like this, Glynnis. I need somebody to talk to." She held up her left hand for Glynnis to see her ring.

"Oh, my good Lord. Holly, you're engaged!" Her hands flew into the air. "Weddings, I love weddings. We will have so much fun planning. Is it that handsome pastor you brought over the other day?" She led Holly to the living room.

"No, Glynnis, it's not Brady." Holly eased herself onto the colorful couch. She was sore from head to toe.

"Oh, well. He seemed like such a nice man. Who is it then?" Glynnis arranged pillows behind Holly's back.

"His name's is A.J. Walker. He's a detective with the Sheriff's Department. He headed up the search for us."

Glynnis sat across from her and looked at her for a long moment. "Somehow you aren't acting like a woman who just got engaged."

Holly covered her face with her good hand. "Well, it all happened so fast. I do know he loves me. He's a good man with a good job. He's handsome, well-respected, and has lived here all his life but—"

"But you don't love him."

"Yes, no, I don't know. He wants me to sell my condo and buy a ranch with him on Santa Rita Creek Road."

"That's what married people do, Holly. Live in the same house."

"*Before* we get married, Glynnis."

"Oh." She fingered her necklace.

"Yes. Oh."

"Why did you say yes to him? Sounds like you two aren't on the same page."

"I didn't say yes. He just assumed I did. Then he put the ring on, and it was done."

"Well, what was done can be undone. Just give him his ring back."

Holly eyed the elegant ring on her hand. "I thought when this happened, I would feel different than I do. I'm not getting any younger, Glynnis. If I don't take this opportunity, I may never get another."

"Being a spinster isn't the end of the world, you know, Holly."

Holly reached over and squeezed her friend's knee. "Oh, Glynnis, I'm sorry. But I do want to be married someday. I'm just not sure I want to be married to A.J."

"Well, that's what engagements are for, Holly, to get to know each other better. Tell this A.J. that you would be happy to sell your condo. You will put it on the market the week you get back from your honeymoon."

"A.J. would never go for that."

"Then I don't think you have any decision to make. Give him back the ring and see where the Lord takes you. From the sounds of it, man's not a believer."

"That's the other thing. I tried to talk about faith issues with him, but he says it's a personal thing. He won't talk about his faith with me at all."

"Holly," Glynnis leaned over and placed her hands on Holly's knees. She looked her straight in the eye. "There is no discussion here. You know what you have to do."

The last tendrils of fog frosted the top of the sand spit across from the State Park Marina in Morro Bay. The morning had been a busy one. Vera and Evelyn had met him for coffee at Top Dog Coffee Bar. The conversation had not begun well but Brady had persevered and eventually Vera had begun to thaw. Both women had a long way to go, but he felt that the relationship would eventually mend.

Brady got out of the car with his Bible and tucked a notepad under his arm, an old pattern from his seminary days that he had resurrected. Some of the sweetest moments he remembered with the Lord had been out in nature with a pad of paper and his Bible. He checked his watch. He had almost two hours before his appointment with Jessica at the County Jail.

He had spied the little point of land across the marina when he had taken Holly to dinner here at the Bayside Café. Pausing briefly to look down at Holly's yellow sailboat tied securely in its slip, he realized a little part of him had hoped she would be there. Most of him was glad she wasn't. He turned south toward the end of the parking lot where he found the trailhead and followed it around the back end of the marina, startling a snowy egret from the reeds. It's great white wings lifted it up and away over the bay.

Brady rounded the end of the point. A solitary figure in a black hooded sweatshirt sat on the large rock where he had planned to spend the morning. Disappointed, he wandered farther along the path in hopes of finding another spot with a dry place to sit. Finding none, he returned to the point. A flash caught his attention. In the person's hand, light danced in the morning sun. A brittle piece of driftwood crunched under his foot and the hooded figure looked up. Green eyes met his, and a wisp of red hair escaped from the hood.

"Holly?"

"Brady?"

Holly stood and turned to face him.

Neither moved for a long moment.

"I didn't mean to … disturb you," he stuttered. I was just looking for a place to have some quiet time." He motioned to the Bible and notepad under his arm. "Privacy is a little hard to come by right now." A smile tugged at the corner of his mouth.

"I can imagine." The morning light twinkled in her eyes. "Yosef and Vera can be a bit, well, let's say inquisitive."

"Nosey would be another word." His smile widened.

"Brady, I never got the chance to thank you for trying to ransom Yosef and me."

"You're welcome."

Holly looked out over the water. "I've been here for a while now. I can go if you want to study. I don't mind." She bent to pick up her Bible from the weathered log and turned to go.

"Holly?"

"Yes?" She looked back over her shoulder.

"Do you have to go?" He took a step toward her.

She turned again to face him. "Do you want me to stay?"

With five quick steps, he pulled her into his arms.

"Yes," he said. "Forever."

ABOUT THE AUTHOR

Born in 1954, Gretchen Ricker grew up riding horses in Palos Verdes Estates, California. She's had a passion for story telling from an early age. Raised by her grandmother after losing her mother to cancer at five years old, she built a world of story around her life. "Fact or fiction?" her grandmother would ask when Gretchen came up with a new story. Drawing from a diverse mix of life experience, she fills her stories with color, passion, and humor.

She currently lives on the Central Coast of California and enjoys sailing with her husband, Dan, and her boat dog, Fred.

To contact Gretchen Ricker, or to be placed on a mailing list to receive updates about new releases, click the "Contact Me" link on her website at www.GretchenRicker.net